STORIES

MY MOTHER TOLD ME

Second Edition

Anne Obert Myers

Second Edition, 2013

© Copyright 2013 Anne Myers

The author intends and has authorized that the Jewell County Historical Society for Jewell County, Kansas will exclusively inherit all copyrights for both editions of this book.

ISBN-13: 978-1502370990
ISBN-10: 1502370999

Printed by CreateSpace, an Amazon.com company.

First Edition 1996
Second Printing 1997

Front cover photograph:
Francis Obert and his wife Frances (Kennedy) September, 1931, shortly after they were married.

Original cover art by Marvel Guy

IN LOVING MEMORY OF MY PARENTS

DR. and FRANCES (KENNEDY) OBERT

and

my grandparents, aunts, and uncles, the wonderful characters in this story who have gone on before us.

DEDICATED TO:

The three remaining "Kennedy Kids"
(at the time of initial publication)

Jessie Muck of Mankato, Kansas

Vivian Ost of Beloit, Kansas

Kenneth Kennedy of Lebanon, Kansas

Acknowledgements

My Aunt Jessie for her patience and wonderful memory.
My Aunt Vivian for her funny stories.
My Uncle Kenneth for kindly filling in the blanks.

To: Norma June Peterson, my loyal friend and support system.

Marvel Guy for always 'being there' when I need help.

Katherine Pettersen for her eager encouragement, friendship and hours of editing.

Barbara Tupper, my mentor and my friend.

Doris Alexander, my cousin, my friend who was always ready to help.

Carroll Obert, my 'double cousin' who spent many hours going over stories, filling in blank spots, and helping to keep the stories accurate.

Linda Siel, a good friend, for patiently helping me through my many computer glitches.

Jim Kennedy, my cousin who did the computer work for the second edition and incorporated information that has been learned since the initial publication.

Preface to the Second Edition

As indicated by the title *Stories My Mother Told Me*, this book is based on family stories I first heard from my mother. These stories were supplemented by stories from my father and stories from others. These stories convey much of the key family history for the Kennedy and Obert families in north-central Kansas in the early 1900s. They may also provide insights about life in general in rural Kansas during that time period. I freely used my imagination to fill in dialogue, details, and continuity for the stories given my knowledge of the events and people involved. Books like this that include both historical information about real people and fictional details are usually categorized as "biographical fiction."

This second edition has many changes from the original book. Much information about family history has become available since I initially collected information for the book almost 20 years ago. This newly available information has been widely incorporated into the book. These updates have included modifying or replacing some stories with newly available information, rearranging the order of some stories to provide a more realistic timeline, and many minor changes to details that make the stories more accurate. The greatest changes pertain to stories about Charlie Kennedy and incorporate surprisingly detailed information recently shared by his son John.

An Appendix has also been added that gives the sources for the main stories and indicates stories that are my surmise about what happened. This book is intended to describe the stories I heard and to provide plausible depictions of the details and context for the stories. In most cases I have not attempted to verify the historical accuracy of the stories. Some names and information about persons outside the immediate Kennedy and Obert families were altered.

Jim Kennedy, my cousin, has taken the initiative to revise and format the manuscript for publication. He has done some editing and significant ghost writing to incorporate newly available information. Only photographs that printed reasonably well and are important for the story are included in this second edition. Several photographs were removed, and a couple of photographs added. Additional information was included in the captions for most of the included photographs.

Anne Obert Myers
December, 2013

CHAPTER 1

Little Francis half shuffled, half stumbled down the dry dirt road. The dust scuttled ahead and behind in little wisps and quickly settled. Lee, his older and much admired big brother, was ahead and turned to motion the little boy to hurry and catch up with him. Francis speeded his steps a little and begged Lee, "You not gonna tell maw, are you Lee?"

"I don't know Stub, she gonna ask me. I can't lie to maw. You know yourself, you been kept in every day so far this year. You haven't been out to recess one time. Every mornin maw says to you, 'Stub, you be a good boy today. You stay out of trouble and get to go out to recess to play with the other kids.' Why can't you just sit still and stay out of trouble one day?"

"I don't know what's the matter with me," the little boy answered. "I get my work done and I get restless and the next thing I know I'm in trouble again. Why does everybody call me Stub?"

"Because," Lee said, "you're so little, so short. You don't grow as fast as the other kids."

"Yeah, but the other kids don't run as fast as me." Stub said defensively. "I'm just as strong, and play ball better than the rest of them, except maybe Charlie Kennedy," and added as an afterthought, "or either of his brothers."

They rounded the bend of the road and lost sight of the little country schoolhouse behind them with the little twisted tree to the side. Incredibly, the tree grew out of some rock and therefore the school was christened the "Lone Tree Schoolhouse." As its name implied, it had a lonesome appearance. The little white frame building, nearly square in size, sat stark and alone in the prairie pasture. It looked sturdy and able to shelter the neighborhood children through all the blizzards and wind storms that can visit this vast midland section of the country. The school was the center of the local social life as well as the center of education. Elections, box socials, and neighborhood dances were held there.

In the distance, the boys could see the Kennedy farm, and both boys thought about the Sunday afternoon ball games in the pasture just south of the big Kennedy farmhouse. It was extremely large compared to other houses in the area. The driveway curved inward from the road, past the barn, which was ingeniously built into the bank. The lower part of the barn was built of yellow native rock so that the cows could enter from the pasture. The top part was built over the bank and could be entered from ground level. The driveway then bent to the left where bushes had been planted around the square two-story house that stood so imposingly on the raw plains. A porch with pillars was wrapped completely around this house with its imperial facade. A lean-to back porch added a handy entryway for the farmers to clean up and store buckets and other such farm paraphernalia.

The three Kennedy boys would be there ready for a wear and tear game of work up, plus a couple of the sisters and the rest of the neighborhood kids. Everyone gathered at Arminta Kennedy's house on Sunday afternoon, partly because the bigger share of the neighborhood kids lived there and partly because they had lots of room and Minty (as she was affectionately called by friends and family) was such a good sport. Minty stirred gallons of lemonade and baked scores of cookies for dozens of kids. The more the merrier was always her motto, and the more children arrived, the more she laughed and smiled.

It was a golden October day in Kansas. The air was crystal clear and cool. The sun's warm rays mixed in with the cool late summer breeze. The sky was brilliant and the countryside was lovely, dressed in its fall colors, as only an autumn day on the prairie can be. The winter wheat was up and shining its gleaming shade of green in fields here and there while the golden ripe corn made a dazzling contrast. The pasture added to the beauty with its subtle shades of lime green and bronzes and its gullies, hills and shade trees intertwined. Kafir corn, the feed crop recently introduced into the area, had matured and its burnt orange color provided a gorgeous blend with the greens and golds all around. The various fields and colors made a delightful patchwork quilt effect of the panorama around them as the two boys walked and looked about in the distance.

They began to drag their pace as they neared home. Both knew that chores awaited them—each had his own cow to milk, the separator crank to turn (after carefully saving enough milk for supper, of course), and then the skim milk to feed to the calves and pigs. Then there was always the last check for eggs in the barn and hen house, feeding and watering the chickens and shutting them up for the night. Also, gathering the dusty cobs and kindling wood for the stove so Maw could cook the supper and take the chill off the house before everyone finally got settled into bed.

At last they reached the driveway and slowly turned to walk toward the house. As they entered the porch, they left their lunch buckets on the washstand and went into the kitchen. There was a little fire in the cook stove and it felt good. The smell of pungent yeast and freshly baked bread still lurked in the kitchen. Maw was turning the butter churn and the bright yellow cream was curdling and getting thick. The process of turning slightly sour cream into the wonderful sweet taste of fresh butter for their bread always amazed the boys. As they watched, the butter slowly gathered together and suddenly became a clump—an island in the middle of a puddle of gray buttermilk that was slushing all around it.

Maw said, "Now, I have to take my paddle and work all the buttermilk out of this butter or it will be sour tasting. I hope the butter doesn't get too warm before I get done. Maybe I should sit out on the back step to keep it cooled off. Come sit with me and tell me about school today." As she said this, Stub's heart dropped. He knew she would find out he had gotten into trouble again.

She put the hunk of butter with the glistening beads of buttermilk into a flat pan and took her wooden paddle and the butter to the back step and sat down. As she began to work the butter with a top to bottom squish of her paddle, the buttermilk would collect in the bottom of the pan. Carefully she would pour it into a jar to be used for pancakes, biscuits, or maybe a treat for Dad after the chores were done. She sprinkled little bits of salt into the butter now and then and worked it patiently.

"How did school go today, boys? Did you get to go out for recess, Stub?"

He hung his head and said, "No," so softly you could barely hear him.

"What did you do today, son?" she said kindly.

"Maw, he always gets done with his schoolwork first, before anybody else, and then he can't seem to keep out of trouble after that," Lee told her. "You know that Margaret Burns, the oldest girl in our school? Well, today she told the teacher that if she would let her stay in for Stub so he could go out and play she would do it. Teacher wouldn't let her though."

Maw shook her head and said "Stub, do you do a good job with your work? Is it well done and all the questions answered?"

"Yes, Maw, and I always get a good grade, most always an 'A'."

She shook her head, gave the butter a final almost affectionate pat, and wondered what could be done about a situation like this. There surely must be something the teacher could give him to do in his idle time to keep him out of trouble.

The incredible prairie sun was getting lower and the sky was changing from a deep blue to purples and roses. The three of them sat watching the giant easel change colors as if a divine painter were creating a masterwork, not knowing what a privilege it was to see a prairie sunset.

Dad and little four-year old Mary came hurrying up the pathway from the barn to the house.

"Be quick, boys, and get about your chores," he said in his thick German accent.

With Father Obert there was never much time for foolishness. His mind only seemed to comprehend work. Stub and Lee scrambled over the barbed wire fence and down the gully. They went on through the pasture to the clump of trees where the milk cows usually stayed when the weather was warm. Sure enough, they were there and they slowly drove the old bossies home.

After the chores were finished and supper was over, Mom ladled out the hot water from the water reservoir back of the cook stove into a dishpan, added a bar of homemade soap and swished it around a little, then ladled another dishpan of fresh rinse water, leaving both on the stove so as to stay hot. She carefully washed each utensil then placed it in the steaming rinse water. The boys and Mary dried the dishes and put them away in the cupboard. After this, they used the rinse water and the bar of soap to wash themselves; then put on their pajamas.

The October chill was in the air in the evenings, warning everyone that the beautiful Indian Summer would not last and winter was creeping down from the north. The fire in the cook stove crackled comfortingly. The evening was spent pleasantly with the boys taking turns reading aloud, Mom mending by the lamplight, and Mary playing with her doll on the floor next to her dad.

Mary adored her father and followed him every place she could. She followed him barefoot up and down the furrows as he plowed behind his horse in the summer, loving the feel of the warm earth beneath her feet and the soft dust squishing between her toes.

Later, the boys jumped into their chilly bed, which was upstairs in the narrow little house—just an attic really. How they dreaded the bitter cold winter nights when their bed was cold and the comforters so heavy it made them ache. Lee still remembered last winter when he hated to change positions because the bed was so cold anyplace but where his body had warmed it. There was no heat in this upstairs room and no rugs on the floor. In the morning they jumped directly from the bed and fell/tumbled down the stairs to the warm cook stove below.

Frank Obert stoked the cook stove, filled the water bin with fresh water for morning, and blew out the kerosene lamps except for the one he carried into the bedroom with him.

Mattie was already in bed and he noted the fresh whiteness of the sheets and pillowcases.

He was still awed by his little Irish wife. Her light auburn hair fluffed against the pure whiteness of her pillowcase looked so fetching. She was small, not quite five feet tall, with a small-waist and slim-hips. She had broad shoulders with a straight back and a full, round bosom. Her eyes were bright blue and merry, showing intelligence and good humor. She always welcomed company; no stranger ever came to her door and she loved to make people comfortable—to feed them and visit a bit. He wished he could be more like her. He loved her but could not understand why he had so much trouble showing his affections to his family. He was not a bad man, he thought as he blew out the lamp and crawled into bed beside her, he just couldn't seem to say the right words at the right time. He did appreciate her efforts in keeping the house so clean and neat, and she was admired throughout the neighborhood for her extraordinarily tasty meals and baked goods. She was enthusiastic about her role as wife and mother. With all this in mind he turned his head toward her and the moonlight was filtering in the window on her face.

She took his hand and said, "Night, Poppy."

He could only lift her hand to his lips and kiss it. He turned toward her, put his big hand on her hair and kissed her softly. As he felt her respond, he gave a shiver of anticipation and knew that she knew how he felt about her without having to say the words.

The morning broke clear and sunny, promising another beautiful autumn day as had been the last ten or fifteen. Mattie was frying potatoes in her big iron skillet and the fresh eggs were waiting in the bowl to fry. Big thick slices of homemade bread were waiting on the table, with the fresh butter from the night before in the middle. She placed a small jar of wild plum jam next to the butter and beside it, a small bowl of sliced tomatoes, the last of the summer garden.

Frank Obert and the boys came in from the morning chores and washed in the warm water Mattie had placed in the washbowl inside the doorway. She broke and fried nearly a dozen eggs and placed them on a big platter. The boys poured cups of warm milk for themselves and for Mary. It was still foaming from the milking this morning. They thought how good the coffee smelled, but knew it didn't taste as good as it smelled.

After breakfast the boys hurried down the road toward school and Mattie picked up the breakfast dishes. She placed the butter in a container, tied it to a rope in the cistern, and dropped it down into the cool water to keep it sweet during the warm, sunny day. Then she tied a rope to the milk bucket with its lid and let it down into the cool water. All the rest of the leftovers went into the slop bucket to be taken to the pigs later, when she went out to take care of the chickens and gather the eggs.

The boys tied their books with a belt and flung them over their shoulders. They started for another day at school in an unhurried pace. Francis gave a kick at a clump of dirt going down the road and said to Lee, "If that bully Fatty Allington pushes me around again today, I'm going to have it out with him."

Lee said, "You in enough trouble already, don't be goin' fightin' too."

"Well, he pushes me to the back of the line when we're waiting to get a drink, he won't let me play in the games, he trips me when I walk by. He's mean to me all the time."

Lee said, "I think he's jealous of you because you're such a good catcher and because you can run faster than he can."

"I don't care," Francis said, "I'm sick and tired of him picking on me."

They arrived a little early and a game of marbles had already been organized. The boys pulled a few marbles out of the pockets of their overalls and joined. Before long, little Stub, with his unusual sense of hand-eye coordination, had won most of the marbles again, including the favorite marble Fatty's grandmother had given him for Christmas last year. Fatty pushed him to the ground with a mighty shove.

CHAPTER 1

"Just because you're way big and fat too," the little boy shouted at him.

"Yeah, and you're a little pipsqueak squirt that cheats at marbles, too."

With that he stomped off and was mean and ornery all day.

Francis got up and whispered to his brother, "I'm going to get back on him—you just wait and see. I am."

Next morning, as soon as chores were done, Stub was out in the barnyard shoveling manure into a little bucket.

Lee asked, "What are you doing?"

"You wait, I'll get mean ol' Fatty Allington."

They started out for school, Stub carrying his bucket and his lunchbox in one hand and his books in the other.

"I'm not helping you," Lee said. "You're gonna get in trouble again and I'm not helpin' you do it."

"Fine," Stub grunted and marched down the road with an unholy purpose in his step. They arrived in the schoolyard a few minutes before the teacher rang the bell for everyone to come in for the first class.

"What you got there, Stub?" the kids yelled from their games.

"Got all the marbles I won from everyone all year. Gonna give 'em all back." He very dramatically laid down his books and his lunchbox. Then he slowly and ceremoniously turned the little bucket upside down.

He announced that he would lift the bucket and everyone could get the marbles they wanted. The fastest ones would get the best. Fatty was waiting impatiently. He was going to be the first and get his favorite marble back. He was bullying the other kids, pushing and shoving.

When Stub pulled the basket up and hollered, "Go," Fatty was the first one pushing both hands in the conglomeration. The marbles were there all right, but all mixed up in the fresh manure from the morning's milk cows. Fatty went into a rage and ran off to tell the teacher. All the children were laughing hysterically and, of course, Stub had to stay in for recess again—but it was worth it.

That evening at supper, Frank Obert announced that the pump would have to be pulled Saturday morning and that both boys would be expected to help. He also casually mentioned that this would be Lee's last year in school.

He said, "You are in sixth grade now and that is enough learning. It's time you stayed home and helped more on the farm."

Mattie protested softly, "But Frank, I was hoping he could at least finish eighth grade."

"School's a waste of time," Frank countered irritably. "Fill their heads with nonsense about old wars in Greece and where to put a period. Won't help a bit to raise a good corn crop or get a herd of good milk cows."

Lee could see an unpleasant situation developing and was a kind little boy who desired peace.

He said, "It's OK, Maw. I would rather be home helping Dad anyway. I love the farm and I love the cows. It's what I really want to do, Maw."

Francis sat quietly, taking in the drama and hoped the same thing wouldn't happen to him when he got in sixth grade—for he really did love school.

CHAPTER 2

Saturday morning dawned bright and beautiful. It was another warm, clear autumn day like the past few weeks had been. The boys were heading toward the barn as the sun began to rise. The sky in the east shined with brilliant rose and gold hazes and the blues and purples in the west slowly turned into bright aqua. As the sun entered the horizon, the whole sky turned into a brilliant blue. The sunrises on the prairies were as phenomenal as the sunsets. After breakfast, Frank and his boys headed for the windmill where the pump was not working.

"I hope it is yust someting broken in the pump," Frank said, "and not that the vell has gone dry. That would be a catastrophe and we have enough trouble trying to keep body and soul together on this place. Mac McCleary is coming to help. He knows a lot about pumps and can help fix it if needs be."

They began dismantling the parts and soon neighbor McCleary came riding into the driveway in his buggy, his wife beside him to visit Mattie while the men worked. The men heaved on the well pipe and took apart a segment, heaved again, and pulled another segment apart, and so on until they got down to the mechanisms of the pump itself. Another heave. Everyone was getting tired by this time especially little Francis.

Dad Obert shouted at him irritably in his German accent, "Pool Stawb, Pool, Gott Dommitt."

He often was testy with the little boy because he was a little disappointed that Francis was so small and especially that he liked to read and study. Stub gave a mighty pull and thought his insides were falling out, but the pump came up and the trouble was evident. McCleary had it fixed in no time and the pump was back in the ground, pulling up fresh sweet water.

After the company was gone and supper over, Mattie began pouring hot water into the big wooden tub in front of the warm cook stove. Little Mary was first to take a warm bath in it, then she was dried off briskly and put into her warm flannel nightie. Mattie added more hot water and the two boys were given their hot baths. Next Mattie took a comforting soak in the tub and last of all Frank relaxed his sore muscles in the tubful of hot water. He helped Mattie empty the tub and sent the children off to bed.

As he watched his little wife cleaning the kitchen, getting clothes ready, and organizing food in preparation for Sunday morning, he wondered at her energy and stamina. For such a tiny woman she had an amazing capacity for work. He felt sorry that so much hard work had been placed on her and wished somehow he could fix it so she did not have to take care of the workhorses in the summertime. It was her job to feed, water, and harness them before he went to the field. He knew at the same time though, that if he allowed her not to do this, his parents would never approve. They believed that American women were far too spoiled and pampered as it was. He also felt some guilt for being so hard on young Stub. He knew how much Mattie's children meant to her. They were her pride and joy—the crowning achievement of her life. He remembered her grief when her baby boy died; her total despair—eyes always red, face swollen , and uncharacteristic lack of energy. Then he remembered her pure joy when the child was replaced with another, her little Francis.

"I must be better to this little boy," he thought. "I have to be more patient with him." Frank was a big man, tall and sinewy, with no fat, just pure muscle. His frame was large as were his hands. He was strong and loved hard manual labor. His face had the chiseled look of the Teutonic race with dark hair and penetrating dark eyes.

He knew his youngest son took after Mattie and made a conscious pact with himself to accept the difference from himself and to be more kindly with the child. Mattie adored her oldest son Leo, who had a stocky build, fair hair, deep-set blue eyes, and a loving, kind disposition. It was Lee that she drew her strength from many days when the hard pioneer life became too much for her. She loved her dusky and brooding daughter as well, for Mary had the dark complexion of her father and a strange moody disposition. Yet when she was in a good mood, she was a happy, loving little girl.

But it was her youngest son Francis that she felt a likeness to, a strange sameness. He was dark like little Mary, but his chocolate brown eyes shown with a merriment and kindness unusual in so young a boy. He was built like Mattie, with her broad shoulders and slim hips, and had inherited her sense of music and rhythm and coordination. Like her, he loved to read and had an unquenchable thirst for knowledge.

Tired from the day of hard work and from so much profound thinking, Frank blew out the lamps, crawled into bed and gave up all his troubles of the day to a soft, soothing sleep.

The whole neighborhood was thankful that the Indian summer remained. Everyone was preparing for the winter, picking apples and storing them in the cellars along with potatoes and parsnips. The shelves were beginning to fill with the canning from the kitchens—tomatoes, green beans and fruit. Outside every farmhouse backdoor sat a mound, like a small Indian hogan with a little chimney jutting out of the top. A slanted door lay in front, and underneath were steps that led down into the underground cellar. These were built more for shelter during the vicious springtime storms, but they were also used as storage for winter supplies. Mattie had dill and sweet pickles on her shelves along with all the other fruits and vegetables she had canned over the summer.

The Obert family felt refreshed from their Sunday rest and the new workweek was going nicely. As soon as the corn was dry the whole family would be out husking for weeks on end. But for now, it was chores and laying up for winter. Frank Obert was making plans for his annual fall trip into town to buy needed supplies to last the winter.

"I'm planning a trip into town, Mattie," he said. "What do you need?"

She sat down at the table and began to carefully write her list. She dare not forget anything as this would be the last trip for a long time.

"Let's see," she mused, "we need kerosene, flour, sugar, coffee and cocoa. Can you think of anything else, Poppy?"

"We can always use beans and macaroni and don't forget lye for our soap."

"Oh, yes," she said, "glad you remembered it."

The boys overhearing the conversation begged, "Can we go too, dad? You goin' into Esbon?"

"No, I ain't going into Esbon and yes, you can go along."

"Where we goin' then, dad?" Lee asked.

"We're goin' into Red Cloud because I need some harnesses fixed and some machinery parts that I can't get in Esbon."

The boys were so thrilled with the prospects of going to the bigger town so far away that they slapped each others' hands and gave a whoop of delight. They rarely got to go clear to Red Cloud, but loved every minute of the long trip there.

"When we goin', dad?" they asked in unison.

"Saturday morning," he answered.

The whole family was up early Saturday making preparations for the all day trip. The horses were hitched to the wagon, the sacks packed carefully to carry the provisions, and everyone dressed in their clean overalls and best shoes. As they were ready to jump into the wagon, Mattie handed each little boy a dime she had saved from her cream and egg money. They gave her a hug and happily thanked her for the rare treat. Finally they were headed down the dirt road toward the gravel highway that would lead out of Kansas and north into Nebraska and the little town of Red Cloud. Francis told Lee he intended to use one nickel of his dime in the bakery for a big ice cream cone and the other nickel on two donuts to eat on the way home. Lee still hadn't decided how he would use his dime.

The wagon lumbered along most of the morning and finally reached the top of the bluffs that rimmed the Republican River just outside the little prairie village. They looked down and saw the misty valley that nestled the town of Red Cloud. On a spring day, the medley of colors blended so beautifully that everyone entering the valley silenced to drink in the beauty of the scene. The Republican River rambled around the outskirts of the town with cottonwood trees, shrubs and brush accenting its beauty. Francis loved the rare trips into Red Cloud because it was the biggest town he had ever been in and because there were so many wonderful shops with goodies. As the wagon continued down into the valley, crossed the river and ambled along the street into the town, the boys were impressed with the greenness of it—particularly the trees and grass in the park south of main street.

Out on the plains of Kansas where they lived there was never so much green grass or so many flowers. In Red Cloud, dozens of children were playing in this lush green park and indeed all over town. Frank let the boys out in the city park and told them to be right here in two hours as he would be starting for home by two o'clock sharp. They quickly became acquainted and joined in the games. They entered the foot race and Francis won easily.

One town boy said, "Let's go over to the icehouse and play awhile. It's cool there and you can chip off pieces of ice to suck on. It's right across the street from here—just don't let the owners see you go in."

The whole group snuck quietly to the back of the icehouse and slipped in unnoticed.

"Shh," one said, and they all fell behind some large blocks of ice covered with straw, peeking out carefully. The men hooked a block of ice each with the large iron hooks and left, not noticing the children in the back.

They soon tired of the confinement of the icehouse and started for main street, where Francis and Lee headed for the bakery. They stared in wonderment at the cases filled with sweets and frostings and at the large and ornamental soda fountain with its mirror covering the whole wall. They crawled up onto the stools, slowly rubbed the smooth marble of the soda bar, looked into the huge mirror, and couldn't believe their good fortune in actually being here today. They each ordered a great big double dip ice cream cone and left the bakery. As they walked out, the rest of the gang of town kids were heading to the movie theater. Tom Mix was playing that afternoon and all the boys were excited.

"Come on and go to the show with us," they hollered as they went by.

"We can't," the Obert boys answered. "We have to head back home in a little bit."

"Have to be home before dark," Lee told them.

"Too bad," said the town boys somewhat carelessly and they took off for the picture show.

Lee and Francis walked toward the theater to peek into the lobby. They stared in amazement at the counter where popcorn and candy were sold. The popcorn smell overwhelmed them so they took their last nickel in and each started back to the park with a big bag of buttered popcorn to meet their father. Frank Obert came along presently in his wagon, filled with winter provisions.

The boys headed for the wagon and asked, "Dad, can we go to the picture show to see Tom Mix?"

"No," he answered not unpleasantly, "we have to be home before dark. We have to start now or we won't make it."

They climbed slowly onto the wagon seats, trying to hide their disappointment, but at the same time understood that dad wasn't being cruel, just sensible. The horses and wagon did have to be home before dark—that much they understood. As the horses plodded slowly out of town, Francis took a final look around this especially pretty green little place in the middle of the grassy prairie and said to himself, someday I'm going to live in this town. Someday, I'm going to have a nice house here like the other town people do—and I'm going to go to the picture show every week—and I'm going to buy something good from the bakery every day.

Lee thought, I'm glad we're heading home where it's quiet and you can watch the birds fly and smell the clover in the fields. It's fun here, but only for a while. The father and his two very different little boys rode contentedly home that afternoon.

CHAPTER 3

As the Indian summer days passed, a chill began to creep into the air. The warm aqua sky gave way to an icy blue with billowing white clouds forming in the west and slowly covering the whole skyline. The cottonwood trees turned a greenish yellow, amidst the golds and reds of the elm and maple trees. The cottonwood leaves rustled metallically in the breeze, giving an ominous warning that the end of plant life for this season was near.

Mattie busied herself preparing the evening meal while Frank and the children finished the chores for another day. Another long cold winter was coming on and soon, she thought. We will be house bound a long time once the cold weather and storms begin. As her family came in and were getting settled for their meal and the evening, she thought one last outing before winter would be nice.

"If you children get your chores done real early Saturday morning, we'll hitch the wagon and go visit Minty Kennedys'," she told them.

"Oh great, oh boy, the Kennedys," Lee said.

"He's tickled to go to the Kennedys' because he's sweet on Georgie," Francis teased.

"Am not," Lee retorted.

"Are so," Francis answered.

"So what if I am," Lee said defensively.

With this to look forward to the three Obert children went happily to bed and couldn't wait till Saturday morning.

When the late October sun came up that Saturday morning, the three excited children were hurrying with their chores so fast they became a blur in the barnyard. Soon the cows were milked, the calves and pigs fed, the chickens taken care of, the eggs gathered, and the kindling and wood laid up for the cook stove for the whole weekend. By 9:00 the horses were brought out of the barn and hitched to the wagon. As the wagon lumbered down the little country road, the family was in a gay mood because at the Kennedy house there were children of every age to play with, and always some kind of fun going on.

They drove into the yard and a beehive of activity. Mrs. Kennedy had her pump style washing machine full of hot water and homemade soap, with all her children taking turns pulling the half-moon shaped tub back and forth. The older boys were wringing and rinsing in an adjacent tub of warm water. The girls were wringing and hanging the clothes on the line that stretched all the way across the yard. Georgie was overseeing the whole event with a benevolence unusual in a girl so young. Arminta Jane Kennedy was pleased to see the company driving in—Minty was always pleased to see company come.

She said, "Mattie, I'm so glad you came to visit today. It's good to have a bit of a break. We'll sit on the porch and visit so I can keep the kids at their jobs, and if we need more hot water, I can be ready to bring it out from the kitchen."

The women settled in wooden rockers on the porch and the children scattered in all directions.

"The washing is nearly finished," Minty said, "and then the boys can go play ball."

About then, a squabble arose around the washing machine and little Kenneth started toward the porch complaining, "Why did we have so many kids? If we didn't have so many kids there wouldn't be so many clothes to wash."

Georgie was right behind him. "If we didn't have so many kids, you wouldn't be here," she answered him solemnly. With that she grabbed his arm and marched him back to do his duty with the pump handle. Minty chuckled good-humoredly, "And we're going to have another next spring."

Mattie patted her hand and said, "You are a strong woman, Minty, to take care of so many children."

Minty answered, "I never had any to give away though."

The two women were comfortable with one another and loved to discuss their children and households, blessedly oblivious to the things taking place outside of their prairie homes. Minty asked how things were going at the Obert household and Mattie answered,

"Going well, except for Francis who gets into trouble every day in school and never gets to go out for recess."

Minty told that her older two, Charlie and Georgie, said that Francis was very bright and finished his work early, then became restless, and next thing you know, he's in trouble. Minty said, "Be glad your kids are bright."

She told Mattie how Mable McClure was visiting the other day and feeling so low because her children were having such a hard time getting their lessons. She said they were barely passing some lessons and not passing others at all.

"Mable told me I was lucky my kids were so booky," Minty laughed.

"Frank is running for school board," Mattie said timidly.

"What would he want to do a thing like that for?" Minty chuckled.

Minty was a good-sized woman, strong and healthy. She had narrow shoulders, short waist and small chest, filling out into wide, full hips. Her arms and legs were long and slim. Her boys inherited these long limbs that contributed to their athletic abilities. She wore her magnificent chestnut colored hair pulled into a bun on the top of her head, and the natural wave in her hair made the plain hairdo quite attractive. At times when she was working, little wisps would escape the bun and fall around her face in curls. Minty was blessed with a good nature and an easy happy-go-lucky disposition. All her neighbors visited frequently. They felt at home in her house as they sensed her sincere enjoyment of their company. After the washing was hung out and the water had been dumped and tubs put away, the boys drifted away to play ball and the girls gathered under a tree to play dolls with empty bottles.

Now the Kennedy girls had large bottles who were the men in their bottle family. The smaller bottles were the women and the tiny bottles the babies. They had three ink bottles all alike who were their triplets. The bottle people were carefully dressed with hats and skirts that the girls had made from scraps. Little Mary sat among them and loved the attention lavished upon her, for it wasn't often she got to play with girls.

Before long, she dropped her little bottle on top of another and it broke. She cried, but the Kennedy girls told her it was all right.

"We have a bottle cemetery, you see," said Frances who acted as the minister for the bottle people. They placed the broken bottle in a matchbox and solemnly buried it in the cemetery next to the other broken bottles. Frances gave such a stirring eulogy that all the children cried and dabbed their eyes. After the sermon they sang a hymn, said a prayer, and resumed playing as if nothing had happened.

Minty Kennedy and Mattie Obert went into the kitchen to enjoy a cup of coffee before the Obert family had to return home. Mattie said she hated to think of all the children walking to school this winter in the extreme cold and stormy weather. Grandfather Kennedy was creating a path through the fields for the Kennedy children, Minty explained. He was building little openings in the fences by placing two corner posts close together, just wide enough to allow little children to squeeze through sideways. He wanted to make their daily trips a little easier she continued.

"You know he planted a melon patch down the little hill from the windmill and horse tank?" Minty asked. "When the tank runs over, the water runs down the hill and waters the melon patch. Grandpa Kennedy raises the best melons in the county. He comes up with the most ingenious ideas."

All too soon the visit was over and Mattie called her children to hurry and get in the wagon. It was time to head home to finish the chores for another day. They waved back to the big family of Kennedy children as the wagon slowly rolled out of the big yard with the long line of clothes waving them goodbye in the light October breeze.

CHAPTER 4

"Not vun fvote, Mattie, not vun fvote," Frank blustered. "Mein Gott, don't I haf vun friend in tis district?"

Frank Obert was devastated after the school board elections.

"Now Frank," said Mattie, "don't get your temper up. Don't get yourself all worked up. You know you get in trouble when you get yourself all worked up."

"I can't help it Mattie. I feel so betrayed. I tought at least Ern Kennedy would fvote for me. I tought Ern was my friend."

"Ern is your friend, Frank," Mattie said soothingly. "Don't take this personal. People probably think you don't know enough about schools. You know yourself, you have never shown much interest in school."

"I'm going over to Ern's and ask him why he didn't fvote for me," and in his frustration, Frank smashed his hat on his head and headed for the barn. He saddled up the horse and rode down the lane at a slow gallop. At the Kennedy farm, he found Ern and confronted him without any preliminary courtesies.

"I tought at least you vould fvote for me, Ern. I tought you vere my friend."

"I am your friend," Ern said, "but Frank, you have to be able to read and write in order to be on the school board. Don't you know that you can't handle finances and paper work required for school board members if you can't read and write?"

"No," Frank answered, "I didn't know that."

"Well, now you do," said Ern. "Now Frank, you just remember this when your younger two want to finish school. You let them go to school as long as they want."

Ern hoped his advice would be considered but felt that with Frank advice went largely unheeded. Ern Kennedy had a quiet manner and was good at peacemaking. His way was subtle and unobtrusive. He was a natural diplomat and was good at negotiating. He usually ended quarrels and misunderstandings peaceably.

"Come inside, we'll have Minty boil us up a cup of strong coffee and have a good visit," said Ern.

They went into Minty's warm welcoming kitchen and visited about the crops and the price of cream and eggs. Soon Frank's mind was off the election and back on the business of daily living and making ends meet.

CHAPTER 5

The steam from the kettle with the old hen gently simmering on the wood stove gave off an aroma that was comforting on this cold winter day. The aroma and steam made the kitchen feel warm and cozy. Winter had set in, welcome or not by the plains' people. Mattie was rolling out her noodles on the big kitchen table with the red and white checkered oilcloth covering, humming the little Irish tune she remembered her mother singing to her as a child. She was reflecting on the stories she had heard of her parents' homeland and wondered why they would leave a home with such a mild climate to settle in this country with its harsh environment. Still, she also remembered the stories of the poverty and lack of work, the sense of hopelessness they felt at the time of their decision to leave Ireland forever.

Her mother, Mary Shannon from Quilty, County Clare, Ireland told of the soft mists floating over the little island and of the fat cows that gave the sweet cream and butter from the rich green Irish grass. Poor Mary had stayed in Quilty with her small daughter, also named Mary, and was pregnant again when her husband James Harkins left for the new country. Mary stayed in Ireland a year before sailing herself with the two small children. She felt alone and frightened. The voyage was so hard that she knew she would never again see Ireland or her family. Mattie, for that matter, knew that she would never see the homeland of her parents either. It was far too expensive a trip for her to be able to afford, and it was much too difficult to ever consider. Even so, she did have a desire to visit that land about which she had heard so much.

The noodles were in large circles drying on the tabletop and Mattie walked to the kitchen window to see how her little family was coming with their winter chores. The sky, she noticed, was clabbering much like the butter in her churn, and beginning to take on the color of the buttermilk. It looked like snow coming and the wind was picking up. Frank and the children were hurrying with their buckets of milk and feed. Little puffs of steam were coming from their nostrils as they breathed in and out and the buckets of milk were steaming. Mattie felt sure a storm was coming, and hoped they could finish before it arrived.

The sky had been so clear in the pre-dawn hours when she went out to clean her chicken. She had gone to the chicken house early and grabbed a fat old hen off the perch before the chickens started to stir. The morning was crisp and clear with no wind, making it seem like a surreal world with the lights of a new day barely showing in the inky blue sky. She had made Frank behead her chicken. That was one thing she could never bring herself to do. She had raised these old hens from chicks and when she laid the head on the chopping block, they had a way of looking at her with that one eye that totally unnerved her. After the beheading, she let the hen bleed a bit then dipped it in the bucket of hot water. The warm feathers felt good as she began pulling them and cleaning the chicken. She quickly burned a piece of old newspaper and singed the bird, then gratefully went in the house to dress it where it was warm. She placed it in a big pan with fresh water on the little porch and deftly cleaned the insides, carefully removing the liver, heart and gizzard. She cut off the feet and placed all the refuse in the bucket to be fed to the hogs and then placed her chicken in fresh salted water to soak and cool an hour or two before putting it on to boil. She walked to the wood stove, added a stick of wood and a few cobs and checked the crock at the back of the stove. The skim milk in the crock felt solid, she noticed with satisfaction, so she placed it in a colander, then poured fresh hot water over it. The sour residue washed away and snowy white cheese curds were left. These she put in a small bowl, added thin cream, salt and pepper and thought how good her fresh cottage cheese would taste with the chicken and noodles.

Later that afternoon the wind howled fiercely around the little frame house and the snow blew and swirled. Inside it was warm and cozy. Frank had fired the stove in the parlor for a

CHAPTER 5

special treat. The family gathered around the stove, the boys playing checkers, and Frank mending his leather harnesses.

Lee said, "This is like another Christmas," for only on special occasions did they get to have a fire in the parlor stove.

Francis said, "Only we don't get an orange today."

"Later I'll make some popcorn," Mattie told them, "it will be almost as good as an orange."

The storm coming out of the northwest was at full strength by early evening. The winds shrieked and whistled and seemed evil as though they were trying to break into the house through the cracks in the doors and windows. The little Obert family was contented even so, as they knew their livestock had been well cared for with the horses in the barn and fed, the cows in the lot with protection on every side, and the hogs and chickens safe in their sheds.

Frank felt a sense of peace and contentment on this stormy winter night. Even though this country could be harsh and the extremities of weather tested a man's endurance, there was something about having four distinct seasons that was rejuvenating. He did realize, however, that you had to be mindful of the seasons—to prepare for the winter and to respect it. The winter, and even the winter storms, gave a body a chance to rest, a time of quiet serenity. The sense of peace and calm during the slower winter months prepared the pioneer people for the busy spring months ahead.

No, Frank thought, I wouldn't trade the milder climates, even with their warm winters, for our four seasons here in Kansas. The changing weather patterns make life more interesting and also break the monotony in an otherwise fairly uneventful life.

"Let's have a game of Rook before we all go to bed." he said.

CHAPTER 6

The next day at the Kennedy farm, Minty finished her early morning routine of preparing school lunchboxes. She had the oven door open on her big wood stove and laid the little mittens, scarves and mufflers on the door. Little boots were all lined in a row in front of the oven to soak up as much heat as possible before the owners started out in the cold snowy world. She had a big kettle of oatmeal simmering on the stove and a bowl of boiled eggs, still warm, at the back of the stove.

"Be sure and put on all your long underwear, you kids," she warned. "You'll need them before you get to school today."

She was braiding Georgie's soft brown hair into tight French braids. When she finished she told her to braid little France's hair while she tended to the baby. Soon everyone was dressed, fed, and going out the door to school. The wind the night before had whipped the snow into swirls along the fence line and ditches like meringue on a pie. It was a cold still world the Kennedy children entered that morning. They had the furthest distance to walk to school, about a mile and a half by road, because their home lay along the northern edge of the school district. The special fences Grandfather Kennedy had built provided a shortcut. It was Charlie's custom to carry one of his little sisters on his shoulders during extreme cold weather as he was a big strong boy.

"Which one wants a ride today?" he asked.

Georgie was shivering with teeth chattering but said, "Carry Frances, she's falling behind and can't walk through the deep snow."

The little column struggled on till they reached Grandpa Kennedy's house, the usual halfway stopping point. There they stood on the porch to warm up a bit and Grandma gave them each a cookie and drink of water before they started out again on their journey.

Grandma Kennedy was a fastidious housekeeper and quite rigid in her approach with the children, yet she was kindly with them and they knew she loved them. She stood surveying the little Kennedy brood in front of her and considering the two little boys still at home. She wondered how many more Minty was going to produce. She marveled at Minty's mild manner and easy acceptance of the trials and tribulations that befell her. As soon as the children were sufficiently warmed and fed, she shooed them off toward school. She did not allow them into the kitchen on those mornings, as she did not want them to track on her clean floors.

"I don't know how Minty manages all those children," she told her husband after they had gone.

"Minty reminds me of an old hen with her chicks," Grandpa Kennedy chuckled. "She clucks and fusses over them and never seems to get tired of those children."

"Yes," said Grandma, "but poor little Georgie just has to work harder with each baby. She doesn't get to play as it is."

"That's true," Grandpa agreed, "but that is Georgie's nature. She wants to stay with her mom and help. She couldn't do anything else."

"I suppose so," agreed Grandma Kennedy. "Minty was the same way. She was the oldest child and did nothing but stay with Mrs. Barnett and help till she married and left home."

The children finally arrived in school where the teacher, Miss Johnson, had a roaring blaze in the old pot-bellied stove and a bucket of fresh water on the ledge. They hung their coats and scarves on the wall and laid their mittens on the table by the stove. The Obert boys had already arrived and were warmed by the stove, waiting for teacher to call the class to order. Lee was watching Georgie carefully, trying not to be noticed when he saw big tears welling in her eyes. She was trying to hold them back but they still splashed in little bits over the big brown eyes.

"What's the matter, Georgie?" he asked shyly.

"I'm so cold," she said, "my feet hurt so bad I can hardly stand on them."

Lee led her to a corner and helped her to a chair. There he bent over, unlaced her boots and removed them slowly from the red frozen feet. He bent over them and gently rubbed each foot, blowing warm breath on them at intervals to bring life back into the soft little feet. Some of the boys were mocking and teasing him for being "stuck" on Georgie. The little girls were giggling softly but Lee didn't care. Georgie was more important to him than what all the other kids thought. He couldn't stand it to see Georgie cry or to see her hurting.

"Shut up, you guys," Francis ordered suddenly. "He's just being a good guy and helping Georgie so her feet won't hurt anymore."

"Time for class," the teacher announced. "Everyone find your seats. We'll start with the Pledge of Allegiance, then our first class today will be English."

By the time school was finished the sun had come out and warmed the world. The snow was soft and melting and the air had lost its bite. The children all headed home exuberantly laughing and playing in the snow along the way.

CHAPTER 7

It was as if spring came overnight. The world in the soft morning light was a green haze of spring. There was moisture in the air that one could almost see and even taste. It felt delicious against the winter-weary skin. The mild warmth and softness of the air were exhilarating. The sky was a clear sparkling blue with white fluffy clouds scudding busily across like newborn lambs playing in a field. Even the birds knew there was something about this bright fresh morning that was different. They sang their melodious songs, warbled and trilled with a renewed fervor.

Minty walked across the yard and into the farmstead, stretching her long legs as far as she could. It felt good to be free, if only for a few minutes, of household duties and children. Her girls were watching the little brothers for a short while to give her this much needed and appreciated bit of freedom. She ambled from the chicken pen to the barnyard and back to the pigpen, breathing in the fresh air and enjoying the broad rolling plains that swelled gently into the rolling hills that were their pasture land. She slowly reached into the air, stretching her arms and gently swung from side to side to relax her upper torso, when strong arms grabbed around her waist and gave her a lift into the air.

"It's good to see you outside again, Minty," Ern laughed. He suddenly twirled her around holding her to him, his big hands holding hers as they crossed in front of her. They stood together for a time surveying their kingdom, both looking in the direction of the barnyard when Ern bent over and kissed her neck, then the back of her head.

"Poor Minty," Ern said. "I never meant to put you through so much pain and trouble."

"I know you didn't, Ern. It's just meant to be and my girls will help me care for all the little boys. We have such good girls, Ern, we should be thankful." Minty put her arm around his waist affectionately and walked with him as he finished the morning chores.

Ern wanted to check the old sow that had been losing pigs one at a time. He told Minty he suspected she was eating them. They neared the pigpen and Ern leaned in to check on the new little pigs.

"Only two left," he said shaking his head in great disappointment. "The only logical solution is that she's eating them."

Minty knew this would lessen his income a great deal when time came to sell fat hogs, but her motherly instincts cringed at the thought of the mother pig eating her own offspring.

"Let's butcher her," she offered with more than a little resentment.

"Good idea," answered Ern. "We'll do just that."

Minty turned and headed back to the house to organize the noon meal. Once inside, she noticed with satisfaction that the older girls had everything quite well organized and the little brothers were playing in an orderly manner. Vivian had been put in charge of entertaining the three little boys and felt quite important. She usually felt left out as she was younger than the other three girls and right in the middle of all the little boys,

"Let's open up a few jars of canned beef today, girls, and celebrate this beautiful new spring day."

Everyone had their own job to do, and the Kennedy table was soon set and everything ready for the noon meal.

"Vivian, go call the menfolk in to dinner," Minty said.

"Why do I always have to do the dumb stuff?" Vivian pouted. "I never get to help cook or do the girl things, I always have to do the dumb errands and go with the boys."

"Well, we never get to go outside and do boy stuff either," answered Jessie. "We always stay in the house and do girl stuff."

"Now Viv," Minty wheedled, "when you get a little older you can help me in the house. Right now, you're too little. And as for you bigger girls, you should be happy you don't have to go to the barn and milk and carry slop to the hogs. Dad says there are plenty of boys to do that work and womenfolk shouldn't

CHAPTER 7

have to go to the barn. He says we have enough to do taking care of the family. Now run on, Viv, before everything gets cold."

The growing family finally got situated at the big long table in the large farm kitchen. Ern had gotten his two benches built on either side of the table so that he and Minty sat at the only chairs at either end. He checked his children quietly and noted with satisfaction that all had washed and the boys had combed their hair back. He said the short prayer that was customary and the table became a rumble of happy conversation along with a little good-natured bumping and teasing.

Ern said, "I'm sure the old sow is eating her pigs. This morning there were only two left. If any of you kids would like to take the two pigs to raise, I'm going to butcher the sow soon as a cool day comes along."

David was up and over the top of the table before Ern could blink and Jessie went underneath. Both children bolted out the back door before either parent could warn them back. Ern was stunned and couldn't decide whether to be mad or to laugh when he heard Minty chuckle indulgently and decided to let it go. Still, there was danger with the old sow.

"Quick, Charlie," he said "run down to the pigpen and help them before the old sow eats them up too. Forrest, you go help him."

As the two older boys arrived on the scene, the sow was chasing the smaller children around the pen with a vengeance. Each child had its baby pig and wouldn't let go for dear life. Charlie and Forrest started beating the sow back with a stick and the little farmers scampered over the fence. They settled their new charges into soft hay in corners of the barn and set pans of water and grain for them. By the time everyone was back at the kitchen table the meal was half over and the baby was crying. I can't remember when we had a quiet dinner with no crisis Minty thought. Ern took the two bigger boys out to build lots around the barn and Georgie organized Frances and Jessie into cleaning up the kitchen. Minty took the little boys into her bedroom to attempt to get them all settled for an afternoon nap.

"Come along with us, Vivian and I'll tell you a story."

"No, Mama, I get tired of all the time being put with all the little boys."

"Well, then go out and play with David," she conceded. Poor little Vivian, she thought. She is right in between all these boys. She is too little to play with the girls and the boys leave her out of their games. She gets in the way of Georgie and the two older sisters when they are trying to help in the house. Well, she'll be older soon and there will be a place for her.

Vivian happily skipped outside with anticipation of all kinds of games on this wonderful warm afternoon. David, her next older sibling, was the only one she could really play with. She found him following the older boys around and no one noticed when the two slipped off to play their games. Jessie escaped outside as soon as the noon meal was finished and the kitchen cleaned. She was a tom-boy through and through and loved to climb trees, run footraces, and play ball. Soon all three were inside the corncrib and pretending it was their castle. David was the King, Jessie the Queen and Vivian her maiden, when suddenly David said, "The invaders are coming, they're on top of our castle. Get your sword and help me drive them back." Vivian soon tired of the war game. She ambled slowly back to the house, formulating a plan in her head to convince Francis and Georgie to play a game with her there.

In the meantime, the other two children stayed at the corncrib. David spotted some birds on the back side of the corncrib and proposed to sneak up on them and put salt on the tail of a bird. Jessie thought that sounded like an adventure and soon had some salt. David got to the top, but as he crawled along the roof, he slipped and started slowly sinking toward the edge. There was nothing to hold on to, only the smooth tin roof that sloped downward. Jessie watched in panic as he hit the ground on some rocks with a sickening thud. She stood frozen with fear, horrified, looking down at the lifeless body of her little brother, and then ran hysterically into the house shouting,

"David's dead, David's dead. He fell off the corn crib and killed himself."

Poor Minty, who had just gotten down for a rest, jumped to her feet. Her heart jumped into her throat and she thought what now?

"My stars," she said. "now what could have happened?" and started on a dead run for the door. "Someone go get Dad, quick!" she shouted to no one in particular.

By the time she arrived at the scene, David was coming back to life and groaning with pain.

"Where does it hurt, sweetheart?" Minty asked softly.

"My leg," little David answered with a muffled cry and tears spilling out of his big, brown eyes.

Minty touched his knee gently.

"Here" she asked?

"No," David answered, "higher."

She felt his upper leg and looked at the boy sympathetically.

He shook his head and said with a little whimper, "higher."

Minty felt sick as she felt his hipbone area and knew instantly that it was broken. When she touched it, David whimpered again. Ern came running just in time to hear the bad news.

"Georgie, go call the doctor, quick," he ordered. "Keep calling till you find one who can come right out."

Georgie stood staring at her little brother with so much concern she was almost paralyzed and then suddenly, as if just waking from a nightmare, she took off on a dead run toward the house. Once in, she grabbed the handle and gave the telephone such a hard turn that it was an unmistakable sound of distress.

"Central, get me a doctor quick." the young girl shouted. "My little brother just fell off the corncrib and hurt himself real bad."

Central said, "Is this the Kennedys'?"

"Yes, this is Georgie and my little brother broke his leg."

"OK Georgie, don't worry, I'll get a doctor out there right away."

Georgie hung up and ran out to the scene to see what she could do to help. Ern was organizing the two bigger boys to make a plank to carry David into the house. Minty had gotten a pail of cool water from the well and was washing his face with her apron.

Soon the doctor arrived and, after feeling the leg and hip area, pronounced it a broken hip. He ordered the men to set up a bed in the downstairs parlor as the little boy would be down for six weeks. They carried him into the house on the plank and set up one of the smaller beds from the little boys' bedroom upstairs. The doctor realigned the hip with quick, confident hands, talking softly all the time to calm the terrified little boy. He told him kindly that he was going to put a splint along the outside of his leg and wrap it with some plaster. He warned him that he must not put weight on the leg for six weeks and that he knew it would be hard for a little boy to lie in bed that long.

"Maybe your brothers and sisters can take turns reading to you and playing games with you," he suggested. "Sometimes big families can come in handy," he chuckled and patted the little boy as he left the room to get his medical bag and find the needed supplies to set the hip. Minty and Georgie quickly made up the little bed in the parlor and Dad and the boys gently lay the small child onto the bed. David was sobbing softly by this time with the pain and trauma, but most of all, with the knowledge of six weeks in this bed all day and all night. It was just too much for a little boy to stand.

The doctor reentered the room, wrapped the hip and covered it with a plaster cast. He gave a bottle of medicine to Minty. Give the little fellow a teaspoon of this two or three times a day, Minty, it will help with the pain. I'm sorry, that's all I can do. David will have to do the rest. Just lie there and heal." Then, the doctor left hurriedly as he had many other calls to make that day, and a baby on the way before morning.

Minty sat down in the chair, exhausted from her emotions, and wondered how in the world she was going to keep that little boy down in bed for six weeks. She suddenly felt overwhelmed and depressed, and was ready to give in to complete desolation when she heard whimpering from the bedroom. Georgie came out carrying her little brother and Minty realized the little girl had been in there all this time seeing over the little boys. With a young girl like this, how could Minty think of giving up? No, she must be at least as strong as her little daughter.

She got up and told Georgie again, "I don't know what I'd do without you, Georgie."

"Mama, there's so much for you to do here, I'm going to stay home from school next year and help you."

Minty sighed and thought how unfair all this was to this little girl with the disposition of an angel and at the same time thanked heaven for giving her to them.

CHAPTER 8

The gentle mild days of spring slowly gave in to the hazy heat of summer. On the plains, the heat seemed to rise up from the ground and join with the rays beaming down from the sun to envelope the creatures in muggy hot discomfort. The women and girls all wore sunbonnets and soft cotton skirts with long sleeves to protect them from the relentless sun, but even so the pervasive warm days seemed unbearable at times. The menfolk viewed the steady heat in direct contrast. "Corn growing weather," they would say or "Can't grow good hay without the sun."

"We'll be putting up hay here tomorrow, Mattie," Frank shouted as he came in the back door and lowered his head into the wash basin. "Better start getting some help and dress a few chickens."

Mattie hurried to the telephone and rang the Kennedys because Minty's girls were her first choice to help when the men worked at their place.

"Jessie and Frances can come tomorrow morning, first thing," Minty told Mattie. "I can't part with my Georgie right now, though," she said with a soft giggle that started deep in her throat and always ended in her characteristic low laugh that sometimes sounded like it began deep inside her. She felt more than a little guilty that the young girl was so confined but knew she could not get through the day without her. Mattie was by far the higher-strung of the two women, her girlish giggle attesting to the restless energy within the small fragile body.

"Jessie and Frances will be fine," she answered. "They get along well and work so nicely together."

"Charlie will bring them over first thing tomorrow, Mattie."

Mattie grabbed her sunbonnet and hurried outside as she had much to do before evening. Once outside, the bright sun startled her and she stood a minute adjusting to its light. She watched in wonderment at the shimmering heat waves slowly rising from the earth, and at the sod covered pasture with its pale lime color warping upward into the broad rolling plains. The cottonwoods all around the homestead were rippling in the summer breeze. These trees were magnificent on this early summer day, with their bright green leaves shimmering and reflecting light like jewels, first silver, then gold when a gust of wind blows through them, and clattering softly like oriental wind chimes.

Mattie suddenly snapped out of her reverie and headed purposely for the hen house. She grabbed four nice young roosters, who immediately began flapping their wings. This stirred up the dust into a swirling cloud and agitated the other chickens from their slumber. The confusion and musty smells that were within the dust cloud made the henhouse an unpleasant place to be. She left hurriedly and began preparations for the meal tomorrow.

Later that evening when the last rays of the summer sun dropped over the horizon and twilight enveloped the world in its pale purple haze, the land began to cool a bit. Mattie took little Mary to the garden and they picked the last of the June pea crop. The whole family hulled the peas before the last rays of light left. She placed the harvest in a big crock, washed them, and then set them in a cool place for the men to enjoy tomorrow.

Early the following morning, the Kennedy wagon bumped into the yard with the two young Kennedy girls. Charlie was driving and feeling mischievous. He drove the wagon a bit too fast and cut the corners short to the delight of the sisters sitting beside him. Although they squealed and scolded, they loved every minute of the forbidden fun. He jumped down and helped them out of the wagon, then headed off to find the Obert men. Charlie always had a little time to visit. He had a quiet, bashful manner but was a good listener and a good conversationalist.

The girls entered Mattie's kitchen, knocking softly as they did. Mattie was delighted to see them. She had a special affection for Minty's girls, especially little Frances. She had a pet name for the little girl who was so different from the rest of the Kennedy clan. She called her Fanny. The other three girls had Minty's oval face, her deep-set brown eyes and light brown hair. They also had inherited her hollow cheekbones and full round lips. Fanny though, like Charlie, had a square face from the Kennedy side. Her eyes were blue and her hair fair. She had high, well-sculpted cheekbones and her skin was very pale, like porcelain in contrast to the swarthy coloring of the other children. Yes, Mattie thought, Fanny with her bashful manner and her slight air of serenity was her favorite.

She greeted the girls and immediately had them sit down to peel apples for the pies, telling them to carry the peelings out to the chickens when they were done and then start peeling potatoes. They were willing and cheerful workers and soon the preparation for this enormous meal was well underway.

Lee drove into the yard about this time with the two blocks of ice Mattie had sent for first thing this morning. They were lying on the clean blankets she had carefully lain in the back of the wagon. Mattie and the girls carried out the two big tubs and with the help of Lee put the blocks of ice into the tubs. They carefully carried the tubs into the little back porch and placed them on the wooden stand just inside the doorway. Mattie then poured the freshly boiled and strained tea over the blocks of ice and immediately poured buckets of fresh well water into the brew until it was the color of clear amber. She then tasted it and was satisfied that the strength would be just right by noon when the menfolk came in to dinner. As an afterthought, she stepped out the back door and quickly picked some fresh wild mint leaves and floated them in the tub of cold tea. This would add a little fresh zing to the refreshing beverage. It was these special touches that made Mattie so admired among her neighbors.

Out in the hayfield, where the neighborhood men were working so hard, it seemed as if the day were heating up by degrees every minute. Frank's two boys and Charlie Kennedy were working the top of the haystack, known to be the hardest and hottest job and therefore usually taken by the homeplace

CHAPTER 8 37

work force. Frank took off his hat, shook off the sweat, and gazed up at the dazzling inferno baring its blistering heat upon the land. He wiped his forehead with his arm and noticed Stub and Charlie were leaning on their pitchforks, talking. He had a good idea what they were talking about and didn't like it a bit. As he was about to holler at Stub and give him a little hell, the water jug came past. He took a long bracing drink of the cool water and looked up again to see the two boys back at work.

The stack was well formed and well packed and, with the good drying weather, he knew it would be good feed for the livestock next winter. He was glad he had not chastised the boy in front of the men. He had a quick temper and he knew it. He was working on controlling this shortcoming and was doing better as he grew older. When the row being raked was finished and loaded onto the stack, Ern Kennedy looked toward the sky and noticed the sun straight up above.

"Time to take our noon break," he shouted. "Looks like noontime."

All hands gratefully laid down their rakes and pitchforks, left their machines, and led the horses back to the farmstead. The horses were watered and wiped down before the men went in for their own respite. This ritual was especially important to Ern, who loved his horses and never let a day go by that they were not curried and brushed. His horses were known to be the most pampered animals near and far, a fact of which he was most proud.

After the noon meal was finished and the men back in the field, the women busily cleaned the kitchen.

"How is your little brother, David?" Mattie asked.

"Oh, Mz Obert," Jessie answered, "he got up out of bed when he wasn't supposed to and threw his hip out a little. Mama just cried and cried cause the doctor said he would walk with a limp, and as he grows up, one leg will be a little longer and he will lean to one side."

Jessie had a prim, very ladylike manner and as she told the sad story she was so intense that Mattie couldn't help but smile. Still, she was sorry about the unfortunate turn for the little boy.

As the sun lowered and the afternoon heat slowly gave way to evening, the men returned and began departing for their own places to do their own evening chores. Mattie told Lee to drive the two Kennedy girls home.

"Sure, Mom," he said, very eagerly.

Stub only grinned. He thought of a remark, but wisely decided against it. Stub rode along and once Frances turned and smiled at him. She is a nice girl, Stub thought. Pretty too. But he was a bit too young to appreciate the opposite sex properly yet; and he was much too shy.

Georgie was in the yard watching the little boys, thus allowing Minty a little rest before the evening chores began. Lyall and Kenneth were chasing a ball. When the Obert wagon drove in the games stopped and the two girls ran to the little boys to play with them a bit. Lee walked over to Georgie and tried to think of something to say that would interest her.

"Sure hot," he said with his slow grin and blue eyes twinkling.

"Sure is," she answered.

They leaned against the wagon and talked for a short time. Georgie telling Lee she felt sorry the men had to work so hard in the hot sun. Lee telling Georgie it wasn't so bad—that the sun actually helped a little, keeping the muscles and joints warm and relaxed. Minty called for the girls to bring the little boys inside and Lee and Francis crawled up on the wagon to head home. It was time for chores and a rinse in the tub this evening.

Frank Obert surveyed his hayfield and the fruits of this day's labor with satisfaction. He noted the stacks were large and well packed. They were numerous this year, maybe even more than most years. This cutting of alfalfa was a good quality with an abundance of green leaves. Before cutting, it was a myriad of purple flowering heads. He took one last lingering look before heading home and thought how the hay stacks looked like giant loaves of bread fresh from the baker's oven, all lined up together against the fence.

CHAPTER 9

Inevitably the summer advanced into July, which always presented the high plains country with a few weeks of the most miserable heat of the summer. The hot dry winds from the south blew relentlessly, grating on the nerves and sucking the energy from the people and from the crops alike. There had been no rain for weeks and the people who relied on the land would scan the horizon every hour or so, looking, hoping for a cloud bank forming in the west. The sky remained clear from horizon to horizon, with the deep blue being unblemished and unending. Minty and the children spent a good part of their day carrying buckets of cold well water to the tomato plants. They hoped they could survive until August when the weather would moderate, the winds settle, and the late gardens produce the final harvest.

"We can afford to lose the cucumbers," Minty told the children. "We can live without pickles, but we have to have our tomatoes for winter provisions."

So they continued carrying the buckets day after day. The early garden was done—the beans and beets picked and canned, and the potatoes and onions dug and put away in the cellar. Saving the tomatoes was the new purpose in each hot summer day.

That evening the Kennedy children thought it was too hot to sleep in their upstairs bedrooms. Indeed, they thought it was too hot to sleep in the house itself.

"Please let us sleep out in the barn tonight," they begged Minty. "We'll take our blankets and pillows out there and clean them all up tomorrow morning," they promised.

Minty was laughing her soft, low chuckle and finally conceded. They all let out a war whoop and headed for their bedrooms. Later that night, after their blankets were arranged in the hay and they thought everyone asleep in the house, they jumped in the horse tank to play and cool off. This was not allowed and they knew it, but it felt so good and was so much fun, it was worth the risk. As the night became quiet, and the dark deepened, the children were not feeling nearly as brave as earlier. A little rustle and squeak could be heard around the feeding area as the children began to settle in their blankets. The girls were queasy about mice and rats getting in their blankets and started fussing. Soon an eerie "whoot, whoot" began to sound somewhere outside. Adding to the strange sounds, a coyote started its spine-tingling song not too far away, then a chorus of yips and howls were added to the medley, followed by a long, terrifying wail. As if on cue, the children all grabbed their bedding and headed for the house as fast as they could go. Inside, they tried to be quiet and not wake their parents, but kept bumping into one another and giggling. Presently dad was standing in the midst of the confusion.

"What seems to be the trouble?" he said with mock irritation.

"Thought maybe it was going to get too cold out there," David answered. "It's too hot to sleep upstairs," he continued. "Can't we make our beds here in the parlor?"

"Oh, all right. We'll try it one night to see how it works out."

He helped them make their beds on the floor and then headed back to bed for a little sleep before dawn broke on another hot summer day.

The following morning everyone was feeling tired and drained from the never-ending heat and sleepless nights. July tended to do this to the mortals living on the plains. It drained the lifeblood right out of a human trying to exist through the worst of the summer. Minty was organizing the bucket brigade again and David was resisting as usual, saying his leg hurt or he couldn't carry a bucket because he was hurt.

Charlie said, "Mom, you baby him. You always have. It's not just since he hurt himself."

The other kids chimed in their complaints in agreement with Charlie. Georgie tightened her lips, gritted her teeth, and muttered to herself as she turned away from the table, clearing the dishes from breakfast.

"Be kind, children," Minty begged. "He hurt himself so bad and he will always have a limp."

The boys turned dejectedly away to go fill the buckets and start watering the large Kennedy garden for another day.

As soon as the Kennedy clan had all dispersed to their bedrooms to get ready for bed that evening, Ern said, "Minty, I want to talk to you." She stiffened a bit and knew immediately what was coming. There had been much complaining and antagonism lately and always about this same subject.

"You have to make David carry his share of the load, Minty," Ern said kindly. "He will have to learn to work with his disability, to compensate and make do. It's no favor to the boy to make him a baby."

"I know, Ern," she conceded softly, "it's not just his injury."

She went ahead to explain that she didn't worry about Charlie. She always knew he would be fine as he is good at everything he tries. He is well above average as a student, an outstanding athlete, and gets along well with people. Forrest also is independent and self-reliant, and she knew he would also be able to care for himself. She went on to confess that she worried about David because he was not the student that Charlie was and now that he was injured, she feared he would not be able to farm or work for the railroad as he had always planned. Ern soothed her worries and tried to convince her that she must let go and let David forge his own path.

"I'll try," was all she could promise for now.

In the evening a few days later, Charlie was wondering when to bring up the biggest request he had ever made. He had graduated from the eighth grade this year and was thinking about his future. He decided there would never be a better time, so took a deep breath and spit it out, "I would like to go to high school this fall, Dad."

There. It was said. Let the chips fall as they may he thought.

"Oh, Charlie, Dad couldn't get along without you here," Minty was the first to react to this surprising development.

CHAPTER 9

"How would you get there and back home again every day. What about stormy weather?"

Ern struggled greatly with this request. He had loved school and wanted more education himself, but had not had the opportunity. He felt like he missed something important and did not want to deny his children the education that he had longed for. But, he also could not get along on the farm without help from his sons. He finally said "If you can stay and work with me on the farm for now, we can try to find a way for you to go to high school."

After some discussion a tentative plan emerged. Charlie would work on the farm for three years until Forrest graduated from the eighth grade. Then Forrest would work on the farm while Charlie was away from home at high school. Charlie might also be able to continue his education at Lone Tree School while he was working at home. The school normally only went to the eighth grade, but schools and teachers were usually flexible in helping students to get an education. Plus, Ern was on the Board of Directors for the school and knew there would be no objections to helping Charlie with his education.

CHAPTER 10

August began just as viciously as July and promised no relief from the miserable heat. The pastures were split with dry ravines and gullies, the grass dry and brittle. To add to their concerns, the cows were not giving much milk and the milk was not rich with cream, making the cream money less. The fields were cracked and dry like spider fractures and even the trees were looking wilted and forsaken.

Ern and the older boys came hurrying toward the house, shouting that a cloud bank was forming in the west. Everyone ran from the house in great excitement and studied the horizon as if their life depended on it. Through the dusty haze the storm clouds were indeed gathering and building quickly. The sky was darkening, the clouds looming eastward in black, billowing masses and now the distant sound of rolling thunder could be heard behind this cloud formation. It began to seem threatening even to the small children.

"Everyone to the storm cellar," Ern ordered.

Wind preceded the storm, sweeping the earth like a heavenly broom, dust and debris flying away with every new gust. Minty and the girls went into the house to shut the doors and windows, then headed for the cellar with the rest of the family. With the door shut to the outside, it was dark and musty. The children became restless and were about as frightened of the cave itself as of the raging storm outside. Dim flashes of sheet lightning could be faintly seen through the chimney and the sound of rain pouring down in a torrential onslaught, sluicing over the mounded cellar, was heard even in their underground shelter. Outside a steady onslaught of sheets of water were pouring from the bloated skies, watering the thirsty land, cooling and refreshing the earth and all its inhabitants.

As the storm had started, suddenly and without warning, it was over. The thunder was distant in the east and overhead just a gentle drip, drip sound could be heard. The family slowly climbed the steps out of the cave, Ern taking the lead and looked around apprehensively. No damage could be seen so far. The frogs were chirping eerily from the creek, giving their approval of the water from heaven. The earth looked fresh and smelled clean with the fresh scent of newly fallen rain still in the air. A rainbow formed across the sky and the sun played peek around the clouds as they rolled eastward, turning vivid purples and mauves as though disgusted with the disruption in their tantrum.

The family entered a world newly washed and refreshed. The garden looked revived and sturdy. The corn had regained its vitality and stood green and strong.

"Truly a million dollar rain," Ern said reverently. "No damage, and yet a good watering for all the crops. It should be a good year."

The Obert family, like all the other families living on the high plains that day, came slowly out of their cellar.

"Glory be," Mattie offered softly. "Our Lord spared us damage again and watered our world at the same time." She slowly crossed herself and whispered, "Thank you Lord."

Frank was always mystified at her personal relationship with her Irish God. He was just as devout in his own way, but his Teutonic God was to be feared and obeyed. He did not have a relationship on such a personal level as did Mattie.

Because there was mud everywhere, the family could spend the rest of the day leisurely. The family took their time finishing up the evening chores, then spent the evening resting and relaxing. Rainy days were a real luxury on the farm as they slowed the pace and gave much needed tranquility to the summertime frenzy. Supper was also more relaxed that evening and Francis thought it a good time to bring up the subject he had been dreading. Frank Obert was in such a good mood this cool, damp evening that the young boy couldn't think of a better time.

"Charlie Kennedy wants to go to go to high school," he said a little tentatively.

"Umph," Frank grunted, "Oldt Grandpa Kennedy came out after the Civil Var and homesteaded his place. He bought the place that Ern and Minty started on and helped them with their first house. When they outgrew that house, he helped build them the big house they live in now. They can afford such nonsense, but our family came out later and had to pay for land that someone vas selling. It took your mother and me veeks to get here from eastern Nebraska in our covered vahgon..., Lee vas yust a baby," he added almost as an afterthought. "It vas a hard trip. Ve can't afford such nonsense in this family."

The conversation seemed to be finished for the time. Stub didn't have the nerve to pursue it any further.

August had mellowed into mild, sunny days with playful breezes blowing whimsically, as if to apologize for the misery July had caused. Frank Obert took advantage of the damp wet earth to have the boys help him fix fences during this respite from working the fields. They were mending fence along the northern and largest of his pastures when he straightened up, put his big hands on his waist and bent his back to relax tense muscles. Frank surveyed his land looking over the open grasslands and gentle rolling hills to the fields of corn and feed. He drank in the warm sunshine and soft breezes on his face, and noticed the boundless blue sky into the distant horizon.

"Life doesn't get any better than dis, boys," his thoughts suddenly formed words and surprised even himself. "To own your own piece of land, to be able to verk it and, best of all, to have your boys verking side by side mit you. You have to verk like a team to make a farm profitable. No, sir, dis is the best life in the verld."

Stub ducked his head and became engrossed in the job at hand, his heart sinking at the sound of the words. The subtle message had been received and carefully filed for further discussion on another day.

Later in the week, the damp earth had dried and dust was again blowing in the August breeze. Occasionally, a dust devil could be seen twirling and twisting up and down the dirt roads or bounding over the fields. Lee and Stub were playing a game of burn-out in the front yard. Each one threw the baseball as hard as he could into the other's glove to see which one gave in first. Suddenly, Lee stood up and stared at the road leading toward their house.

"Look at all the dust, Stub," he shouted excitedly. "It's a car, Stub, it's an automobile and it's coming this way."

Stub ran to the corral fence and crawled up to see the road a little better. Lee crawled up a way on the windmill.

"It's Uncle Jim," they both shouted together and began to wave in wide arcs as if swimming in deep water. Uncle Jim jolted the machine into the driveway and jerked to a sudden halt. He was waving back and hollered, "Hi Ho, Buckaroos," as he climbed out of the automobile.

"What kind of car is this?" Lee asked excitedly.

"It's a Ford car and her name is Lizzy, Tin Lizzy," Jim answered with a laugh.

"Can we have a ride in it?" the boys asked in unison.

"Sure you can and real soon, but first I want to see me sister, Mattie," and Jim headed for the house to surprise Mattie with his unexpected visit. Inside he crept up behind her and blinded her eyes with his hands, "Guess who?"

"Jim." she shrieked and at that he picked her up and swung her around.

"Mattie, me darlin'," he said, "it's good to see you again and those boys of yours are growin' like weeds to be sure."

Jim had not lost his Irish brogue as had Mattie for he had stayed close to the original immigrant group. His speech was melodic and lilting. He was built like Mattie, short and rather sturdy and had a devilish mischief in his eyes. Wherever Jim Harkins was, fun was sure to follow.

"I'll be takin' the lads into Red Cloud to the picture show tomorrow, Mattie," he announced. "Tom Mix is playin' there and I know they'll love seein' him."

The next day, Jim and the two boys headed down the road towards the Nebraska border with a holiday attitude, for indeed this was the biggest thrill the Obert boys had experienced in years, maybe their whole lives. As they rode along the high plains of Kansas in the open automobile, they felt as though they were riding on top of the world. Along the bluffs that lined the valley, Jim stopped and parked. He sat quietly enjoying the scene ahead of him, the gentle slope from the bluffs into the valley ahead and the little town sprawling along the river. The hazy mist that enveloped the area muted the colors of the summer scene. Presently, he snapped out of his reverie and called the boys to get back in and they headed down into the valley toward Red Cloud.

The boys proudly sat in the front seat beside Uncle Jim and hoped the uppity town kids would see them make their entrance in the newfangled machine. Just as they hoped, their arrival did not go unnoticed. They saw some of the kids staring at them going down the main street, eyes wide and mouth agape. If ever two boys enjoyed sweet revenge, it was this summer day entering this small town in Uncle Jim's wonderful machine.

Uncle Jim parked along the street and the boys jumped out excitedly. He gave the boys some money and told them to meet him back at the automobile at five o'clock. They weren't used to such freedom or to so much change in their pockets. Both boys headed for the picture show building as fast as they could go and stood in front of the building until the doors opened for the afternoon matinee. They were waiting for Uncle Jim at five o'clock sharp when he came into view, his step lively. He had another surprise for them, and when he told them, they couldn't believe his words. They thought he must be teasing them.

"Eat in the cafe?" they both asked. "What will we ask for? How do you do it?"

"I'll show you," he assured them and headed them toward the fanciest restaurant in the area.

The boys studied the white cloth on the tables, the fancy glassware and silver in wonderment. The waiter came to take their order and they could only look at Uncle Jim in total exasperation.

"Three steak dinners with all the trimmings," he ordered. "Oh, and bring the boys some soda."

Going home that evening, the boys thought there could never be a more exciting day than this had been. The Tin Lizzy bumped along the narrow gravel road back toward the Kansas plains with two very happy young boys holding a memory they would never forget.

Uncle Jim ushered the tired little boys into the house and brought out the gifts from his suitcase for the three Obert children. A doll for Mary, and a Macmillan Classic for each of the boys. He showed them how the books were small enough to carry in the bib pocket in the front of their overalls.

"Carry them with you all the time," he told the boys "and read them every time you have a spare moment."

Lee's book was 'The Virginian' and Francis' book was 'Oliver Twist.' They agreed to trade books after each had finished reading his own and trundled off to bed happily with their new treasures.

Mattie and Jim stayed up for a few minutes of private conversation after everyone else had retired. They had been the last of a large family. It had really been more like two families—the first eight all close together, then a space, and then Jim came along and Mattie soon after. Their father had called them the "caboose." They grew up looking after one another and protecting each other. They were very close and confided everything.

"I see why you and Frank love this country," Jim told Mattie. "I used to wonder because it is so different from eastern Nebraska where we were raised." He told her how he had admired the grasslands rippling in the wind like the sea, with waves rolling over the hills. He also told her how the country was not monotonous as most people believed, but that the land had an inverted beauty. The little creeks and many gullies and ravines cutting deep into the grassland were beautiful, meandering across the low flat pastures that were lined with trees as far as the eye could see.

"I especially love the valleys with their luxurious bottom lands," he added. "Things seem to be going well for you, Mattie." It was more a question than a statement.

"Things have been real fine lately," she assured him. "Frank has not let his temper run away with him since his bad trouble with old Stan Leeds." She explained how Leeds had pressed charges and Frank had been put in jail.

"It was hard times, Jim," she said quietly.

She had walked all over the neighborhood, holding little Lee's hand and carrying Francis in her arms, to get a petition to get Frank out of jail. The good neighbors all loaned money to put up a peace bond and the men took it to the courthouse and brought him home. The case went to trial and the jury found Frank guilty, she related to Jim. She had not talked of this incident to anyone since it happened and gave a little shudder even now as the memories returned.

"Well now, what did Frank do to make this Leeds so angry?" Jim asked gently.

Mattie tried to explain the situation to Jim as well as she could but confessed she had not really understood herself what had brought all the trouble about.

"It seems as though this Stan Leeds is a wealthy and prominent cattle buyer. He goes through the country buying cattle and then drives them home to his place to fatten and sell for quite a profit. He was driving a herd home one day and passed through our pasture and apparently a couple of milk cows got in with his herd. He just took them along with the rest of the herd and never offered to make it right with us," she explained. "When Frank tried to get his cows back or force Leeds to pay him for them, he denied he had taken the cows. Frank had no way to prove that they had been taken and eventually they were sold with the rest of the fat cattle."

"Later," Mattie continued, "Frank was helping the neighbors, the Sullivans, butcher. To make matters worse, it was Christmas day," she told Jim "and they had just killed the critter and laid the loaded gun in the wagon when Leeds drove his fancy carriage into the driveway."

CHAPTER 10

As was explained to her, Frank just lost his senses and picked up the revolver and took after Leeds, shouting threats to him. When Leeds ignored him, Frank shot over his head. "Not once," Mattie said with tears in her eyes, "but twice." Leeds panicked and ran into the house and, of course, everyone there panicked as well. Leeds had Frank arrested and put in jail, and pressed charges against him. Some testified in court that Frank had tried to kill Leeds and had shouted at him, "You son of a bitch, I want my money," Mattie told Jim with a quivering voice. "It was such a humiliation. I could hardly hold my head up for such a long time. Our good neighbors stood with us and helped us out of the trouble, even paying Frank's bail."

Jim put his hand on Mattie's shoulder and patted her, "It's all behind you now, little sister. I think Frank has learned a lesson here and seems to have his temper a little more controlled."

"Yes," Mattie agreed, "Maybe it's God's will and in the end will make Frank, and myself too, better people. Maybe we needed to be humbled. I'm sure we are stronger for the experience now."

They went on to more pleasant conversation and shortly said their goodnights and headed for bed, tired but content. It seemed good to have one another to confide in again. Mattie knew she would miss Jim when he left in the morning, but she had her memories of their childhood and carried their close friendship in her heart.

The next morning the Obert family all stood waving goodbye as Uncle Jim rumbled out of the yard in his Ford Tin Lizzy. They felt sad to see him go but had a warm afterglow from all the fun he had brought into their lives. It was late in August and school would soon start again for Mary and Francis—if Frank would allow Francis to attend another year. Francis felt sure that he would be allowed to as there had been no mention of it and even Lee had been allowed to finish sixth grade. After that, "heaven knows" was Francis' attitude.

CHAPTER 11

"The year's at the spring
And the day's at the morn;
Morning's at seven;
The hillside's dew-pearled;
The lark's on the wing;
The snail's on the thorn;
God's in his heaven-
All's right with the world!

—by Robert Browning" Stub muttered so fast it was unintelligible, and then slammed his book shut with a resounding kerplop, partly to entertain the children and partly to make certain they wouldn't suspect that he really did like poetry. He knew that if the boys, particularly the bigger boys, knew that he liked poetry they would tease him mercilessly. The teacher frowned at him and he only grinned back with that impish look he knew she could not resist. His black eyes were sparkling with gleeful mischief; his whole demeanor showed his delight in this being the last day of school. He would soon be outside in the glorious spring day—free for a whole summer.

Miss Johnson sighed and said with a smile, "Class dismissed. See you next fall." The children let out a whoop of joy and headed for the door and freedom. They had spent the morning playing the customary last day of school games: three-legged races, sack races, marbles, jacks, ball throwing, and foot races. After lunch they were each assigned to recite a poem about spring, and then this year was over.

Miss Johnson had at some point determined that Francis needed more work to do and had started him working ahead. This solved the problem of his disruptive behavior, but she could clearly see another problem arising. He would more than likely finish 7th and 8th grade simultaneously next year at twelve years old. If he should go on to high school, and she was certainly encouraging him to do so, he would start while he was still twelve. That seems very young for a boy to leave home and live on his own all week she pondered to herself.

Well, she decided to shrug off all the problems from the schoolroom for this year and enjoy the summer herself. She pushed all the worries of her students from her mind for now, cleaned the room and her desk, and headed for the house where she had roomed and boarded all year long. She intended to pack her things quickly, have the host family drive her to Esbon where she would catch a train home—home for the whole summer. The thought was intoxicating after the responsibilities of managing the schoolroom, keeping the fire going, washing the windows, and caring for the whole student body all year. The students scattered, skipping happily, each along his path toward home. The Kennedy brood all cut through the pasture to shorten their trip and Francis and Mary Obert scuttled in the opposite direction along the narrow dirt road leading to the Obert farm about a quarter of a mile away.

CHAPTER 12

The summer days gave way slowly to the cooler shorter days of autumn. Indian summer continued well into the fall with its warm breezy days and cool starlit nights. Frank kept Francis home from school one week to help Lee plant the wheat in the bottom field just east of the home place. He was afraid the fall rains would come and the bottomland would not get planted on time.

"Harness up Babe," he told them, "and plant dis field extra thick." If we get some rain, the bottom will grow a good crop of wheat." The boys led Babe and the planter slowly down the dirt road toward the wheat field. When they go to the field, Stub looked the situation over carefully. "I don't see why Babe can't plant this wheat all by herself," he told Lee.

"What," said Lee in surprise.

"Well, here's how we can do it. We can each get at one end of the field. The field is flat and straight. We can read the books Uncle Jim brought us that way. When Babe gets to one end we'll just turn her around, slap her on the rump and send her the other way."

"Oh, I don't know, Stub," Lee answered. "If Dad catches us, he'll kill us, or worse."

His eyes were wide with excitement for a plan that could be risky, but could be fun, and the element of danger made it that much more appealing.

"Uncle Jim told us to read our books every chance we got, Lee, don't you remember that?"

"OK," Lee finally agreed, "but if we get caught, don't whine to me cause you remember it was your idea."

The boys situated Babe in the direction of the first round of planting, one boy on each side of the field. Lee set sites down the field, made sure everything was in working order, and gave Babe a sharp slap on her rump. She headed slowly, but surely down toward Stub who was comfortably propped against a shade tree and already reading his little book. When Lee was satisfied that Babe was pulling the planter and this thing might work after all, he settled himself with his book and thought this was not such a bad idea after all. Before long, Stub heard Babe snorting and looked up to see her heading for the edge of the field where he sat. He got up, turned the big workhorse around, slapped her rump and started her back toward his brother. The afternoon passed slowly, with the boys reading their books and Babe planting the wheat.

Unfortunately, Frank Obert finished mowing his hay patch earlier than expected and decided to walk over the hill to check on the wheat field the boys were planting. As he approached the top and the scene on the bottom patch became visible, he exploded into a sudden rage. The old uncontrollable temper that he had struggled with all his life was unleashed. He headed toward the house with a vengeance in each step. Mattie was startled as the back door flew open in a fury as if a vicious storm had suddenly blown up and attacked her house. She knew immediately that something was wrong and that Frank was in danger of getting himself in trouble again. She could tell by the determination in each step and the dark, threatening look on his face, "Where are you going, Frank?" she demanded.

"I'm going to get the BB gun and shoot at doze two boys," and he headed for the bedroom where he kept the guns safe in the closet. Mattie's heart skipped a beat and she felt dizzy. "Now Frank, you come here right now and sit down. I'll get you a glass of cool water," Mattie said sternly, her tone of voice startled Frank as he wasn't used to her giving him orders. He walked slowly to the chair she was pointing to and sat down like an obedient child, a bit bewildered by her sudden commanding manner. She brought him the water and moved behind him a bit in order to massage his shoulders, and then his neck in an effort to relax this distraught man. As she rubbed the back of his neck she coaxed in a softer voice. "What did the boys do, Frank?"

"The boys made Babe plant the veat all by herself," he nearly shouted. "Dat damned brother of yours and his books, doze boys were sitting on the side of the field reading doze books and Babe vas planting the veat."

Mattie had to suppress a smile and was glad she was standing behind him for he would be furious if he could see her smile at his predicament.

"Let's think of another way to punish them, Frank. Remember the other times you got mad and got yourself in trouble with a gun?"

"I vasn't really going to shoot dem, Mattie. I vas yust going to shoot in the air and scare them."

Mattie managed to calm Frank down and they reached an agreement as to the manner of punishment that would best serve the situation. Frank walked back to the hay field, brought the horses and mowing machine home. He rid himself of much of his frustration by currying and brushing the horses, after which they were fed and watered and the evening chores started. Soon the two boys returned, leading Babe and the planter toward the barn.

"How did the planting go boys?" Frank asked.

"Fine." Lee answered but sensed something ominous in his father's voice that made him suspicious.

"Dat's goot and now you boys von't have to vorry about vat costumes to vear at the Halloween party at the schoolhouse next veek."

Francis' head jerked spontaneously, his eyes wide. "Why?" he asked suddenly.

Lee was glaring at his little brother and only muttered under his breath, "I told you so."

Francis hung his head with the realization that he not only was in trouble with both his parents, but also with his big brother Lee. This next week is going to be long and hard he thought. To miss the party was bad enough. To be in bad standing with his parents would be miserable, but to have his big brother mad at him all at the same time was going to be unbearable. Oh how he dreaded these next several days.

CHAPTER 12

CHAPTER 13

The winter had been kind to these prairie farmers, the weather mild and the snows gentle and soft. The snows lay on the fields like a soft comforter, protecting them from the cold, and when melted would provide needed nutrition for the coming growing season. The spring planting was well under way and many farmers were in the process of beginning the haying season. Life was busy but the farm families were contented as the crops were looking good, especially the winter wheat. Frank Obert took the boys into Esbon one afternoon in late spring, and after the supplies had been purchased, stopped into the local feed store for a short visit.

The feed store was the local hang out for the men of the area. Out of habit, they gathered around the wood stove, even in summer when it was not used. Chairs were set around the old stove and a counter behind it served for the overflow to lean against. Many of the regulars there were older, retired farmers who had moved into town, but still liked to talk the "farm talk." They never tired of hearing the news from their former neighbors and enjoyed watching the young boys grow up and begin their farming careers. Of course, they loved most of all to give these young people advice. Many of the Obert neighbors were among the group this afternoon and the topic of conversation as Frank and the boys walked in was the fine condition of the wheat this year. Emmett Johnson was discussing the unusually mild weather the Midwest had been enjoying this year.

"Weather in this country is as fickle as the village whore," he offered.

As the men laughed, Lee and Stub looked at each other, a little unsure as to what their reaction should be. They didn't know quite yet if they were expected to understand these grown-up jokes, or if they were still expected to be innocent— too young. They grinned a little, looked down and then around the room. No one was paying any attention, so they concluded that they were now considered old enough to join the society of men. Amid the laughter, old Henry Dobbs was not to be outdone.

"Yeah, weather in Kansas is like a woman, teasing you all day with soft, warm breezes and then changing suddenly to a storm."

"It can be cold as a spinster's kiss at noon and within an hour hot as a firecracker," offered Carl Young, grinning with satisfaction at the laughter he received.

Stub considered all this good-natured banter and decided men liked to entertain each other when they gathered in conversation. Each one seemed to encourage another and they all competed for the last laugh. He decided it was going to be fun to be a man someday.

Old Grandpa Snow was leaning against the wall, smoking his pipe thoughtfully and enjoying the raucous group. He had long ago rented his farm and moved to town, but stayed alert through his keen interest in the current crops and in the young people growing up in the community. Grandpa Snow never missed a baseball game and knew every boy on the team, what position they played, and how good they were at it. He admired the Obert boys, not only because they were good ball players, but he recognized a fine character developing in both of them. He also liked their devotion to each other.

"Best field of wheat I've seen this year, Frank," he suddenly joined the conversation. "That field on the bottom just north of your hay field."

Frank Obert turned his head toward Grandpa Snow with a gleam of pride in his eyes.

"My boys planted dat field," he said a little arrogantly. "Going to be fine farmers, doze boys."

Francis shot a look at Lee, his dark eyes flashing in anger. Lee only grinned, his blue eyes twinkling in amusement. How can Lee always be so good-natured about everything, the little brother wondered. I wish I were more like him. I will be more like him he decided and grinned back at this big brother he respected so much.

Later, the father and sons were loaded into the wagon and heading home. Father Obert, singing his old German songs, was happy as he could be. The two boys jostled and joked most of the trip home. Typical of children their age, they had long forgotten the ordeal of the past wheat planting and were looking forward to the spring planting.

At home, Frank suddenly announced, "If you children vant to go to the barn dance at the McCarty place next Friday night, you vill haf to catch up on all the verk you missed this veek."

The three Obert children looked in astonishment at one another, not believing so much fun could happen in one summer. Frank explained to Mattie that the barn they had been building for the McCartys would be finished towards the end of the week and they planned to have a big dance there, while it was still clean.

CHAPTER 14

Dinner at the Kennedy house was unusually quiet and trouble free. The family knew there was going to be a new baby any day. Kenneth and Lyall were being unusually good. The rest of the children had long ago learned how to behave at the table so Ern and Minty were enjoying a relaxed conversation and carefree respite. Charlie had something on his mind and recognized this as being a fine time to ask for favors with everyone in such a good mood.

"Are we going to get to go to the barn dance at McCarty's, Dad?" he suddenly asked, a little too loudly and persistently.

"Well, Charlie, I hadn't thought of it. Mom can't go and I wouldn't go without Mom. I don't see anything wrong with Charlie and Forrest taking the wagon to the barn dance, do you Minty?"

Ern looked at Minty to see how the idea set with her. Minty sat up a bit as the idea of her children growing up and being old enough to go to a dance by themselves was a little hard for her to accept. After careful consideration, she answered, "I don't see a thing wrong with it, Ern, as long as they're home by 12:00." She noticed Georgie lower her head and sensed her disappointment. "I think the boys should take Georgie along, Ern." Minty suddenly suggested. "She never gets to play or go anywhere. She stays here and works all day."

"Sure Mom," the two boys agreed in unison. They didn't mind taking Georgie. All the children loved their gentle, kind Georgie.

"OK, then kids, just be home by twelve," Ern told them.

Georgie raised her head and her big brown eyes sparkled radiantly. "What will I wear? How shall I fix my hair?" A million other questions were dancing in her young head.

A jolly mood prevailed as the three Kennedy kids bumped along in the wagon, dressed in their Sunday best. Georgie, with ribbons in her hair and sitting between her two brothers, was proud as the Queen herself. The two boys were so excited at being out on their own and given responsibility for their sister that they were feeling carefree and very grown up. They arrived at the McCarty place, tied up the team and wagon, and helped Georgie down from her seat. The barn was alight with lanterns, and the cheerful music from the band wafted throughout the warm night air. They entered and immediately got caught up in the atmosphere of celebration.

The Obert family had already arrived. Frank and Mattie were whirling and marching to the rhythmic commands of the caller. He called the square dancing much like rappers of a later date would chant rhythmically to the music with their messages. Lee was standing aside and leaning against a post watching the merriment when he noticed Charlie, Forrest and Georgie enter through the side door. He was so startled to see Georgie that he jerked slightly, and then composed himself and headed in their direction. He intended to try to give the impression that he wanted to talk to the boys, but when he neared their corner he blurted, "Want to dance, Georgie?"

"I don't know how to dance, Lee," Georgie lowered her eyes and blushed.

"It's easy. I'll show you." Before long the young couple was one-stepping back and forth in rhythm to the music. Frank and Mattie danced alongside them and each gave them an encouraging smile, then spun away in a swirl as the waltz music swelled into a crescendo. I'll never be able to dance like that Georgie thought. Mattie was known to be the best dancer in the neighborhood. She had a style and grace in her movements and impeccable rhythm.

The band consisted of a fiddle player, a guitar, a harmonica, drums, and special for tonight: a piano. The McCarty's were exceptionally well-off and even owned a piano. The McCarty boys had carried it to the barn for this special dance tonight and it added a real touch of class to the evening.

The caller now announced another square dance and the people began forming squares. Georgie told Lee that she couldn't possibly square dance so they ambled off toward the refreshment table. It was made of two barrels with boards laid across that were groaning under the weight of all the food brought in by the neighborhood ladies. Each dish was the household specialty so a finer assortment couldn't be found in even the grandest dining establishment. The children filled plates and went off to a corner to watch the next dance set. The night air seemed to thicken as the evening advanced, gathering up the aroma of Mrs. McCarty's petunias and the wild roses growing around the barn and in the pastures. The soft scents wafted in through the open barn door and at the same time the lamps' glow diminished to a soft flicker that gave a surrealism to which the young boy and girl were unaccustomed. Neither child knew what to say and began to pick at their food and shift uncomfortably on the bench.

Fortunately, the square dance began. The music had a lively rhythmic beat and gave the two novice socialites a diversion. They both looked up to follow the marching, twirling couples go through their sequences when the call for the grand promenade was given. The couples marched proudly, men taking short strides to accommodate their ladies, and ladies with their heads up stepping lightly on their toes with an imperial air as if they were European royalty. Indeed, no grand ballroom in the eastern United States or Europe could have seemed finer to these Midwestern farmers than this newly built barn in northern Kansas with straw strewn slightly to make dancing easier and this little hometown band playing happily throughout the night.

Too soon it was time for the Kennedy children to leave. The boys brought the wagon around, helped Georgie in, and lit the lantern they had brought to help guide them home. A bright new moon streaming its white light along the roadside helped them make their way along the narrow country road. Charlie and Forrest had fared quite well with the ladies and were feeling quite proud of themselves. The big Kennedy boys with their quiet bashful manners were well liked by the local girls.

Most of the rest of the revelers stayed throughout the night and didn't try to get home before the first rays of daylight could help them find their way. The young people and adults were not the only ones having a fine time this night. Upstairs in the haymow the younger children were enjoying wild and boisterous games. Stub and Mary were in the midst of the melee, shouting and running and sometimes jumping into the stack of hay off to the side. It was good to be able to yell and run wild without adults reproaching them every minute or two. The games ran their course and by midnight the children were wearing out and beginning to tumble one by one into the hay and to fall asleep. Stub was among the last to give up, which was characteristic of this little boy with the restless energy and enormous stamina. When finally all were asleep, quiet prevailed in the haymow. By this time the dancing had toned down to mostly waltzes and polkas, leaving the last dance to be the most intricate square dance they knew.

After the last dance was finished, the women began to bring out pots of hot coffee and rolls. A large breakfast was served before the families loaded children and empty dishes to return home. These young pioneers never tired. Their bodies were accustomed to long days work and they were also capable of playing as hard as they worked. Their conversation throughout the early morning meal was lively and animated. The families enjoyed being together, as it was very seldom a party like this occurred. The wagons were loaded as the first rays of light began beaming from the eastern horizon. Children were carried down from the haymow and placed still sleeping in the back of the wagons.

The Obert family began their journey home, tired but happy, each one feeling the contentment of laughter and happy times. The music, dancing and merry-making gave a release from daily pressures and worries. Lee was especially feeling a sense of exhilaration. It was the first time in his life he had spent a whole evening with a girl, and for the girl to be Georgie was the best part of it.

Francis and Mary were sound asleep, worn out from their wild games. Soft fingers of daylight began to dance in the horizon in shades of pale oranges and mauves. The air took on a lighter, fresher texture as the morning breezes began to stir.

The dew sparkled as if handfuls of gems had been sprinkled on the leaves, plants and grasses in the pastures. Off in the distance the Bobwhite sang its good morning song. Before long the robins joined in and the meadowlarks sitting on the fence posts added to the chorus. From the treetops the little wrens added their soprano obligato and the turtledoves gently cooed rhythmically like a muted percussion section, completing this burst of harmony on the plains. Their music was as lovely as a symphonic orchestra and seemed to be created just for this special morning.

Suddenly, a crow burst into the concert with an insistent harsh caw-caw as if an out of tune musician had suddenly invaded a well-practiced orchestra. This intrusion startled the audience in the wagon and seemed to inspire Frank to add his own music. Perhaps it was the off-key crow that encouraged him or maybe it was the lovely summer morning, but soon his rich baritone echoed over the hills and valleys:

Ja, Ja, Ja, Ja, weisst nich wie gut ich dir bin.

And then a little softer he sang the first verse:

Du, du liegst mir in Herzen,

Du, du liegst mir in Sinn.

Du, du machst mir viel schmerzen,

Weisst nich wie gut ich dir bin.

The rousing chorus had awakened Francis and little Mary and when the verse was finished, the whole family joined into the chorus: Ja, Ja, Ja, Ja weisst nich wie gut ich dir bin.

The family finished their journey home in this gay mood. As soon as they arrived the morning chores had to be done. The whole family changed clothes and finished chores as their remaining energy allowed. After completing the morning work, a light lunch was eaten and everyone rested an hour or two in the afternoon. Restored by the short rest, the work was finished for this day and all were eager to submit to an early bedtime, even the children who usually resisted going to bed.

The next afternoon, the Kennedy children found Minty was lying down. She announced that it would not be long before they had another brother or sister. "Dad has gone to bring Mattie here to stay with me until the doctor gets here," she told them. "If the doctor can't make it, Mattie and I will have to do this by ourselves. Dad has started the fire in the parlor and opened the door to our bedroom so it will be warm in there. Before long I will go to the bedroom. Georgie will fix your supper. Frances, you help Georgie with the baby, and Jessie you help take care of the two little boys."

Soon Ern appeared with Mattie right behind carrying her little carpet bag that she kept ready by the front door at all times. The three disappeared into the bedroom, leaving six little children sitting at the big kitchen table in wide-eyed astonishment—a little frightened and full of anticipation. By the time Ern returned to the kitchen they all knew the baby was in the process of being born and all wondered how this thing could happen. Ern looked at his growing brood of children and felt amazement that he and Minty had brought this about.

The doctor arrived right after supper was over and disappeared into the mysterious room. Very shortly he emerged again and announced that the Kennedy clan had a new baby brother.

Ern gathered them around the warm kitchen stove and told them that the new baby would be named Byron.

Whatever am I going to do with another little boy, Georgie wondered.

Little Vivian was disappointed. "All I ever get to play with is boys." She was nearly in tears.

Ern laughed. "You can be my playmate, Vivian," he said gently. "Now let's all go to bed. We've had a big day."

Georgie looked up as the kitchen door opened early the following morning and was relieved to see Grandma Kennedy coming in to help the family get off to school. She tried so hard, but could not quite cope with the enormous responsibilities of this large family.

"Georgie, you just get yourself around for school now, and I will take care of the little ones, dear," she said kindly. She then put the little boys at the table with a firm yet gentle admonishment:

"You stay there now, til I get the baby ready for breakfast." She then washed and dressed the baby, put him in the high chair and placed breakfast in front of the three little ones.

The school children were bundled and sent off to school and another day was beginning.

Grandma surveyed the task at hand, shook her head and wondered where to start. She went into the bedroom where Minty lay with the new arrival. Grandma looked the baby over carefully. "It's another fine healthy little boy, Minty. Grandpa came along to help Ern outside and I'll take care of the house today."

"I don't know what I'd do without you, Mother Kennedy," Minty answered, and closed her eyes for a soothing nap while the baby slept beside her. Grandma tiptoed out of the bedroom and began the tasks of kitchen work and caring for the children.

Outside, Ern stopped to scan the horizon and reflect on the past years that seemed to be an endless parade of babies. They were a big happy family—the children all with loving dispositions. Minty had instilled a sense of sibling affection and loyalty; he was grateful for that. Yet, he wondered how many children were to be their lot.

Grandpa Kennedy walked up behind him, "Ern, I came to help out today, whatever you need. Congratulations on the new baby boy."

"Thanks, Dad," Ern answered.

They both knew this was enough babies for one family, so the thoughts between them remained unsaid. The men worked outside caring for the livestock and Grandma Kennedy worked in the house caring for the babies. Later the school children returned home and changed into their chore clothes and were soon helping finish chores for this day. And so another day on the prairie ended, peacefully and without incident.

CHAPTER 15

Charlie Kennedy packed his bag as he prepared to return home for the summer after his freshman year at Mankato High School. As his father had wanted, he had worked at home for three years after graduating the eighth grade. After Forrest graduated the eighth grade and started his turn working on the farm, Charlie finally was able to attend high school.

Charlie stayed at the YMCA in Mankato during the week and took the train to Esbon on weekends. By the time Charlie could go to high school, he knew that he wanted to go to college and needed to go to school in Mankato. The Esbon High School did not have the classes needed for college. He had taken the ninth grade at Lone Tree School, but was taking it over again to get the education he would need for college.

He was staying an extra day in Mankato to attend the Honors Convocation as he had an inclination that he was going to receive an award or two. He knew he had done well in his schoolwork, and also that he had done unusually well for his freshman year. He didn't take all the credit for his successes. He was older than most of the boys and much larger. He was by nature large framed and tall, with long legs and arms like his mother, and muscular from the farm work he had done as soon as he was old enough to hold a pitchfork or carry buckets. He packed his school clothes into his old carpetbag, left the YMCA, and headed for the high school auditorium in a light and cheerful mood.

As he neared the high school his schoolmates were arriving from all directions. Soon the happy chatter of teenagers floated in the warm springtime air. The lovely mild morning with its soft mists veiling the bright sunshine only added to the exhilaration the young people were feeling this day. They entered the auditorium and slowly their lively conversations softened and then ceased altogether as the faculty members began to take their places at the podium.

The students were systematically seated according to class, group affiliations and all the things that make up the high school hierarchy. Charlie sat with the other boys who played on the athletic teams. The music students mostly sat together, the popular girls sat together, and so forth. The teachers brought the program to order and began the ceremony. Charlie was pleased when his name was called for the honor roll for the freshman class and more so when they awarded him a letter in every sport for his first school year there.

The superintendent was very lavish in his praise for this young man and mentioned that to his knowledge no one had ever lettered in football, basketball, baseball and track his first year. He left the auditorium in high spirits as if nothing could spoil this most perfect day of his life. As he boarded the train for Esbon, he could not wait to show his parents what he had accomplished his first year of high school.

Though he was in a great hurry to get home, he decided against calling his father to come pick him up. Somehow that would spoil his moment of glory when he told his good news. He wanted the whole family to be there, at least both his parents, so he decided to hitch a ride to the end of the highway and walk the last few miles home. He thanked his benefactor as he jumped out of the old truck that had picked him up outside Esbon and bumped and jostled him along the highway to the turning off point as the highway bent westward. He slung his bag over his shoulder and walked eagerly down the narrow dirt road that led to the Kennedy homestead.

It was a beautiful day and he drank in the fresh early summer air as he rehearsed his speech so that everyone would be properly impressed. His long legs striding steadily made the walk in half the time most others could manage. He entered the driveway and quickened his steps, feeling excitement and anticipation both at being home again for the whole summer and for the story that he had to tell.

Now that his attention was not focused on school, he realized how homesick he had been for this big house and this big family, even for all the little brothers that sometimes were a

CHAPTER 15

nuisance, wanting him to play ball or games with them. He entered the warm kitchen where Minty and his sisters were always occupied at some task or another. When they noticed him enter they surrounded him all at once.

"Charlie, we're so glad to have you home," Minty told him. "It seems like something's wrong when you're gone. Sit down and we'll fix you some milk and cookies. Viv, go tell dad Charlie's home."

This time Vivian did not complain but headed out the door as fast as her legs would go. Charlie sat at the table and watched the girls and Minty flutter around the kitchen. He noticed for the first time that Minty had grown thicker around the middle. Her face had lost its youthful firmness and there were strands of white in her thick, rich chestnut hair.

About that time Ern came strolling in the kitchen door. Charlie got up, but somehow the exuberance of the day had suddenly disappeared and his reunion with his family lost its luster. Perceptive as Charlie was, he failed to notice the dark and introspective mood that Ern seemed to have acquired.

Ern had always accepted life with an acquiescent attitude. He had long ago learned to be satisfied with his lot and to make the most of it. Even Minty hadn't noticed the change in Ern, during the past year or so. She was so busy with her children and kitchen that one day blended into the other and nothing seemed to change for her. He sat down at the kitchen table across from Charlie and said he wanted to hear about how his first year at high school had ended.

Charlie told them all to sit down that he had some good news for them. He said that he had made the honor roll and that he had lettered in every sport in the high school. Minty looked puzzled.

"Lettered? What does that mean, Charlie?"

Charlie laughed and explained to her how when you get to play enough in all the games they reward you with a letter to wear on your sweater.

"And honor roll? Does that mean you got the best grades?" she asked, her eyes sparkling with tears forming and trying to hold them back so he wouldn't think her an old fool.

"No, Mom, just among the top bracket in the ninth grade."

"You've made us all proud, son," Ern offered.

That evening when the whole family gathered around the big table with the two benches along each side, the younger brothers were insatiable in their curiosity about high school sports. He had become their hero and all were asking questions at once until Ern had to bring some order to the table. The Kennedy household was for the most part fun-filled but organized.

When the din quieted down some, David told Charlie that Pleasant Plains school over toward Mankato was bragging all the time about having the best baseball team in the county.

"They haven't been beaten this year," he said "and they think they're really something wonderful."

"We could beat 'em," Kenneth piped up. "We have a great team at Lone Tree this year."

"Yeah," all the others agreed. "Teacher told us we could challenge them to a game next Sunday afternoon if you would coach us." Forrest suggested, a little timidly. "I could pitch, and Stub Obert could catch. He's turned into a really good catcher this year," Forrest added.

Charlie thought the situation over a bit. He knew the pitcher for Pleasant Plains threw the ball like a pistol shot and for that reason everyone called him Gunner. He also knew that if they could get onto that fast pitch the ball would go clear into the next county. His two little brothers could play outfield and the other boys could play the bases. Yes, he reasoned, I think I could put together a real good team.

"OK," he answered, "tell her the game is on for next Sunday afternoon, and I want practice Saturday afternoon with everyone there."

Pure pandemonium broke out at the dinner table with even the girls joining in. Maybe Jessie thought, Charlie might be short a player once in a while and put me in. Frances just liked

CHAPTER 15

to go watch her brothers play ball, and Georgie hoped that maybe she could go along that day to watch. Minty made popcorn that evening and let the children stay up a little past bedtime to play cards and games.

Saturday morning broke warm and still, just as if the young ball players had special ordered it for their practice day. The Kennedy boys all loaded into the farm wagon and headed for the schoolyard. They worked the first hour to mark off the bases and clean the debris from them, then built the pitcher's mound and made the catcher's place nice and level. Soon the other players began arriving. When young Stub Obert came hustling around the driveway Charlie was surprised at how the boy had filled out. He still had a small frame, but had grown wiry and strong. He was muscular from the farm work he had done since a small child.

"I'm going to make you catcher, Stub," he announced right away.

"Oh, great," he answered.

Stub loved to catch and he had a good arm. He only wished Lee could be here to play second base. He and Lee were so used to catching for each other that he knew he could put more runners out if Lee were there. Charlie worked the boys, practicing basic plays over and over again. He also had batting practice with him pitching to them. He had a fastball like the Pleasant Plains pitcher, but with much more control. If the boys could get used to batting his pitches, he knew they could win this game. In the meantime, he had Forrest over near the outhouse, throwing a rubber ball to a circle he had drawn. This should give him more accuracy in his pitches and, hopefully, throw more batters out.

After a good practice, Charlie sent all the players home with the instructions to wrap up their day early and get a good night's sleep. Sunday morning broke murky and damp. There was a chill in the air as if winter were trying for a comeback. Now and then a warm breeze slipped in from somewhere attesting to a power struggle between the two seasons. Later, the incessant prairie wind that blows during the spring and early summer whipped up from the south, gathering strength and keeping the air filled with wisps of dust. Charlie intended to tell his team this would be a benefit to them. Even though it would make playing the game a little uncomfortable, the wind would make it hard for the opposing team to get a good hit from them, but if they connected with Gunner's fast pitches, their ball could still sail.

The Lone Tree team arrived early, excited and nervous, and started warming up the infield to settle their nerves. Charlie was hitting balls to the outfield. Before long the Pleasant Plains team arrived in cars and wagons and gave a war cry that made the Lone Tree boys cringe. The purpose was to intimidate them and it worked. Charlie called them over for the final pep talk and told them he would forgive any errors they made or any outs they made, but he would not forgive them if they did not hustle. For that matter, he told them he didn't want to see any of them merely walking to and from their positions between innings. He wanted hustle all the time, to the field and off the field.

The umpire arrived, pulled his hat around, ceremoniously wiped home plate, stood erect and cried, "Play ball!"

The Lone Tree team took the field first. Stub Obert wore his overalls, work boots and old felt hat to keep the sun out of his eyes. Forrest, the pitcher, took pitcher's mound in a pair of Charlie's old dress pants, now worn out and too big around the waist. He pulled his belt real tight, pulling the pants askew, and puckered. His old work shirt was too big and he also wore his old chore boots. The McCleary boy headed for first base in a pair of hand-me-down pants that were also too large. He had suspenders to hold his pants up and an old work shirt and hat. They were a rag-tag team that looked like orphans from a far distant war. When the Pleasant Plains team took their place around the batting zone, they were uniformly dressed in old uniforms purchased from some town team. They were mostly too big and ill-fitting, and somewhat worn out with patches and loose seams, but to the Lone Tree boys they looked like a professional team from a faraway city.

CHAPTER 15

Charlie gave the nod to Forrest, he took a deep breath, a big wind-up and let go the first pitch. It was right in the pocket, surprising the first batter, and popped right into Stub's glove. Stub grinned at Forrest, rose and fired the ball back to the pitcher with a very decisive pop as it landed in his glove. This also surprised the batter. Maybe this game isn't going to be as easy as we thought, he mused. Forrest wound up again and threw the ball with deadly accuracy, the batter swung and missed. "Stree-ike two," shouted the umpire. Another pitch, the batter swung, hit a little whiffle ball directly to second base. It was caught and one batter down. The next batter hit a high ball directly to center field, it was caught and two were down. The third batter hit a slow grounder between first and second, it was picked up by first base and another runner was out.

Elated, the Lone Tree boys lined up to bat while the Pleasant Plains took the field a bit dejectedly. Stub was leadoff batter as he was fast and a good base stealer. He was also hard to pitch to because of his small size. He watched the ball closely and drew a walk to get on base. Forrest was next batter up and got a little grounder toward first base. It was scooped up easily and he was thrown out, but not before Stub had advanced to second. McCleary came to bat next and struck out, which brought up David, the power hitter. He hit a hard grounder to the outfield that was too hot to handle. The center fielder bobbled a split second, enough time to allow Stub to steal third base. The fielder was a bit rattled by the error and threw the ball so high it sailed over the catcher's head. At that moment Stub saw his opportunity to steal home plate. He put his head down and started running madly like a mindless machine and slid into home plate safe. Lone Tree had one run on the board. The next batter was Kenneth, quite small and scared to death. He hit a soft little pop and it was caught. Thus ended the first inning, with the score Lone Tree 1, Pleasant Plains 0.

The next two innings were scoreless for both teams. There were a few errors on each team and much good fielding that made the game exciting for the spectators. In the fourth inning a Pleasant Plains batter hit a high fly to outfield, which the fielder misjudged. With a series of little hits and errors the runner eventually made his way to home plate. After four innings the score was Pleasant Plains 1, Lone Tree 1.

At this time the game ceased to be fun and took on a purpose. Both teams were determined to win this game. The inning ended with no score for either team. In the fifth inning a few Lone Tree boys got on base but couldn't make it clear around to home plate. Nor could the Pleasant Plains team. They were beginning to get very worried. They had not even considered that this little team of unknown country boys could beat them. The sixth inning was much the same—the score remaining 1-1. The top of the seventh inning showed Pleasant Plains threatening, but the inning ended with no score. They felt they could hold the Lone Tree team in the bottom of the seventh and beat them in overtime. The Lone Tree boys were no less worried. Someone had to do something to get them out of their hole. The first batter up was McCleary, who popped out.

Then it was Dave's turn, he took the bat with confidence, stepped to the plate and closely watched the pitch. It was a hard fastball and Dave hit it square. It had so much momentum that it became evident right away that the ball was going out of the playing field. Dave motioned to his little brother Lyall to run the bases for him and the game was over. Lone Tree 2, Pleasant Plains 1.

The celebration and jubilation were so spontaneous that the opposing team climbed quietly into their wagons and headed home, their heads between their knees. They were very nearly heartbroken. Ern had walked to watch the game so that he could drive home with his brood of children.

Charlie hunted for Stub after the game and found him in the middle of the celebration.

"Good game, Stub," Charlie said sincerely and patted his shoulder. "How is school going?"

Stub told him that he had finished seventh and eighth grades together this past year.

CHAPTER 15

"I sure would like to go to high school with you next year, Charlie," he told him. "My dad hasn't said a word about me quitting school. I know he doesn't like it, but maybe he'll let me go if I want to."

"Stub, you're only twelve. Could you get along away from home? If you think you can manage it, you could live in the YMCA like me and come home on week-ends."

"Yeah, sure," Stub answered. "I'll get along just fine."

He headed off then for home, wondering where his funding was going to come from to pay his bed and board for a whole school year in Mankato.

The weather had turned decidedly chilly with a cold mist blowing in their faces. They only now began to notice the weather with the excitement wearing off a bit. None cared though. There was nothing that could dampen the spirits of this new championship team.

Ern Kennedy loaded his brood in the wagon and headed home. He tended to be quiet and withdrawn, but was kind and caring. He was first and foremost interested in his large progeny of offspring and enjoyed each of his children. He was especially proud of David today. The boy had outgrown his resentment toward his disability and had blended into the family unit again. He was also proud of Charlie. He had done such a wonderful job with the children. Somehow he knew that Charlie was going to be successful. In what direction, he had no idea, but he knew it deep down.

The wagon slowly plodded home as the clouds began to roll in, dark and boiling. The rain picked up strength, but the wagonload of Kennedys didn't seem to mind at all. As the wagon pulled into the yard, the weather was becoming blustery. The rain was falling harder and the wind blowing.

Ern said, "Let's get the chores done quickly and spend the evening in the house. We'll start a good fire in the parlor and celebrate this fine day."

The Kennedy tribe entered the kitchen and found that Minty had ham and bean soup simmering toward the back of the cook stove. The warmth from the stove felt so good and the aroma of the soup was in every corner of the kitchen. There was a sweet smell lingering in the air as well. The children examined the kitchen and found two big applesauce cakes sitting on the pie cupboard.

Minty had the two little boys washed and ready for bed before feeding them. When the family arrived, she was in the middle of stirring up pans of cornbread to go with the bean soup she had given them.

Charlie looked around the big homey kitchen and thought how sad it made him to leave this wonderful family—this comfortable home where he had a deep sense of belonging. And yet, he knew he must leave. There was something driving him. There were things he had to do and he didn't quite understand why. Minty was overjoyed to hear all about the game and thoroughly thrilled at the Lone Tree boys' victory.

Ern soon delegated the chores. Kenneth and Lyall were to carry the firewood onto the back porch. He would start the fire in the parlor and Jessie and Francis were to keep the fire going. Georgie and Vivian were to help Minty in the kitchen, and the three older boys were to help him finish the chores. Before long, the family was seated at the table. The conversation was of course going over every detail of the game as the Kennedy family enjoyed a happy evening.

CHAPTER 16

After the baseball game, Lee and Stub started walking from the schoolyard toward home. Stub explained how Charlie Kennedy had suggested that he attend Mankato High School with him next fall.

"I think you can manage, Stub," Lee told the little brother. "Dad's satisfied that I'm home helping. Why don't you talk to Mom alone when you get the chance?" Lee had grown into a strong sturdy teenager by this time. Frank Obert was pleased with Lee. He saw him as a good farm hand to help enlarge his operation. He did not at any time consider that Lee might grow up and leave.

"Do you think Mom will help me?" Stub asked hesitantly. "Most of all I need some money to help pay my board and room."

"I think she will, Stub. She has a little money put away from her eggs and butter."

Mattie jigged for joy when the boys told her about the wonderful success that afternoon. Frank, however, merely listened politely. The only thing that really impressed Frank Obert was a good day's work.

Later that evening, after the chores had been finished and supper over, Stub helped Mattie with the dishes while Lee and Frank started the fire in the parlor stove. He carefully explained to her the chance he had to go to Mankato with Charlie Kennedy and the need for cash for his rent in the YMCA, a little food during the week, and train fare to and from Mankato. Mattie assured him she would take care of "Poppy" and that she had some money put away from her eggs and butter. She told him she would make a little more butter to sell and keep more laying hens for the following winter for a little extra cash money.

Stub accepted this with a great deal of relief, but wondered what she was going to say to Father to bring him around. After thinking about it a bit, he still couldn't imagine, so he decided to let it be and to let Mattie decide how she would handle this situation. He never was to know what Mattie did to take care of this situation, but father Obert never fussed after that about Stub continuing his education.

For the rest of the summer Stub worked hard and did everything Frank asked him to do. He felt some apprehension that he might at any time tell him his schooling was finished, but toward the end of the summer nothing had been mentioned. Stub began to relax a bit and make plans with Charlie for the adventure soon to come.

CHAPTER 17

All too soon the glorious summer was over with its freedom and special summertime occasions. Stub and Charlie were on the train heading east toward Mankato amidst the splendor of autumn. Both boys were quietly looking out the window watching the countryside slip by. Young Stub Obert was apprehensive. He had never been away from home, least of all to live and to take care of himself. He watched the homesteads on every corner of the section with happy children playing, the chickens, the houses, and felt a real pang of homesickness already. Finally Charlie broke the silence, "Your brother and my sister Georgie seem to really have a romance going. They spend the whole evening together at the neighborhood dances and when there is a box supper, Lee always buys her box. They find a corner and seem to have eyes only for each other."

"Yeah," Francis answered. "Lee really does like Georgie. I've known that for a long time."

"My other two sisters, Frances and Jessie think you are cute too," he grinned at the little boy.

Stub hung his head and blushed. He was too young to know how to react properly to these things.

They soon arrived at the Mankato depot, picked their bags up and headed toward the main street in the county seat of Jewell County, Kansas. Other boys got off the train with them, but they were all strangers to them. They were coming from all parts of the county. Young country boys like themselves from every corner.

All of these young farm boys found the YMCA about the same time. They introduced themselves and felt relief to have so many boys like themselves, feeling somewhat lonesome already. The younger boys were more frightened and unsure. They each claimed a cot in the big dormitory room, made up their beds, unpacked their few meager clothes and looked the building over. It was an oblong red brick building with four steps leading up to the door. It seemed quite intimidating to the boys who were used to their own warm homes with family waiting as they entered the door. They found a kitchen in the back where they could cook their meals if they wished, at least breakfast. Maybe they could figure a way to get a meal now and then somewhere else.

The following morning, after a restless first night away from home, all the boys headed for the high school building. Stub and Charlie stopped to look the big brick building over before entering. It was the biggest building Francis had ever seen, with many big, wide steps leading up to the front door. The anxiety for young Francis increased as he sized up the situation. He couldn't imagine how he was going to find his way around in that big building. How am I going to know where I'm supposed to be and how to find it, he wondered. Charlie headed toward the stairs with confidence and a very timid little boy following right behind.

The new student body spent the first day signing up for classes with the teachers advising which classes each student would need. Charlie was ready for some advanced courses. Francis was advised to take first year algebra, first year Latin, English and history. They were shown where each class would be held and then introduced to all their teachers. All the boys were feeling better by the end of their first school day. Most crawled into their beds early and fell asleep from sheer exhaustion and stress.

After the first day, school quickly became routine, every day the same thing, the same classes. The new became normal. They were kept busy and for the most part happy. Charlie joined the athletic teams right away, but Stub was too small and too young. He did, however, get to scrimmage with the older boys. Charlie would laugh during his visits home and tell how Stub could scamper around the field, "like a little mouse. He would go over us, under us and sometimes between our legs. We couldn't catch him." He thought it was too bad the boy wasn't a little older and a little bigger. He would make a fine football player.

Mid-way into the first semester Stub established himself as the top of the Latin class. He didn't understand it himself, but the conjugations, the changes in adverbs and adjectives, plurals and possessives, all fell together for him. He did study, but not much more than the other students. One day during class, he managed to translate the whole lesson both from English into Latin and then from Latin into English. The whole class stood, put their arms high in the air and bowed, "Hail Caesar!" they chanted in unison.

Amused, the teacher also stood up, put her hand to her forehead and bowed saying, "Hail Caesar."

After that, the little boy who had become known as Stub throughout the neighborhood suddenly became Caesar. By the end of the year the whole student body knew him as Caesar.

Toward the end of the semester, Charlie was home for the weekend when his beloved grandfather Kennedy died. He died sitting in his chair on a winter Sunday afternoon. The clock in his house happened to stop at about the same time. Charlie had helped him dig potatoes just the day before. Charlie and his siblings were inconsolable. Their grandfather had always done for each one of them considerate and special things. He was available to them for help with their problems, big or small. He had made their little wooden wagon with the big iron wheels, fixed up the donkey cart, and created hundreds of other little bits of memories. Ern was devastated. This was the father he had worked with all these years, who had always supported him and never let him down.

Ern was the child his father, Charles Kennedy, had brought out to the Midwest on the train after the end of the civil war. The train line went as far as Red Cloud, Nebraska and there they spent the night in the livery stable. They took a wagon into Kansas and homesteaded on land that was still part of the family farm.

Grandma Kennedy did not know what she was going to do without him and had a most dismal outlook on life. It was decided that for the time being she would spend a few months at a time with each of her children, until she could decide what she wanted to do.

Stub Obert suddenly felt lonely and afraid the first night that Charlie stayed home with his family. After he had finished studying his lessons, he went outside to sit on the steps and morosely ponder life and death. He pondered about all the strange things that happen to make people go their own separate ways and find different things to do with their lives. His thoughts were most profound this winter night as he looked up at the sky, wondering where God lived and where the angels stayed.

The winter sky was an inky blue. A waning moon made it very dark, with a myriad of stars twinkling out of the dark sky. A marvelous world like this attests to a God in the heavens doing what it takes to keep this world running right, he thought as he got up and headed to his warm bed and soothing sleep.

Charlie took a week off from his studies and returned, weary and blue, but ready to get back into life again—knowing he must. The semester passed, a vacation for the holiday seasons, and then back again to a new and exciting second semester.

At the end of the semester, the boys packed, boarded the train and headed home for another glorious summer vacation. They watched the countryside passing as they rode, and the meadows tinged with green gave them both spring fever with no small amount of excitement for the summer activities yet to come.

They hitched a ride and then walked the country roads to their homes. Francis entered the driveway leading down to the farmstead. He immediately noticed the large flock of chickens Mattie had managed to accumulate. He felt more than a little twinge of guilt for making his mother work so hard to help him through high school. Mattie loved her flock of chickens he knew, but he also knew she had a heavy workload and didn't need the extra work.

About that time the big black rooster that Mattie called Sultan came strutting proudly around the corner of the hen house.

CHAPTER 17 83

His feathers were shiny, blue-black with white tail feathers and a bright red comb. His color was dazzling and his demeanor comical. He protected his harem of white hens like a maharaja from India. He was proud of himself and did not care who knew it. Francis laughed out loud at the pompous rooster and headed for the house. Mattie was in the kitchen stirring her famous chocolate cake that she only made on special occasions. She considered this, the homecoming of her second son, a special occasion.

"Mom, I've got a job for next year working at the soda fountain in the drug store. I can work after school, and on weekends. Maybe sometimes I can come home Saturday night or Sunday mornings."

"Stub, I really don't mind, but if the extra money will help, I think it would be fine," Mattie answered.

He explained to her how the other boys were playing football and basketball at those times, and he was too young and too small and would just as soon be doing that anyway. Thus, the second year of high school was beginning to be lined up.

Stub, like Charlie, noticed for the first time that his mother had thickened around the middle and had sprays of gray in her light auburn hair that was thinning. She still wore her hair up in the little bun, but she was aging and it was noticeable. She had lost the spring in her step, although she still was quite spry. She could do nearly the same amount of work in a day, but she moved slower and showed exhaustion more quickly. He hated to see Mattie grow old. He would have liked to keep her always young, always the young mother with so much spirit and fun. He resolved that this could not be and grudgingly accepted this new phase in his life.

The next year of high school was much like the previous. Both boys were now comfortable in their new lives. Charlie was taking more advanced courses. Francis was taking his second year of Latin and chemistry was added to his curriculum. Algebra was not easy for him, but chemistry came as easily as his Latin.

The teachers were taking great interest in this little boy with such a fine mind. He seemed to enjoy learning and had a very curious mind. The more he learned, the more he realized he did not know. This began his life-long quest for learning and searching for answers to virtually all the questions the world inspired. His social life was successful, as he was well liked, got along with everyone, and the boys found him fun to be around.

Their families were adjusting to the absence of a child. The boys were becoming self-reliant and, for the most part, were over their homesickness.

In March, when Charlie was home for a weekend, a new baby brother named James was born. Another little boy, Charlie thought. That makes four in a row after Vivian. I hope this will be the end of it. Mom and dad are getting worn down with eleven children.

The Arminta and Ernest Kennedy family circa 1918.
Back row left to right: Charles, Forrest, Frances, Georgia.
Middle row: David, Ern, Minta holding baby James, Jessie.
Front row: Lyall, Kenneth, Vivian, Byron.

CHAPTER 17

CHAPTER 18

Georgie came down stairs early one spring morning, the house still chilly from the long winter, and headed for the warm stove in the kitchen. Minty was alone, with the exception of the younger boys popping in and out of the kitchen, playing their games.

"Mama," Georgie said suddenly, "is it a bad thing for a Protestant and a Catholic to go together?"

Minty answered, "Some of my best friends are Catholic, and I think they are fine people. I have nothing against the Catholic Church; their faith is the same as the Protestant churches. Their rituals are a bit different, but I think if people understood them, they wouldn't be so threatened."

"But Mama, Grandma Kennedy talks so bad about Catholics and some of my friends in school say they do strange things in their church and chant a strange language. Grandma says it is just wrong for Protestant and Catholic to get married."

Minty thought carefully. How could she answer this question? She did not want to undermine Grandma's authority, yet did not agree with her philosophies.

"Grandma was an Irish Protestant. There is a lot of hate between the Catholics and the Protestants in Ireland. Grandma was raised that way and she can't help it, but I don't altogether agree with her. Maybe though, it would be better if young people married within their own faith. It would take some stress out of the marriage. Married life is hard enough at best," she added almost as if she were thinking out loud.

Georgie considered this dilemma all throughout the weekend. The following Friday night, Ern drove the older children to the dance. Lee caught Georgie before she entered the building and asked to talk to her before they went inside. They walked a bit away from the festivities and Lee carefully took Georgie's hand, "Georgie, I want you to be my girl," he asked with much emotion in his voice.

Georgie looked up at him and answered, "Lee, I can't. You're a Catholic and I'm a Protestant and it would never work."

Lee looked dazed with so much hurt and pain showing in his eyes that it broke Georgie's heart. He got up slowly from the bench and said, "I'm sorry Georgie. I didn't know you felt that way."

He slowly walked away toward the building, his heart so heavy he didn't know if he could live with it. Georgie also felt pain and confusion and was immediately sorry. Why did she do that, she asked herself. But she knew that the prejudices were there and would make it very difficult for them to be happy. She ran into the outhouse, leaned against the outside wall and let the tears fall in trickles. How could she live without Lee there by her side, she wondered? He makes me feel so safe and protected. He treats me like a queen. There will never be another man to make me feel so carefree. And with that she let her tears fall until she was overcome with exhaustion.

Both she and Lee sat on the sidelines during the dance and returned home heavy-hearted and troubled. Each family noticed the unhappiness in their child, but wisely said nothing. Mattie was sure there was trouble between Lee and Georgie, but could not imagine what could possibly have gone wrong. She held her silence for a week and then found a good time to gently ask Lee what was wrong.

He told her, "Maw, Georgie quit me because I'm a Catholic."

Mattie could not believe her ears, sweet, good Georgie being so cruel. She was stung, feeling betrayed by her good friend Minty and the whole Kennedy family.

"Lee, if you knew the cruel things the Protestants did to the Catholics, the harsh way the English treated us in our own land, you would be afraid to get involved with a Protestant girl anyway," she explained.

Mattie still held her grievances as a result of the stories her parents had told her about the Orangemen who came into their country, made them slaves and took away their lands, letting many starve and die. Lee wasn't much interested in the troubles in far away Ireland. He was more concerned about the

CHAPTER 18 87

here and now, about losing Georgie. He committed his energies and thoughts entirely to his farm work and stayed home the rest of the summer to heal his wounds. They were deep and he knew it would take much time to overcome this, the biggest disappointment of his life.

His younger brother sensed Lee's melancholy immediately, but said nothing. Lee was quiet, the joking had ceased and his merry, sparkling blue eyes looked sad and serious these days. When Francis got a chance to talk to Mattie alone he asked her what was wrong with Lee.

"Georgie quit him because he's a Catholic," she said simply and turned away to her chores in disgust. Francis sat in a daze, not understanding how something like that could make a difference. He couldn't believe the Kennedys, and especially Georgie, could treat Lee that way for such a silly reason.

He spent the summer working beside Lee, trying to help him overcome his deep sadness. By late summer Lee was showing signs of returning to the boy he used to be. He felt an impulse to go to the social functions again and be with young people his age. When the Obert boys learned of the dance to celebrate the end of summer and to welcome harvest time, Francis urged Lee to go with him. Reluctantly, Lee finally agreed and the brothers ventured off in the wagon after the work for the day had been completed.

The older teenagers and the more adventurous departed their neighborhood and attended dances in the next township, at the Bohemian Hall. It was big and built just for dances. The potbellied stove sat at one end with a little raised platform where the band stood. The band consisted of a fiddle, piano, drums, and another instrument. Twilight was descending as they slowly rode along the winding dirt road toward the dance hall where all the merriment took place. The sky was streaked with purples and rose hues and blended into shades of blue toward the east. It was the time of day when young people feel at their best.

They arrived amidst music already started and the laughter of young people enjoying the social moments of these neighborhood festivities. The horses were tied to the railing, watered and both boys entered the building where the dancing had already commenced. Lee caught a glimpse of Georgie, sitting alone on the side benches, looking forlorn and lonely. He felt his heart leap, then settle. Without acknowledging her, he headed toward the stag line. Georgie felt a constricting lump of emotion in her throat. She was sorry she had broken their courtship so abruptly. I should have at least talked to Lee about it first, she told herself. If only I could take it back, turn it around and make it like it used to be. She was however, positive that she could not change things now. Lee probably hated her.

Little did she know that Lee would have welcomed a change of heart and done most anything to take her back as his girl. The evening progressed and nothing changed. Georgie stayed alone on the sidelines and Lee began the rounds of girls, dancing with each one that he saw alone.

For the last dance, he asked a cute little round-faced girl with red curls fluffing around her face, big bright blue eyes and an unusual sense of fun. Before the dance had ended she had Lee chuckling in his old good-humored way and he felt she had an interest in him. She did not keep him at arm's length, but instead seemed to melt as they danced. Her warm reactions to his conversations and her interest in his likes and dislikes were very comfortable.

She told him that she was a teacher and had taught a year at Lone Tree School, but she also loved farm life and wanted to live on a farm. Georgie saw this new romance developing from the corners of her eyes as the dance ended. She noticed Lee and his new friend, Nita, talking after the dance ended. She went home with a heavy heart and felt it was getting time she left the shelter of her home and went out in the world to see if she could make it on her own.

CHAPTER 19

Another school year rolled around with Charlie moving into his senior year and Stub into his junior year. Frances and Jessie started high school together in Esbon. The two girls planned to transfer to Mankato to finish the last two years. Frances carefully explained to her parents that she wanted to be a schoolteacher, and they needed to go to Mankato for that. Of course, Jessie would go with Frances. Jessie was also thinking she might want to go to college. Since childhood, very seldom did one of the girls do anything without the other. Jessie's interest, though, was in business. She was patient and methodical and loved numbers and figures. She enjoyed keeping track of money.

In the middle of autumn, Georgie told her folks she intended to go to Mankato, find a room and a job, and try to make it on her own. Minty hated to see her go, but resolved to allow her wishes, telling Ern that if anyone ever deserved it, Georgie did. They both agreed on that point and reluctantly gave her permission to try it, but made it well understood that she was welcome to return back home anytime and to visit as much as possible.

Right after the holidays Georgie took the train from Esbon to Mankato, found a job in a business on main street, found a room, and started her new life with much apprehension. She knew that Lee and Nita had become a couple and felt she could not stay in the same neighborhood and watch them grow closer. It hurt too much. She did well in her new career and began saving a little money each month, which made her feel that she was achieving something.

CHAPTER 20

Ern had been to a farm sale down the road a few miles in early fall. He came home with the wagon filled with odds and ends that could help in a pinch if something broke around the barn or the house. Trotting along behind the wagon with much self-importance was a little gray donkey. One child in the yard noticed and the news quickly spread throughout the Kennedy farmstead. The children converged on the donkey, yelling and screaming in excitement, like kittens on a mouse.

"What'cha gonna do with it, Dad?" they shouted, and, "Can we play with him, Dad?"

"That's what I brought him home for," Ern smiled tolerantly. "You can name him whatever you want."

He went to unpack his newly acquired items, while the children began the process of training their new pet. "Let's call him Lucky." "No, let's call him Pal." "I got it, let's call him Happy," could be heard all over the barnyard. The donkey sat on his haunches as the children crowded around him and refused to budge. Minty hurried out when she heard of the new purchase, excited as her offspring. *I knew Ern was crazy over horses,* she told herself on the way, *but I never thought he would take it this far.*

When she arrived the little boys were behind, pushing the donkey's rear to no avail. The older boys were pulling from the front with an equal lack of success. Another was atop the donkey's back, kicking his sides, shouting "getteeup, getteeup, donkey." Minty stayed a short while and watched the circus, then shook her head, giggled softly and went back into the house. The children labored until chore time with the little beast, then one by one gave up and wondered off. Ern put the donkey in the barn for the night after the chores were finished.

That evening at the supper table Ern inquired with a grin, "What did you kids name the donkey?"

There was a deadly silence around the table, one child looking at the other when suddenly little Kenneth spoke in his squeaky voice, "We're not going to name that dumb old donkey anything."

Everyone convulsed into helpless laughter and from that day forward his name was "Dumb, Old Donkey." Each day for the rest of the summer, the children worked to break the donkey to ride but accomplished very little. He would follow them when they had pocketfuls of grain, and they would feed him a handful now and then. In this way, they lured the little donkey to follow them and learned that he would carry them home at a fast trot. Dumb Old Donkey at least knew where home was and that home was where he wanted to be. He did submit by the end of summer to pull the little cart Grandpa Kennedy had fixed for them. The Kennedy children traveled throughout the neighborhood in their little donkey cart. They spent many long, sleepy summer days playing happily with Dumb Old Donkey and the cart.

CHAPTER 21

The school year ended with Frances leaning toward English, drama and poetry and Jessie taking her business courses. Charlie graduated that spring as valedictorian of his class and Francis still continued to do well in his schoolwork. The four young people from Lone Tree School in the middle of the Kansas prairie were making everyone in their district proud. During Easter vacation, Charlie told his parents not to buy him clothing for graduation as he would be enlisting in the army. The year was 1918 and the war in Europe was raging. America had entered the war in the spring of 1917.

"No," Minty screamed and immediately broke into tears, almost hysterical. "Why should our boys go to Europe and fight for them? It's not our fault if they can't get along over there. Not my boy, my first born, not my Charlie. I won't have you being killed in some strange country in Europe. Their troubles have nothing to do with us," and Minty continued to cry and plead.

"Minty," Ern tried to soothe his distraught wife, "America is in this war now. All the young men are going and it's natural for a young man to want to be a part of it."

"But I don't even know what it's about," she countered.

"Well, Minty, it's about one little country in Europe named Serbia wanting to dominate other little countries called Bosnia and Herzegovina. A patriot from Serbia killed the Archduke from Austria-Hungary and the whole of Europe took sides. The leaders of some of the countries were committing atrocious war crimes, all in the interest of conquering territories to expand their own countries."

"But what has that got to do with us, with America, with Charlie?" she sniffed softly into her handkerchief.

"It got so bad that America had to join to protect her own country and to fight for the weak and old, the women and children that were being killed and abused in the occupied territories. Strong and healthy young men feel it their duty to protect the innocent citizens that are suffering and dying," he added.

Minty still did not approve but knew she could not argue anymore. Charlie's mind seemed made up. She just wept quietly into her apron, dabbing her eyes now and then and said no more.

The May morning Charlie was to leave for boot camp, Minty was again weepy. She sat at her kitchen table, cradling her head in her circled arms, sobbing softly. Charlie touched her hair, leaned over kissed her on the cheek and told her good-bye very gently and that he would write right away. His sisters were standing together in the corner sniffing softly into their handkerchiefs. All the little brothers were lined up with big questioning eyes. Charlie shook his older brothers' hands, kissed his sisters dutifully, ruffled the disheveled hair of his little brothers, and turned to leave.

Ern came in at that time and said, "I have the wagon ready, Charlie. Guess we better be on our way." The two men arrived at the train station where Charlie immediately packed his things on board the waiting train. Ern shook his son's hand warmly, patted him on the back and then forgetting decorum, suddenly grabbed the boy, gave a warm hug and turned to go with wet shining eyes.

CHAPTER 22

The following spring, Georgie met a young man named Paul Morgan who also was working in Mankato. He was an accountant, but aspired to move to a larger city and to get a better job. They courted through most of the summer and grew very fond of one another. Georgie would never forget Lee and had a special place in her heart for him where she kept the happy memories of their times together, but she knew she must move on. Paul had decided long ago that Georgie was the girl for him. She was so gentle, so kind it brought out the best in him. He liked himself when he was with Georgie and liked the feeling of peace he felt with her.

By the end of the summer Paul was making plans to leave for Denver to find a career for himself, promising Georgie that he would send for her as soon as he was settled and they would be married in Denver. He gave her his new address and promised to write every day. She accompanied him to the train station, saw him off, and immediately felt loneliness creep into her heart. She returned to her room and wrote her first letter to him that very evening.

The war ended that summer and Charlie returned in June without having left the United States. He had trained and served on guard duty and attained the rank of Corporal. His duties included transporting prisoners, and he testified in three trials. He had experienced life outside of Kansas when he was stationed in Utah and Illinois, and his travels had included New York. After returning home, he wanted to attend college and applied to Washburn College in Topeka. He did not have money and knew he would have to find work to support himself, but he was definitely looking forward to playing sports in college.

Minta was again expecting a baby. She accepted it philosophically. Minty told herself she kind of expected it. She somehow always knew she was destined to have a dozen children.

Somehow eleven seemed an odd number and the twelfth child was more or less bound to happen. Ern too accepted it as one of those things. They managed eleven children, what difference could one more make? Ern did, however, hope this would be the last one. Minty was at the end of childbearing age and he was surprised at this late pregnancy.

In late summer, baby Donald was born to Minta and Ern.

Young Obert was making plans to finish his last year of high school. He was still amazed that he had been allowed to finish this much school. Lee was courting Nita, and Francis was certain that he had marriage on his mind. He worried a bit about Lee. When Papa Obert found out that Lee intended to marry and leave to make a home and a place of his own, he didn't know what would happen. He felt guilty to leave Lee and not be there to help him when the time came. Lee had always been there for him when he needed help. He wouldn't be in school today if it weren't for Lee. Lee sacrificed his schooling for his little brother, and the little brother never forgot it. The days passed swiftly until suddenly it was the day to meet the train and begin Stub's final year of high school.

It was toward the end of the first semester that the principal left word for Francis Obert to come to his office. When Stub learned of this development, he was terrified. What did I do, he asked himself. I seem to be able to get into trouble real easy, but I really don't know what I did this time—or do I, he mused. He was breaking out into a cold sweat when the principal walked by, noticed him and came to his desk. The boy's heart skipped and his throat went dry. The principal noticed the alarm in the young boy's demeanor and laughed, patted him on the back and assured him that what he wanted to talk about was no cause for worry. He stressed that he was not in any trouble but he wanted to visit with him a little when he had time.

"I have a free period now, sir," the boy stammered, the words tumbling out.

"Fine," the principal answered. "Come into my office when you can."

Francis slowly put his things away in his desk, stalling for time. He needed to think, to be ready for whatever the principal wanted. He could not imagine so gave up and headed slowly for the office, wondering what was in store for him and feeling more than a little apprehensive. Could this be about the conspiracy to see how many music teachers we could get rid of this year, he wondered. But, why would they pick me first. I'm not the ringleader of this thing—a willing participant, yes—but not the leader. It was true they had already chased out two young music teachers and the new one was leaving class most days in tears. They knew it would be just a matter of time before she left. Their new plan was to divide up into small groups, each group picking a different song. When the teacher raised her arms to direct, the cacophony of the various songs unnerved her. She would patiently explain to them which song she wanted sung and very condescendingly they would all agree, then again each group would switch to another set of different songs and the whole situation would begin again. This usually ended with the teacher leaving in tears. Or could it be the thing with the mouse? He couldn't help grinning when he thought of the English teacher opening her drawer to find a mother mouse and her nest of babies.

When he entered the office, the principal motioned for him to sit in the chair by the desk. He, of course, was behind his enormous desk which made him look even more intimidating.

"Obert," the principal began. "I've been wanting to talk to you for quite some time now. You have shown much promise in the academic area and we, the faculty and administration here, would like to know your plans after high school."

"Umm, I really haven't thought about it, sir, I don't have any plans for sure."

"We think you would make a good candidate for college," he continued. "You show promise in the fields of science and languages. You would get along fine in say, medicine, research, biology, any of those things."

CHAPTER 22

"Where would I go, where would I get the money?" the young boy stammered with surprise.

"Kansas University in Lawrence would be nice, son," the principal answered. "You're young, only 16. You have time to take jobs, save your money and at least get started. You think about this next year, OK?" This ended the conversation but the boy did not quite know how to answer.

"OK," he finally said, "I'll think about it," Francis left the office a little muddled and confused.

This was an idea that changed the outlook of his whole life. Suddenly there was another dimension added to the life of farming or working out as a farm hand. Could he really do this thing, he wondered. He finished the year showing more fervor in his approach to his studies, especially in the field of chemistry and biology. A seed had been planted in his mind and, to his alarm, the seed seemed to grow each day.

CHAPTER 23

Francis "Caesar" Obert packed his belongings for the last time, said good-bye to his classmates, and started his journey home. He was now a high school graduate but more confused about his future than ever. He had no real goal or purpose at this time, only the nagging idea the principal had put in his head last semester. The idea of going to college intrigued him, but how to get the funding was the biggest problem. He arrived home and, without any further ado, fell into the working routines of the family farm.

That fall, Frances and Jessie started their last two years of high school in Mankato. Arrangements had been made for the girls to stay with Widow Wilson, working for their room and board. They were expected to cook, do dishes, clean and iron for Widow Wilson in exchange for their keep. After the train had arrived in Mankato and they had gotten settled in their room at Widow Wilson's, the Kennedy girls began to confide in one another.

Jessie said, "Stub Obert is a cute boy, don't you think, Frances?"

"Yes," Frances answered, "but so young. He's still a little boy in a lot of ways."

Jessie challenged, "I think he's going to grow into a fine-looking man and be successful too."

About then, Widow Wilson called the girls to come and get their routines and to tell them what she expected of them. She was a short woman, built like a robin with skinny little legs, slim hips, and gradually increasing into a disproportionate size upwards toward the top of her body. She had an enormous bosom, a big abdomen and shoulders like a buffalo the girls whispered, giggling when she couldn't hear. They noticed that she even moved like a robin. She seemed to hop around on her little skinny legs and wobble from side to side. They didn't much like Widow Wilson, she was bossy, cranky, had a sharp tongue, and was not at all kind. They knew they must get along with her, though, if they were to go to high school. In the Kennedy manner, they said nothing, treated her with respect, and made the most of their situation.

Georgie and her two sisters enjoyed spending time together in Mankato. Georgie needed support and solace as she had not heard one word from Paul Morgan. She mourned this inexplicable circumstance and discussed her fears with her sisters in their free evenings together. Neither sister could understand what could have happened with this young man who seemed so fond of Georgie. Both sisters tried to play the situation down.

"Maybe he got sick," they would say, or "maybe he doesn't have any money."

Yet, all three knew they were kidding each other. He had obviously found another girl and forgotten all about Georgie.

"Let's all go home this weekend and help Mom get ready for Thanksgiving," Jessie said suddenly. All three girls agreed this was a good idea. We'll clean and help with the laundry they all decided at once.

Minty was delighted as they walked through the door that next Friday late afternoon. "I am so behind with my ironing," she confided. "Vivian tries hard to help, but just the two of us trying to take care of all these men," and with that she grinned, thinking of all the sorts and sizes of men she was speaking of.

Saturday morning Minty was up early, with a good fire going in the cook-stove. She had the ironing board set up and the flat irons lined up in a row along the hottest part of the stove. They were soaking up heat for the enormous ironing that she had placed along the wall in baskets. She had rinsed the outer clothing in a starch mixture and hung them out to dry with the rest of the washing. When the washing was brought in, the starched articles were sprinkled with water, carefully rolled up and placed in baskets with a towel covering them, waiting to be ironed a day later. The damp material and the extremely hot irons could be a risky situation, so the girls had to check carefully before touching the irons to the good clothing. A wooden clamp was used to hook onto the hot metal irons. After a short time, the irons would lose their heat and be put back on the hot stove, and a fresh hot iron picked up with the clamp. Then the cycle would begin again, continuing until all the ironing was finished. It was hard, hot work, and the irons were heavy.

The girls took turns as one would tire and rest while another took over for a while. By mid-afternoon the ironing was finished, the noon meal over, and the kitchen cleaned. Georgie fell right into her role as eldest daughter and Minty's solid partner. She began to feel a bit homesick and wished she had never left. She was not as lonely and disparate here as she felt in her small room in town. Maybe I will consider coming back home for a short while she thought as she finished her household duties for her mother later in the day.

The holidays came and went uneventfully. Minty cooked several old hens in her big cookers, and vast kettles of mashed potatoes and vegetables to fill her hungry family. Then the two girls went back in high school and Georgie back to her job in town.

Georgie's spirits were falling daily and a slight depression was beginning to set in. She felt she was wasting her time here. The cold, dismal winter wasn't helping her outlook. Outside, the scene was like a charcoal etching, with the stark trees black against the gray sky, the white snowy ground only adding to the drabness. She made her decision to return home for a short while in February, and by March was settled back into the routine of the Kennedy household as if she had never been gone. She spent much time discussing the Paul Morgan situation with Minty, telling her she had written letters for one whole month before giving up. Minty finally offered advice.

"Georgie, some things we never understand. These things we have to put away and forget. You just have to give it up and go on with your life."

Georgie accepted this, and did try to forget and start again. She felt though, that she was not cut out to be married. I will never have anything to do with another man in my whole life, she told herself.

At Washburn, Charlie was taking classes, playing football and working at any job he could get. His various jobs included carrying newspapers, janitorial work, and sometimes being a professional pall bearer.

CHAPTER 24

Frank was pleased to have both boys home on the farm and life was relatively trouble-free for over a year. However, neither Lee nor Francis wanted to stay on the farm working with Frank.

Lee confided in Francis his plans to marry Nita, find a small place to start with and farm on his own. He knew Frank Obert would never approve and admitted to his brother he had not yet found the right time to talk to him about it. That evening Francis convinced him to broach the subject and said he would back him up. Frank behaved as expected, but Lee did not back down. Though shaken, Lee tenaciously held his ground.

Suddenly, Francis said, "Dad, I'll stay home and farm with you for a while," and then immediately wondered why he had agreed to this. Still, he knew he owed his brother the years he had been allowed to go to high school. He did not resent this commitment any more than Lee had resented his years staying to keep their father happy. It was just part of family life on a farm. He intended to make a little money from the farm work and from odd jobs around the neighborhood, and see how much money he could save in a year's time.

Lee had been negotiating for quite some time with an older couple who were ready to retire into town. Their farm was further away than he would like, but about the right size to begin his operation. A small farmhouse went with the property, and also a barn, hen house, and shed. The farm was east of the Odessa Township several miles, and the owners were ready to retire after the holidays next year, leaving the place ready to move into by summer. Lee's only problem was to get a team of horses, some rudimentary machinery, a flock of chickens, milk cow, and a hog or two to start with.

He and Nita were making plans every time they were together. Their money was not growing fast enough, but they were slowly gaining a small nest egg and felt confident that soon they could be married and start their own home.

The following March, Lee made the break and moved onto his newly acquired farm. The terms were cash rent, which was fair enough. Nita and her mother spent much time fussing over the little house, putting up curtains, finding used furniture, and cleaning the kitchen. Their wedding plans were set for later in the summer and Nita's parents committed to give them a team of horses as a wedding gift. This left Lee free to spend his savings on a plow and planter.

They were not married in the Catholic Church, which nearly broke Mattie's heart. Her church was the single most important thing in the world to her. She had raised her children as good Catholics. Her boys had been altar boys and all had learned their catechism devoutly. Mattie wisely said nothing, preferring to keep good will between herself and her children.

After the wedding the neighbors gave the young couple an old fashioned shivaree. They came in the night, woke the young couple up banging pots and pans, and generally "raising the dead," as the old saying went. They brought chickens, flour, kitchen utensils, canned goods and an assortment of things to help them get started. Now, they only needed a milk cow and they would be substantially on their feet. Nita and Lee were happy in their new life, and happy with their little house and little farm. They still enjoyed the dances at the Bohemian Hall and the social life in the neighborhood, but were equally happy just being together and enjoying their own little home.

CHAPTER 25

The Bohemian Hall in the township to the north was not only a large building with good music, but more important, the Bohemians who settled in that area knew how to have a good time. It was understood that Ern would take his girls in the wagon to the dance and be there to bring them home at a decent time as well.

The first Saturday after the homecoming, the girls were happily dipping rainwater from the rain barrels. These old barrels were placed strategically in the corners of the house where the rainwater and snow would drain into them, then the dirt and particles would settle to the bottom. They washed and fixed their newly styled bobs with the latest thing, a permanent wave, then pressed their best dresses, cleaned their shoes, and when finished put all the shampoo water together to rinse off and freshen up for the festivities. After the supper meal was over, the kitchen cleaned, and the little boys bathed and ready for bed, Ern came in to let them know he had the horses hitched and the wagon ready.

Frances, Jessie and Vivian merrily jumped up on the wagon. Georgie declined, saying Minty needed help for the evening. She still was not prepared to meet the old crowd socially or to cope with young men wanting to dance with her. She felt wounded and vulnerable yet, and the girls understood she needed more time to heal. Ern dropped his daughters at the front door of the dance hall, turned the wagon around, and slowly clip-clopped home.

The evening was soft and mild. A full moon hung in the sky and radiated a silver glow that brightened the royal blue sky. All this led to some deep meditation. He wondered if Minty regretted all the dancing and parties she had missed with the many children to be cared for. He remembered how they used to love to go to the dances, riding double on his horse when they were young. He decided that he would not trade any of his children for the fun and parties. Minty, he knew, would not either. They enjoyed their children, each with a unique personality and corresponding differences, and wouldn't change anything if they could. When he arrived home, he tied the horses to the post by the barn, watered them, brushed them briefly, and returned to the house for a little nap before going back to get the girls.

It was his habit to rest on the day-cot in the kitchen so as not to disturb Minty before everyone was home. He set the alarm for twelve midnight, lowered the wick to the kerosene lamp and lay down for a short rest. Too soon the alarm rang. He got up wearily and started out to take the wagon back to the hall. As he neared the dance hall, he could hear the spirited music and laughter coming from within. He smiled, knowing the good times these young people were having, and did not mind at all. Too soon they will have families and responsibilities of their own, and the dancing and parties will be over.

He tied up the team and walked toward the front door to enjoy watching a bit before it was time to load up for home. His habit was to stand just outside the door and peek in without being seen by the young people inside. The dancing couples were whirling around the floor. Some of them doing the newfangled dances that he considered not to be very ladylike, but kept his own council on that matter. It didn't do to quarrel over small matters he had long ago learned. With his large family, he had to concentrate on the important matters and let the trivialities go as they may. Ern had a way of dropping his head downward and to one side in a manner of humility.

His youngest daughter came dancing by with the Sloan boy from the neighborhood north, circling and swirling. At the end of the dance the boy dipped Vivian low to the floor, both laughing gaily. They were so well suited, both tall and slim, with happy-go-lucky dispositions, and both loved to laugh. Ern's head bent a little lower upon seeing his youngest daughter with a boyfriend. Well, he thought, Minty and I were about the same age when we started seeing each other, I guess.

The dance ended and the participants went to their wagons and buggies. All three of Ern's girls had other ways home that evening, even little Vivian. Ern pulled his wagon out of the yard and started once again down the familiar narrow dirt road, awash in the moonlight—harboring his own thoughts of long ago.

He entered the house, lit a second kerosene lamp to help him find his way upstairs, and left the other lamp for the children. He did not worry about the boys. They would find their own way home. He tiptoed into the bedroom, holding the lamp high. "You awake, Minty?" he whispered.

Minty turned over and leaned on one elbow, "Just sleeping lightly, Ern," she answered.

Minty never slept soundly until all her children were home and safe. "Little catnaps" was how she referred to her sleeping habits.

"Did you come home alone again?" Minty whispered.

"Yeah, got stood up again," Ern told her. "It looks like our little Vivian has found that playmate she's been wanting for so long," he informed his wife. "She was dancing with Wiley Sloan and Minty, they look enough alike to be brother and sister. They dance like vaudeville stars, and they laugh and seem so happy together. They are both blessed with a vivacious, fun-loving spirit."

"But Ern, Vivian's so young," Minty complained.

Wiley Sloan and Vivian Kennedy circa 1929

CHAPTER 25

107

Then immediately considered, "I guess about the same age we were when we started going out together." She smiled, turned over and tried to go to sleep. She knew the little boys would be bouncing in before too long to start another day.

The days slipped by and too soon the older children were preparing to leave. Charlie was to go to the train station first, to be in Topeka by the end of August. Frances would begin her first year teaching at a country school in Odessa Township. Ern especially appreciated this. He had a great respect for teachers, and especially for good teachers.

Jessie, however, deviated from the usual and expressed her wish to study stenography and bookkeeping at Fairbury Business College in Fairbury, Nebraska. Ern disapproved of this intensely and made his feelings known. Minty was quite in agreement with him. Fairbury was too far away and women did not as a rule go into business. They both thought Jessie should become a teacher. Jessie, however, was a young woman who knew her own mind and held resolutely to her goals. Ern's final word was that he would not take Jessie somewhere for some tomfool idea she had come up with. She could find her own way. Frances slipped away to her room to pack because she did not like unpleasant situations. She agreed with her sister, but did not dare speak against her parents. Jessie shortly joined her in the room they had always shared, lay down on the bed, and wept bitterly. "Mom and Dad have never been so obstinate and narrow," she told Frances between sniffs. "What has gotten into them now?"

The following morning Charlie said his good-byes and left with his father to catch the early train for Topeka. Frances was to leave the day after next. She was packed and ready and fretful of her willful sister, who had not as yet given in to their parents' demands. The morning she was to leave, Frances bid her farewells to all the little brothers, the sisters, and the rest of the family. Jessie remained in her room, so Frances kissed her good-bye as she left. Ern had the wagon waiting outside and another child was gone. Jessie did not leave her room the whole day and evening.

Early the following morning Ern tapped softly on Jessie's bedroom door, "Can I come in?" he softly inquired. He entered the room upon hearing a soft, yes, from within. "Jessie, I'm sorry I took such a harsh attitude with you. I didn't sleep all night and it suddenly came to me that the reason I couldn't sleep was because I was wrong. There's nothing wrong with you wanting to do bookkeeping," he continued. "I think my reasons were selfish. I think I didn't want you to go so far away and that I wanted you and Frances to stay together. You have been together since you were little girls. I hated to see you separate."

Jessie sat up in the bed in wide-eyed surprise. "You mean I get to go to Fairbury?" she asked incredulously.

"I will have the Overland gassed and ready tomorrow morning. Get packed. We'll start early in the morning."

Long before noon the following day, the two were bumping and jostling along the highway north toward Fairbury, Nebraska. Jessie still could not believe her good fortune. Her parents were the best, she thought as she rode along toward a new school and a new life.

They arrived at the school in Fairbury right after lunch and Jessie began moving her things from the car to her room on the top floor of the dormitory. Ern was not allowed in the girls' dormitory so he waited beside the car outside the building. When the last of Jessie's things had been carried up, she kissed her father, thanked him for bringing her, and climbed the stairs slowly up to her new room—to her new life. Tears were sliding down her cheeks as she went to her room, crying into her handkerchief.

Her new roommate entered the room and said, "Well, here you are crying up here, and down in front of the dorm a man was standing beside his car crying."

Jessie looked out the window in time to see Ern wipe his eyes. She waved a sad good-bye and watched her father get into the old car and drive away. Ern reached home in time to help finish the evening chores, and felt more than ready to retire early.

CHAPTER 25

Georgie had decided that it was time for her to go back to Mankato and get on with her life. That evening she explained her plans to her parents.

"Everyone is leaving us all at once," Ern complained. "It's like another Exodus."

Minty laughed her hearty giggle, but felt every bit as abandoned as Ern.

Jessie soon found an arrangement where she lived with a family and worked for her room and board. In a letter to Charlie, she wrote "School life is great here-(I love everything but the boys!) Typewriting comes very easy for me and, so far, I have been able to keep ahead of my class. Our work is handed in by Budget's, a certain number of perfect sheet; and I have handed in Budget 14. AHEM. A boy from Concordia is gaining on me; he is on Budget 13, but he has several advantages over me; as he gets to work on Saturdays and he is'nt taking Shorthand. Otherwise he would never see the day passing me." She also described a boy that "is my man but I'm not very crazy about him; even tho' his hair is nearly red. I am crazy about his musical ability tho'; he plays and sings very well. When he comes to see me I always make him play for me. He is a Sophomore." She signed the letter Jessie Le, which is the name she used during her school days.

CHAPTER 26

Alone on the train Georgie wondered if she would ever know the mystery of her engagement to Paul Morgan. She felt sure she would never learn the true story. But in fact she would, later in her life. Paul returned to a local celebration during their middle years, and he and Georgie happened to encounter into each other during the parade. He was quite embarrassed and stammered as he tried to explain.

"Georgie," he spoke softly. "There was a girl who lived in the same apartment house as myself when I arrived in Denver. I guess she had a crush on me because she took your letters from my mailbox and mine to you. I thought you had forgotten me and found another. You probably thought the same. Anyway, she and I were married. She kept all those letters and only showed them to me a year or so ago. If she had shown them to me earlier, I would have left her. But now, after all these years, it really doesn't matter anymore."

No, thought Georgie as she walked away from this encounter, it doesn't matter anymore at all.

In February, Ern and Minta received a letter from Charlie with a clipping from the Topeka newspaper that described what he was doing. The headline was "CHARLES KENNEDY GOES TO KANSAS UNIVERSITY." The article said Charlie was transferring to the University of Kansas to study medicine and described what a loss this was for the athletic program at Washburn. In his three years at Washburn, Charlie had lettered all three years in football and was chosen all state tackle last fall. He also lettered in baseball two years, basketball one year, and track two years. He was treasurer of the junior class and treasurer of the "W" club. The news was a surprise to the coaches at Washburn. Charlie had kept it a secret until all the arrangements were made. Charlie wrote to a friend, "They probably think I am a good one for leaving the way I did, but it seemed the easiest way for me."

CHAPTER 27

Warm spring breezes tantalized the countryside capriciously during the middle of March. The people knew spring had not really arrived, but Mother Nature was teasing them unmercifully. They knew she would send a winter storm before spring just to show them who was really in charge. Minty decided nevertheless to take advantage of the warm days. She told her family that it was a good time to clean the upstairs.

The following Saturday morning she organized all the young boys to help. In the closet of each room was a chamber pot, which was the duty of the inhabitants of the room to empty and rinse each morning. Minty set the boys about emptying out all the closets and taking the chamber pots out to the pump to be scrubbed and rinsed thoroughly. The boys sullenly carried the pots downstairs, mumbling complaints just within earshot of their mother all the way out the backdoor. Minty ignored the complaints with good humor. She and Georgie then cleaned the empty closets with their mops and scrub rags, piling all the dirty clothes found in the corners and under the beds out in the hallway. The boys then were given the job of shaking the bedding and rugs out the windows and letting them air over the windowsill a while.

Minty called from a bedroom down the hall for someone to come help her take down the curtains in that room. Everyone ran at once and the curtains were down in no time. Minty looked around the room and cried, "Where's the baby? Where's little Donald?"

Everyone looked around at one another, and then as if on cue, reality hit and the group turned together like an army unit and rushed to the room they had just finished. They entered the room just as the baby was crawling up onto the windowsill. The screen was still loosened with bedding in between and Minty screamed, "There he goes," and covered her eyes.

They all turned toward the stairs and ran down with Minty in the lead.

"He's dead, I know he's dead," she screamed all the way down. "What a dreadful mother I am. I can't even keep track of the baby."

The group hit the front door all at once and squeezed through to the front porch. Minty could not look. She hid her face in her apron, the little boys behind her hiding their faces in her skirts, and Georgie behind them hiding her face on her mother's shoulder. No one could bear to look at the scene they knew was waiting for them. Georgie was the first to regain composure, took a tentative peek around Minty and saw a movement. Instinctively she ran toward it and found Donald crawling in Minty's perennial flower garden. It was somewhat soft from the remains of last summer's flowers.

"He's alive, Mom. Donald's not hurt," Georgie called and ran toward the baby.

Minty pulled her head out of her apron in time to see the baby look up, sit on his fat little haunches, throw his little arms in the air and say very clearly, "Do again."

Minty grabbed her baby gratefully and sat on the front porch examining him carefully.

"An angel had to catch him," she mumbled over and over again. "I know an angel had to catch this baby and save him from the terrible fall." Minty had always been a bit superstitious and this last episode only encouraged her beliefs more.

CHAPTER 28

Forrest had been regularly seeing Goldie Gibbs, a pretty young girl who was in her last year of high school in Esbon. Her dark hair curled around her young round face, and gave the effect of fern and baby's breath surrounding a beautiful bouquet. Her dark brown eyes sparkled and lent an alert appearance that brightened her whole being. Though young, she portrayed a womanly attractiveness, and possessed a lively sense of humor and fun. Forrest loved to dance, and they had met at a dance. By the holidays, they had become quite inseparable. By Easter it had become apparent that Forrest and Goldie would someday be married. Forrest liked working outdoors with his hands and was planning to farm, but knew the low productivity of the family farm was making it difficult for his father to support his family. Forrest had been talking to an uncle near Otega about going to work for him.

Minty was beside herself with excitement at the prospect of all her children coming home for Easter. Charlie and Jessie would arrive in Esbon at the same time. Jessie's train would also stop in Mankato where she would board and be together with her brother. Frances would drive over in her car from where she was teaching in Odessa Township. Vivian would be home from high school. It would be like the old days when the family still lived together at home. Minty was preparing chickens to be fried, hams to be baked, eggs to be boiled and deviled, and all the favorite things her brood liked. Suddenly, after the noon hour the back door opened and in walked her three adventurous older children.

"Well, there ye are," she smiled and straightened up her stiff back. "Have ye et yet?"

Charlie looked at Jessie, and Jessie looked at the floor. Frances smiled knowingly. Minty had always spoken in a country dialect, but the children had become so used to it that they hardly noticed. Now, after being away from home, her speech sounded so foreign that Jessie didn't know quite how to react. Her first instinct was to correct, but instantly knew that she could not embarrass Minty. She could not hurt her feelings. All smiled immediately and told her they had a sack lunch on the train.

Vivian, of course, had not noticed. She had never been gone from home long enough to become aware of Minty's habits of speech. She closed the oven door oblivious to the reaction of her older siblings.

"I can remember always wanting to help in the kitchen and being mad because everyone told me I was too little. Now, I don't know why I was in such a hurry. I'm the only girl left and I have to do all the helping."

She gave a breathy giggle that lilted into a melodious cadenza, and giggled again in her good-natured playful manner. She had a laugh that was positively infectious. Everyone in the room had to join Vivian when she was amused.

"I have an idee that you'll be pretty hungry for supper then," Minty offered. "I have an idee" being another of her favorite sayings, "idee" pronounced to rhyme with tidy. "We'll just cut off some pieces of these Easter hams and fry them tonight."

Easter Sunday morning dawned bright and mild, a perfect Easter day. The Kennedy clan all dressed in their Sunday best, loaded onto the wagon and attended church. The hams had been placed in the oven with the fire carefully banked and low. The chickens were ready to fry, the potatoes peeled and in the pan of water ready to boil. When they arrived home, the kitchen became a bustling madhouse with Minty giving orders and making a bit of sense of the madness. The dining room table was stretched and set, as was the kitchen table. The younger boys would eat at the kitchen table. Since Forrest was bringing his girl to dinner, all the older children would eat in the dining room. They were all carefully instructed not to embarrass Forrest.

"This is the first time he has brought Goldie to our house," Minty carefully explained, and threatened at the same time. Before long the aroma of frying chicken was tantalizing the family. The pies and cakes were placed side by side on the pie cupboard. Soon the little boys entered the kitchen, having changed their Sunday clothes into play clothing. Byron and James where growing rapidly and promised to be large and tall like Charlie. They were playful and full of vinegar. They were dancing with each other, dipping one another and twirling around the other.

"Here's Vivian and Wiley," they giggled.

"You stop that now," Vivian ordered, but couldn't help a small giggle.

The boys gave a play hug and kiss to each other and announced, "This is Forrest and Goldie."

"All right now, that's enough tomfoolery," Minty ordered. "You boys get outside and play ball until we call you in to dinner. Forrest, you better be on your way to get Goldie so we can all get settled when the meal is ready."

Minty did not at all mean the testiness she had displayed. She loved every minute of the teasing and high-spirited tricks her children loved to play on each other.

The meal was finally prepared and ready to be served. Georgie had been home since Friday so had helped with this enormous meal all day Saturday. Everyone was seated at their place.

Goldie became wide-eyed at the size of this family and the good-humored fun they all seemed to enjoy. The little boys stared at her as she walked in, but said nothing. The sisters made her feel very welcome, as did Minty. She was treated as another Kennedy sister from the first minute.

Minty felt so fortunate to have her whole family together once again, everyone happy and healthy. Three of my children with some college education she told herself in disbelief. I didn't hardly finish eighth grade and here my children are in college. She knew there would be very few times when they would all be together like this and that she would savor this day and its memories for the rest of her life. The little boys in the kitchen were devouring everything they could get their hands on, and the others were enjoying the relative peace in the dining room. The three oldest took turns telling the family about their recent experiences away from home. Charlie began by describing his classes in biology, chemistry, and algebra.

"Dad, I just can't get the hang of algebra," he pled.

"Maybe after dinner we can sit down and look at it," Ern offered. "I used to be pretty good in math."

Then Charlie made an announcement that pleased Minta and Ern. Charlie said he needed to take some time off from school to earn money. He was hoping to teach and maybe coach at Esbon High School for a year and then go back to school. Ern liked the idea of another one of his children teaching.

Frances said that she had more opportunities for teaching jobs now that she had a state teaching certificate. Grade school teachers could get a teaching certificate from normal training in certain high schools or from County Normal Institutes held in the summer by the local county. But attending a summer program at a college to get a state teaching certificate was the best. She had a one-year state teaching certificate after attending a summer program at Fort Hays Normal School, and planned to take more summer classes at Hays until she had a three-year teaching certificate. Vivian listened intently to this.

Jessie thanked her parents for allowing her to study business.

"I'm the fastest typist in class and just love to balance my pages," she explained to them. "There is something about bookkeeping that is so satisfying to me."

It took nearly all afternoon to clean the kitchen. The younger boys wandered outside with their balls and bats. Before long many of the neighbor boys appeared and they got a lively game going in the flat field just south of the sprawling farmhouse. Kenneth was showing promise as a pitcher, with a good accurate ball and good speed. Lyall was a bit too gentle; he could play ball, but did not have a consuming interest in sports like his brothers.

Byron and James were showing the most promise of all the Kennedy boys at this time. They had already played so much together that they thought alike and seemed to know what the other was going to do.

CHAPTER 28

Little Don was now behind the outfield, gathering the lost balls and throwing them into the fielders. He thought he was really a part of the team and was so proud. Each time he would throw a ball in the players would praise him and make him feel important.

After the confusion and noise had quieted down in the kitchen, Forrest, Goldie, Jessie, Dave, and Vivian went for a horseback ride into the pasturelands. Goldie was not the horseperson that the Kennedys were. Ern said she should ride the most well trained horse, which was Jessie's horse Queen. Jessie had raised and trained Queen since Queen was a foal and was very attached to her. Jessie objected to Ern's request; however, Ern was insistent so Jessie reluctantly agreed to ride another horse. Goldie also had a saddle, while the Kennedys rode bareback. After all were mounted, the riders set off.

Minty went to her bedroom to lie down a bit because she tired more easily now. The many children and all the work had taken their toll on her. Her offspring were very aware that mom did not have the same energy and spring in her step that they remembered.

Ern and Charlie sat at the kitchen table, lit the kerosene lamp and Charlie opened his algebra book to explain to his father how this was supposed to work. Ern looked the book over carefully, digesting information from page one on to the problem at hand. He finally, took pencil and paper and told Charlie, "I think it should be set up like this," he said as he set up the equation using X as the unknown. They worked quietly, Charlie listening intently to his father in wonderment. Where could he have learned this, he asked himself. How could he have learned all this math? Finally he asked "Dad, where in the world did you learn to work math problems like this?"

"I don't know," the father answered thoughtfully. "I just always had a knack for math. I never really wanted to be a farmer, you know," he confided. "I never liked farming the way most of the neighbors do, and I'm not as good at it as my dad was. I wish I could have done something else, like teaching."

Charlie sensed more than heard the distress in his father's voice. He had lately noticed his father's melancholy and wondered what was bothering him. Maybe it is all us kids leaving he mused. Maybe he is feeling old age approaching and feels despondent about it. Whatever it was, it saddened Charlie, but at the same time he knew there was nothing he could do now to help.

The horseback riders returned after a generally pleasant ride, with only one noteworthy incident. Jessie had taught Queen to take off running when Jessie let out a war whoop. As the riders were ambling along, Jessie let out a war whoop and Queen took off, much to Goldie's dismay. Later, Jessie accepted Ern's reprimand, but she also knew she had made her point—Queen was her horse.

Minty woke and joined the family, and delighted in the good times her children seemed to have when together. The ball game ended and the neighbor children drifted away as twilight fell. The magic spell was broken; Minty's family would soon leave and she knew it. She was still basking in the joy of the day with her whole family home together one more time as the holiday ended and the grown children returned to their respective places.

After the holiday, the young children again walked together to their one-room schoolhouse down the road, leaving only young Donald home alone. He spent most of his time following Ern as took care of the horses and gathered eggs for Minty.

CHAPTER 28

Kennedys and friends going riding probably in 1923. Their large wooden house is behind them. The man in front is Forrest Kennedy and Goldie Gibbs is right behind him on Jessie's horse Queen. Jessie is on the white horse to the right and David is standing holding a horse. Vivian is mounted on the far right. The Kennedys are all riding bareback, while the others have saddles.

CHAPTER 29

When Lee decided to leave the Catholic Church, Mattie accepted his decision. It hurt her deeply but she held her tongue. She prayed fervently to her Friend and Master in heaven each night and had faith that he would bring her son back to his church.

She knew as well that things were not working out for her second son Francis. He was not happy farming with his father. That was apparent to everyone but father Obert.

Her life had not been a bed of roses nor did she expect it to be. Her Irish parents had known much hardship in the Auld Sod and had not given their children any false hopes about life for the working class people. Her great happiness now lay in the knowledge that she would become a grandmother soon. A new baby in the family was a cause for great celebration. For the new baby to be the child of her firstborn son gave her a special satisfaction.

The long awaited spring was welcomed by all the farmers and their families as the winter had been long and wretchedly cold. Frank was anxious to get into the fields to plow and prepare them for the planting. Planting season was always the most gratifying time of the year for him.

"Stub, you better wrap up all those outside jobs and get ready to settle down and plant our own place," he warned the unhappy young boy. Francis was not amassing the fortune that he had hoped. In fact, his little coffer was not much healthier than it was last fall at the end of harvest season. Nevertheless, he prepared for the new season and readied himself for the fifteen-hour days that Frank Obert demanded.

Somehow I've got to figure a way out of all this he told himself nearly every day. But how, another little voice would ask from somewhere deep inside him. The one bright spot in his new life was that his big brother seemed for once completely happy. He and Nita were well suited and enjoyed each other's company.

Now that the baby was expected, everything seemed to be going perfectly for Lee. Lee deserved happiness Francis thought to himself. He has suffered so much grief during his young adult years, not to mention the long hours of hard work he endured while Francis was allowed to go to high school. The planting season approached with the father and his young son readying the ground to a fine, smooth planting bed. "Obert's fields are like a fine garden in town when they are ready for the seed" many of his neighbors would say about his love for the land and for growing crops.

The same could not be said of Frank's care of the livestock. He had little patience with animals. Fortunately, Mattie enjoyed the cows, horses, chickens and other barnyard animals. She cared for them as much as she could to save Frank from losing his infamous temper.

Spring was a delight with the rains coming just often enough to allow the fields to soften and be worked down to a fine top layer. With very little effort all the planting was done and the farmers settled in to get the cultivators ready and the threshing machines in perfect working order.

The rains suddenly stopped. All through June and July the rains did not come. The land was drying up with open cracks developing everywhere. The crops were wilting, even beginning to turn brown. The hot southerly winds were unrelenting and sucked the green life out of the crops. Each day one could see them wither a bit more, turn a little browner.

"If rain doesn't come soon," Frank told Mattie, "we won't have any crops to harvest. I don't know how we can get through the year without some cash crops," he worried.

"If we have to, Poppy, we can live on our egg and cream money," Mattie assured the poor frustrated man.

"This country, dis vast Midwest, is so unpredictable," Frank muttered almost as if talking to himself. "You can't count on anything, rain, varm veather. It could be cold in Yuly and warm in Yanuary. I tell you, Mattie, if we could figure out a way to bring water into dis country either from the mountains or the rivers, to pipe it in somehow, we could raise all the food this country vould ever need. We could make money and prosper."

Still the rains did not come. By August it was a full-fledged drought all through the plains states. It became evident to all the farmers that there would be no need for harvesting. The corn shucking would not take long and this year would be considered a total loss.

By early fall the paltry crops had all been harvested. The dry, brownish stalks of corn produced ears with a kernel here and a kernel there. Even the wheat crop was a complete disaster—the little kernels all dried and shrunken in the heads, the pitiful whiskers drooping and withered.

The corn would not have been worth harvesting if not for the free labor from the farm families. The farmers reasoned that free labor made the corn worth keeping for feed for the horses this coming winter and the wheat worth keeping for chicken feed. Before the decision was made to harvest, the farmers stood on the edges of their fields in complete despair, surveying the dismal crop failure that represented the culmination of their labor for a year—and more significantly, their primary income for the year. Some felt they could not continue and began making plans to sell out and move on. Others worried that the bank might not carry them another year if they could not make their payment again.

Ern Kennedy scrutinized his situation and felt even more desolate than the others. He had so many children to take care of.

One autumn evening as the chill began to filter through the warm sunshine, Ern was sitting at his kitchen table with the kerosene lamp turned high and dejectedly thumbing through the pages of the latest Sears-Roebuck catalog. All the pretty things he would like to order for his family were unattainable, even the small toys he would like to order for the young children for Christmas. He sat there in his overalls, smudged with the day's work, his head hanging a bit lower. He looked so dispirited that Minty stopped her kitchen work for a short

CHAPTER 29

minute to watch and worry. Of late, she had noticed his preoccupation and melancholy. She wondered if he were sad because the children were leaving.

"Ern, what's bothering you?" she asked abruptly.

"Oh, nothing really. Just feel sad lately," he finally admitted. "Guess all the children leaving all at once kind of got me down this year." He continued, "Minty, Charlie's gone to college, Forrest is going to be married soon, Georgie is working in town, Frances is teaching and Jessie will soon have a job. David wants to go to work for the railroad, he always loved the trains, you know, and little Vivian is ready to finish high school and has a boyfriend."

Minty considered all this information and decided maybe this would be the time to break her news to Ern. She had dreaded this moment and could not seem to find the proper situation. "Well, Ern, I don't think you're going to run out of children for awhile. I'm expecting again."

Ern looked up abruptly, his chin quivered and his eyes were sparkling with unshed tears.

"How could this happen?" he nearly choked. "Minty, you're past the child bearing stage. Too old."

"I know Ern. I don't know myself. It must be some kind of miracle," and then noticing that Ern put his head on the table, cradled with his arms and wept she said, "Ern, I'm sorry, we can make it through this. Somehow I know it will be another little boy. That will make us six little boys for our old age," she laid her hand on his shoulder and patted softly.

"No, Minty, I'm sorry. It's not your fault." With such a strong woman how could he cave-in now. He knew he had to buck up to give her strength for this unfortunate condition. "You're right, Mom, we'll make it and bring another healthy young boy into the world."

Across the section in the Obert household, the lamplight shined brightly from the kitchen window in the old farmhouse. The night was dark with the light from the window the only thing that could be seen. The buildings and house were only outlines in the darkness. Frank Obert sat at his kitchen table in much the same dejected state of mind as Ern Kennedy. He had worked hard all his life and what did he have to show for it. This was not the way he planned things to be when he was a young man eagerly starting his farm operation.

"Mattie, a lot of the trouble in this country is that families don't stay together anymore. In the old country the boys stayed with the father and kept the family farm going from generation to generation," he complained. "Here Lee is off on his own place, trying to be his own man, Francis is pulling on the bit to get away and go to school. Little Mary is off in high school. We will be alone one day soon and lose our farm."

"I know, Poppy," Mattie answered soothingly, "The children today want independence and maybe that's not all bad. They seem to need to establish their own lives and try to make it on their own. Maybe it's right, maybe it's progress. I don't know the answers but these are new times and things are changing."

"Umph!" was his only answer, so she continued her kitchen work, and when she finished sat with the handiwork that was her only comfort of late.

CHAPTER 29

CHAPTER 30

Minty was struggling uphill with a bucket in each hand, one to fill the reservoir behind the stove for hot water and the other for fresh drinking water. She was experiencing the most miserable pregnancy she had yet endured. She felt as if all her insides had dropped and wondered if they had stretched with her earlier pregnancies or if it were her age. Then she decided ruefully it was probably both. Ordinary activities had become challenges.

The little cold outhouse had become a dreaded encounter. She chilled easily nowadays and was forced with discomfort to frequent this little house again and again. Ern and the boys had been cutting wood all morning and were now splitting the pieces to fit the stoves. He looked up just as Minty set her buckets down, reached toward her back and stretched in a vain effort to relieve the pain there. He dropped his ax and started toward her, his distress in her discomfort as strong as her own aches and pains. She stumbled a bit as she reached to pick up the buckets again just as he arrived. He grabbed her shoulders to steady her, then drew her to him.

"You go on in, Mom," more a gentle order, than a request. "The boys and I will see that there is water in the house every day." Minty nodded, trying to hold back tears that were brimming in her eyes. She started for the house immediately with Ern right behind carrying the two buckets of water. He set one bucket in the entryway where the fresh water was kept because it was cooler there, then poured the other into the compartment in the wood stove.

"This will be the last child, Minty," he solemnly promised. "There will be no more babies. No matter what it takes there will be no more babies." He dropped his head, left the kitchen and soon the steady tap of his ax could be heard echoing throughout the farmstead. Outside, Ern was in deep contemplation. I wish I did not have to spend so much time cutting wood, he thought. The big family demanded more than others, with more stoves to feed and the cook stove never resting. With all the girls gone, and even Vivian ready to finish high school, it is more difficult for Minty to care for the five little boys. And now another one on the way, he reasoned despairingly. If he and the boys didn't have to spend so much time gathering and chopping wood, they could spend more time helping her.

Inside, Minty poured hot water into the dishpan. As she swished a bar of homemade soap around in the water, the tears she had so valiantly held back earlier started to slide down her cheeks, then spilled in uncontrollable streams. She hated self-pity and rarely gave in to it, but her misery was so complete she had to seek relief somehow. She stared at the dishpan and the stacks of dirty pots, pans, and dishes. Her legs and back were aching and longed for Charlie and Georgie. They could clean up a mess like this in fifteen minutes. Charlie's big, strong, nimble hands would spread out dinner plates like a freshly dealt hand of cards, wash them one at a time, dip them in the hot rinse water, and hand them to Georgie who would dry them and put away as speedily as Charlie washed. They washed the silverware in the same manner. Charlie would spread a handful of them apart, wash, rinse, and hand them to Georgie. Minty felt a deep sob wrench through her body. She sighed, wiped her eyes with her apron, and began the task of cleaning this big kitchen—again.

After releasing her emotions this day, Minty drew on her inner strength, regained control, did her chores one slow day after another until she finally finished her term of pregnancy. She was a strong and healthy woman with enormous recuperative powers. She was delivered of another baby boy, as she knew she would, and named him Morris. Her remarkable constitution allowed her to be on her feet earlier than most new mothers and she was soon doing the lighter chores around the household. The neighbor women from far and wide had brought food as well as staying to help with the work. Minty felt an aching appreciation for these caring neighbors who helped her through this difficult time.

CHAPTER 30

In Lawrence, Charlie carried his mail to his room. He opened the letter from his father first. He read slowly the news of a new baby boy, his new brother, and dropped his elbows to his knees, then his head lowered a bit, letting the letter slowly float to the floor. Poor Mom, he thought sadly, I don't know how she is going to be able to stand all this. All the older kids are gone, especially the girls. I wish dad would hire a girl to help her, he pondered. He couldn't understand why he did not.

At the Obert farm, Francis knew it was time to have a talk with his father that he had been dreading. Stub timidly broached the subject of his pay for the year.

"Dad, I've worked for you all year now. We've planted the crops, harvested, put up hay and I've helped with the chores twice a day. When can I get my pay?"

Frank jerked around in surprise, a scowl invading his face. "Pay?" he shouted, "how can you ask for pay when we didn't have one decent crop. Nothing brought in a profit this year and you want me to pay you?"

"Well, Dad," Francis insisted. "I did work, after all. It's not my fault that there was a drought and nothing grew."

"The conversation's over," Frank hissed furiously at the outrageous request of this ungrateful son of his. "That's the way it goes on the farm, you'll just have to get used to it."

This formally ended the conversation, and Stub knew in his heart he would never see a penny for his labor for this past year.

CHAPTER 31

Mattie received the call in the early hours on a cold February morning. Lee sounded distressed when he explained to his mother what was happening.

"Nita has felt a little sick for a few days, but we did not think it was anything to worry about and she needed to take care of the baby. Now she has severe pain in her stomach" he explained. "Can you come and stay with her while I get the doctor?" Nita had given birth to a baby boy, Glenn, just three months before. Things had seemed to be going well for family.

"I'll be there as soon as I get the horse and buggy ready," she answered.

As soon as Mattie entered the house and quickly assessed the situation, she realized that Nita was severely ill.

About this time Nita's parents entered with worried looks on their faces. Nita had requested that Lee call them too. Shortly, Lee entered with the sleepy doctor right behind, carrying his little black bag. His clothing was crumpled as if dropped on the floor before he retired, then picked up again, and hurriedly climbed into in the dark. It did not take long, however, for the doctor to regain his alert expression.

Dr. Diele began his examination and was soon gently pushing on Nita's lower stomach, which caused severe pain. Finally, he took Lee aside and said "I think she may have a ruptured appendix. This spreads infection inside her body. I'm sorry, but there isn't anything I can do."

Lee felt anguish that he could not have imagined. It was all so sudden and unexpected. The doctor told the others, and then left, saying he would return the next day.

When the baby began fussing, Mattie was most able to respond. Soon Nita's mother offered to take the baby and appeared to need the distraction.

For the next two days Mattie and Nita's mother continued the agonizing tasks of attempting to comfort Nita, take care of the baby, and console Lee, as well as deal with their own overwhelming grief. When Nita's final moments came, Francis sat beside Lee, said very little, but intended to be ready to help whenever Lee needed him. He silently wondered what he could do, or even say if the need arose. He felt entirely helpless and hated the feeling. At this moment, he resolved to find a way to go to school and learn as much as he could about the art of healing. Then he would be able to help these misfortunes as much as modern medicine would allow.

 Nita's parents insisted they take the baby with them to allow Lee to make the funeral arrangements and have time to recover. Lee requested Francis stay with him a bit longer and Frank allowed this because his feelings at this time were rather tender. He felt Lee needed someone with him for a while.

 It was a murky morning, when the funeral day arrived. A fog developed early in the morning that clung like a ghostly shroud and made the occasion even more sorrowful. The families accompanied Lee back home and stayed until early evening when Nita's parents insisted they take the baby until Lee could better care for him. Lee, benumbed with exhaustion, loss, and fear for the future, agreed but with much anxiety. Francis again scowled at his brother, then at his parents, and again felt helpless. This was Lee's business and his alone he told himself. It is not my place to interfere. The boys finally returned to their routines with Lee coping as usual by withdrawing. He had as little contact as possible with neighbors and worked steadily the next few months. It was good for Lee to have his brother with him. He asked him to stay permanently and offered him to share expenses and profits. They could even rent another field or two to farm for added income.

CHAPTER 32

Lee and Francis were in their second year of planting. The first year had not been very productive. The drought seemed to have settled in for the plains country. However, with pioneer determination and the enthusiasm of youth, they readied their fields to be planted again.

Francis noticed with satisfaction that Lee was beginning to recover from his loss. He was again interested in events around him and showed some desire to attend public functions. He also had begun to enjoy being with friends and neighbors again. Still, the grandparents did not feel he was able to care for little Glenn. Since the baby was nearly two years old, Lee thought he could manage.

The end of the summer proved to be a carbon copy of the previous year. The rains came early, but shut off completely during the long hot summer. The stocks stood in the fields, dry and nearly dead. The pasture grass was brittle as were the hay fields. The two boys stood looking forlornly at the field of corn that had completely dried and withered. The dry, fitful wind seemed to hold the rich dark soil in suspension.

"Just as well turn the cattle in this winter and use it for feed," Lee suggested. "Won't be enough hay to feed them anyway. "

"Yeah," Francis agreed. "It's not worth the trouble to harvest."

They both looked toward the ground, knowing there would be no cash crops again this year. Each hated to be the one to bring the subject up first.

"Lee, if we're ever going to get anywhere, I've got to go to school," Francis told his brother in a decisive tone of voice. "I'll apply to Kansas University in Lawrence right away."

I'll never save enough money to put myself all the way through at once, anyway, he told himself. I might as well begin with one semester and attend school as I gather the money. At least I'll have a start that way.

He was accepted in time to enroll for the fall term. He packed his few clothes, tucked his small savings away in his suitcase, and was ready to leave the weekend before enrollment day. Lee held out his hand and Francis grabbed it gratefully, both trying to be manly about this separation. Then abandoning proprieties both reached for the other in an affectionate bear hug.

"Remember, Stub, this is still your home. You're welcome here anytime," Lee reminded him fondly, reverting to his childhood nickname.

Lee drove him to the train station where Francis boarded the train to Lawrence, Kansas. As the train chugged out of the station, he quietly pondered the unknown he was now entering. Where will I live, he wondered. How much is this going to cost? Can I even learn all the subjects I will have to take? He watched the landscape slowly change from central Kansas into eastern Kansas. The terrain transformed from hard surfaced windy plains and rolling hills, to thickets of low bushes graduating into wooded glades, then into forest covered rolling hills. The rains were obviously more frequent in the east than in the central uplands where he lived. Here the countryside was green with wet meadows and sheltered lowlands. Francis slowly gathered his luggage as the train entered the Lawrence platform area. His thoughts were in disarray and he felt much apprehension. His deliberate steps belied the dread he felt for his first encounter at the college.

The same feeling that overcame him on his first day at high school was again plaguing him as he surveyed the huge complex that was Kansas University. "Home of the Jayhawks" was inscribed on top of one prominent building. What are Jayhawks he wondered as he walked around the campus, trying to get acquainted while biding his time. He did not even know where to go first.

"Where do you go to sign up for classes?" he asked one student who seemed to be more sophisticated than others and was probably an upper classman. The student kindly stopped to show him which building to go to first and then patiently explained where the freshmen dorm was and many other helpful bits of information. This gave him courage to begin his enrollment.

The weather was still warm for autumn and he discovered that he could save a little money by sleeping in the park for a few days. He was shocked to learn that he must buy his own books and many notebooks, paper, pencils and pens. This was a hidden expense he had not counted on, so the savings in dorm fees would help. The first evening he unrolled his blankets and pillow and slept on a park bench. It was not too bad he decided and headed for the public restroom to freshen up for the day. The biggest problem was his white shirt. He only owned one and it needed to be done up each day. He decided he would rinse it out in the restroom the night before and then press it with the school's public laundry services early the following morning. Thus, began young Obert's college career.

After he got settled at the freshman dorm, he soon realized that his money was not going to last as long as he had expected. He inquired around about jobs and learned that there was an opening in one of the prestigious frat houses down the street. Sigma Phi gave him the job of waiting tables and washing dishes for his meals and a portion of his room rent. This allowed him to finish the first semester. He wrote Lee that he would drop out the second semester and take the train with a large group of students to eastern Nebraska to pick corn there. "They have more rainfall and rich, flat farm ground the guys here tell me," he added at the end of the letter. Lee hated that Francis could not continue steadily through college, but Lee was in no position to help.

After the crops were harvested in Nebraska, Francis returned to Lee to help get the spring work started and the planting finished. Then with a little money again saved, he started for Lawrence and the second semester of his first year.

Lee by now was noticing his own loneliness. After Francis left for school, he decided a trip into town would do him good. There were supplies he needed anyway, including some shirts, socks and work clothing. He hitched the wagon and drove the horses toward the road into Mankato one exceptionally warm day early that winter. He shopped, visited with other young farmers at the local hangouts, then as an afterthought remembered he still needed shirts and socks, so he walked toward the dry goods store on main street. Georgie Kennedy looked up from the shelves she was stocking just as the young farmer entered. She felt the sadness and loneliness in this young man even before she recognized who he was. Lee on the other hand immediately knew Georgie. *She hasn't changed since I last saw her*, he thought as he started inspecting shelves for socks.

"Can I help you?" Georgie asked politely.

"I need some socks," Lee shyly answered, his heart doing a cartwheel inside his chest.

"Why, Lee," Georgie suddenly exclaimed. "I didn't know who you were at first. Lee, I'm so sorry about Nita," she whispered in sincere sympathy. "Do you have the baby back, yet?" Lee had almost forgotten about Georgie's immense capacity for caring and was caught a bit off guard.

"No," he answered hesitatingly, "his grandparents still think he is too young for me to care for."

They reminisced for time about the old days, the neighborhood and each other's families. Lee fell into the same comfortable feeling from the pleasure in her company that had experienced before with Georgie. *It is like I found the lost mate to my most comfortable pair of slippers* he thought to himself in some confusion. It was nearly closing time when Georgie finished wrapping his package and tied it neatly with white string.

"Would you like some ice cream?" Lee blurted impulsively, then wondered why he had even suggested such a thing. He knew she would reject him again. "I don't go to the Catholic church anymore," he added, and immediately felt he was making things worse.

"Lee, I...I'm sorry about that. It was a mistake and I don't know what got into me," she stammered uncomfortably, her wonderfully expressive eyes showing true remorse.

"It's OK, Georgie," he answered good humoredly. "Just forget it. How about the ice cream?"

She agreed, put on her coat, turned the lights out and locked up the store. As they walked down the street together she wondered what she was doing. *I promised myself I would never have anything more to do with men and here am I going out with my first boyfriend.* After this simple ice cream soda date, Lee inquired if she would be willing to spend time with him again sometime. She blushed, nodded slightly and encouraged him to call her again.

CHAPTER 33

Ern stepped into the kitchen one day on a cold winter afternoon. His color was pallid, his appearance more depressed than ever before, his manner that of complete hopelessness.

"I have been trying to conciliate with Mr. Grant, the banker, for the past three years," he began, a slight quiver in his voice. "I didn't tell you Minty. I didn't want to worry you, but I was forced to sell this farm. I had mortgaged it, but couldn't keep up the mortgage payments. Mr. Grant offered an alternate plan. He bought the whole farm, all 360 acres, and then offered to rent it back to me. He promised he would never sell it as long as I paid my share of the crops to him. I have done that, Mom, but it seems he went to Canada on business and died there. It seems his wife, Mrs. Grant, did not share his views. Before I had a chance to bargain with her, she sold it. She's a hateful woman, Minty," he finished softly.

"What will we do, Ern?" she asked as she dropped into a chair, picked up her apron and began to weep bitterly into it.

"We can move to the rock house and eighty acres my dad left. I'll farm the eighty. I'm so sorry to bring you down like this, Minty, but we have six boys left at home. They can sleep in the upstairs in the small house and we'll make it somehow."

"Oh, Ern, my big house. I hate to leave my big house. I love it so much," the tears spattered as she blinked her eyes to shake them away.

Ern had taken over most of the family farm. His father Charles had expanded the farm from the original 160 acre homestead to 560 acres, all paid for. Then Charles sold some of the land and distributed 360 acres to his children. Ern accumulated the farm from his siblings. Now he had lost all of it except for his share the 80 acres his father had kept for himself and his wife in their last years. After his father died, the 80 acres were inherited by his five children.

Ern could only collapse in a chair, hang his head in total despair and look toward the floor. Their first house had been a small house like they would soon move into. There was no comfort for him and he could not gather enough strength to comfort his wife this time. The two sat in their kitchen, each suffering in his own way, for much of the afternoon. The five boys in school all arrived home just as little Morris was awakening from his afternoon nap. The dismal scene did not go unnoticed by them. They looked at each other curiously, then immediately went to their rooms to change into their work clothes. That evening at supper, the situation was explained to them and they finally understood they would be leaving their home to a much smaller house.

The rock house Minta and Ern Kennedy moved into after leaving their large wooden house. This photo was taken in 1927. They moved about 1924 or 1925.

Minty awoke the following morning; she had found some solace from her night's sleep. Minty was by nature adaptable, and had learned over the years to endure many unhappy occurrences. She bore this latest setback with uneasy acceptance.

She told her family as they entered the back door from the morning chores, "We will thoroughly clean up the rock house,

CHAPTER 33 137

fix any loose boards and windows, put up curtains and the like, before we move in."

She had long ago lost interest in life's amenities. We will get along just fine in the rock house she told herself.

Ern had never loved his wife as he did at that moment. He was overcome with wonder at her indomitable will and her strength of character. How like Minty to react like this, he thought, and felt teary-eyed at her calm acceptance of their many misfortunes.

As expected, Ern's siblings turned over their part of the land to Ern, but Ern started their new life with a $1200 debt on the land.

The Kennedy family spent the early spring cleaning and repairing the old rock house. Georgie and Vivian came when they could to help. Frances and Jessie could not be there, but sent small items to help the transition. Frances bought a rug for her mother to place in the parlor before they moved in. Minty was so delighted with the rug she felt it almost worth the move. The first day Georgie arrived to help her mother, she noticed with alarm how Minty had aged. She was ashamed that she had been so preoccupied with her own life that she had not noticed before. Minty had become stooped from carrying babies and buckets, her once splendid, rich brown hair now a steel gray. It had lost its spring and much of the natural wave, and was now wiry and brittle. Georgie put her arms around Minty's shoulders and hugged her affectionately. "Poor Minty," she mumbled softly. "You have had some hard times."

Minty patted her daughter, "There have been more good times than bad, Georgie. Always remember to count and balance the good with the bad before you give up," she counseled. As she scanned the homeplace scene before her, Georgie noticed the look of defiance Minty acquired when she met adversities. She looked at the world as if to say, "Bring it on. I can take it."

The two women entered the house to appraise the situation. Georgie was surprised that the house was so nice. Minty had forgotten how sturdy rock houses were. They were cool in the summer and warm in the winter with very little draft slipping through. Both women gazed in admiration at the construction of this house.

"Grandpa Kennedy built this house for him and grandma after his children were grown. He and grandma lived here until he died," she explained to Georgie. "Dad and I first lived in a small house with stone walls and before long we had too many children so all the Kennedy men worked together, plus a neighbor or two, to build our big house on the hill. It's a lot of work, to build rock houses, Georgie, but they are wonderful buildings when completed."

She went ahead to explain how the procedure worked. The rock is found in layers underneath the sod, especially on hills. The men dig up the sod and literally mine the rock right from its layers. They mark off the size of block they want, chisel it and lift it out of the ground like huge bricks of native rock. It is all the same color, a pale mustard yellow, and is rugged enough to build large buildings such as the courthouse in Mankato. It can be used for whole business districts and even for posts for fences.

The women both felt a new sense of enthusiasm for the rejuvenation of this wonderful house. The kitchen extended the whole width of the house. There would be room for Minty's table with the benches at either side, they noted with satisfaction, but very little space for cupboards for storage. The parlor with the wood stove gave added living space. There was a downstairs bedroom. Upstairs was one large room with wood floors, much like a college dormitory.

"We will put beds up here in a row for the boys to sleep," she told Georgie. "Maybe even a curtain to divide the room, so the girls can have some privacy when they visit," she added as an afterthought.

In this way Ern and Minty moved into the rock house that was like when they had started their life together—but now they had much less land.

CHAPTER 33

Ern and Minta Kennedy circa 1928 at their stone house in Odessa Township.

CHAPTER 34

It felt good to be finished with at least one year of college and Francis knew his grades were above average—very good, really. He felt confident at this point that he actually might finish college. He had heard through the dormitory grapevine that the state was doing roadwork on the highways and was hiring young men at an unusually high pay scale. He applied and got a job driving mules during the long, extremely hot summer. He was able to ignore his aching back and muscles by counting his savings each week. This was the most pay he had made since his graduation from high school. He would be able easily to finish the next semester but decided to stay with the job throughout the fall and save even more money.

When he signed up for the second semester he felt assured that he would be able to conclude this semester without financial worries, but then he suddenly remembered all the semesters he had yet to complete. Rather than take this semester in easy comfort, he decided to work ahead and save money for later. He inquired at the business office and learned there was a job opening for a student to stoke the furnace and he also would be allowed to sleep in the furnace room to save dorm fees. He gratefully took this job, lived in the furnace room where it was warm and well lighted, and was able to study in peace and quiet. When the semester was finished he actually had money left over and could hardly believe it.

CHAPTER 35

Ern walked slowly toward the house, balancing his two buckets of water. He was always happy when the children came home for a visit in the early summer, but it sure took a lot more water he admitted to himself. He set the buckets down and stood by the door to hear the latest news. Inside, Frances, Jessie and Vivian were enjoying a most animated conversation. Minty thoroughly delighted in having her girls home. She enjoyed the female company and catching up on the new experiences taking place in their lives.

This was a big year for Vivian. She just finished her junior year of high school at Esbon and played on the girls basketball team that won the district championship. Next year she would graduate and planned to become a teacher.

Jessie felt proud when the Kennedy girls did well in sports. Jessie had been a left-handed pitcher on the girls' softball team both years at Mankato High School.

Frances was going to teach at a school in Esbon Township this fall. She had taught every year after graduating from high school, first in Odessa Township for three years and then a year at Otego. She continued to take classes at Hays during the summer and was working on getting a three year teaching certificate. She was now making $85 per month during the school year.

Minta was pleasantly surprised by Jessie's news—as Jessie told stories of Fred, the youngest son in the family she worked for. After finishing Fairbury Business College, Jessie had taken a job as bookkeeper and secretary with the Muck Produce Company in Clay Center, Kansas. This was a family business for the Muck family. She applied for the job and was accepted through the mail without actually meeting the family. She took the train to Clay Center with her small suitcase and had no plans for where to live.

"When I got off the train," she related, "A daughter in the family was there to meet me. She offered to let me use the spare bedroom that night and also invited me to share the evening meal with them. They were so nice to me. The following day Mrs. Muck invited me to board and room with them permanently."

Jessie said she quickly became like a member of the family. Fred was a broker for the business and lived at home, but traveled much of the time. The Mucks were more formal and religiously conservative than the Kennedys. The parents did not like dancing or popular music. Jessie said Fred was the scallywag of the family and had a playful relationship with his mother. He smoked, liked to dance, and would sing popular songs to tease his mother. Soon Fred was passing notes to Jessie under the door of her room. Jessie did not mention that he also started playing footsie with her under the table during the rather formal family meals.

As Minta listened to Jessie enthusiastically talk about Fred, she thought this sounded like a good match. A man who was independent and responded with playfulness could be good for Jessie. When Ern was asked how many children he had, he often replied "I have nine boys, three girls, and Jessie." He was not trying to be funny; this was how he thought about it. Jessie was hard to categorize. She had insisted on going hunting with her brothers, whether or not they wanted her joining them, and shot rabbits from the back of her horse. In terms of independence, pure determination, and competitiveness, Jessie could hold her own with any boy. Fred sounded like someone who could appreciate Jessie and get along with her.

Minta suspected she would soon be hearing that Jessie had gotten married. The way most young people got married had not changed much since when Minta and Ern married. Weddings were usually considered private. At most, only one or two very close friends or siblings would attend. Parents normally did not attend and often did not learn about it until it was over. Of course, in most cases the parents were not surprised.

Jessie continued, "Fred's mother complimented me on my fine manners. She asked if we all had manners so fine. I told her we did," at this she smiled at her mother.

"Do you remember, Mom, when we were teaching the little boys their manners?" Vivian smiled at her mother. "Jessie asked Byron one day at the table if he would like the mashed potatoes. He looked up with his most polite expression and said, 'yes, please and thank-you, ma'am.' He nodded his head with every word and batted his big, brown eyes around the table. He was such a cute little boy."

Minty giggled, relishing the memories and agreed. "I remember. He was a darling little boy."

Minty had news of her own. "Forrest and Goldie are expecting a baby soon. It will be so close to Morris' age, it kind of embarrasses me," she timidly admitted. "My grandchild and my own child will be playing together. I suppose people will snicker behind my back."

Ern looked into the yard and silently watched the boys at their afternoon game. Kenneth was becoming a fine pitcher, he noticed. He throws a nice accurate ball with a lot of speed. Kenneth was also a switch hitter. He was left handed as a small child but broke his left arm and learned to use his right arm. After the arm healed, he was recklessly playing on ice one day when Minta warned him to be careful or he would break is arm again. He continued and soon slipped and broke his left arm again—which gave him more opportunity to develop his right arm. Ern noted that Lyall has all the coordination and ability the others have, but does not show the aggressiveness. He isn't as interested in playing ball as the other boys, he admitted.

Byron and James (now known as Moose and Pete) were showing the most promise of all. They were gaining muscle and coordination every month. Ern was still dismayed at their nicknames. James had picked up the nickname Pete when he was a small child learning to talk. His brothers teased him that he sounded like a neighbor named Pete who had speech impairment. James started saying his name was Pete, and the nickname stuck when he went to school.

"Byron and James are going to be the best ball players of the lot," he suggested suddenly. "Kenneth is a fine pitcher, but

Lyall doesn't seem to have the same enthusiasm as the other boys."

"Lyall is my gentle boy," Minty explained. "He has the heart of a poet."

"That's right," Jessie agreed. "He is so kind to his sisters and to his little brothers."

"He loves books, Dad, and wants to go to school to become a teacher someday," Frances added. "He told me he was going to work and save money after graduation to go to college."

Ern left to start the evening chores and Minty retired to her bedroom for an hour's rest before starting the evening meal. The girls were cleaning up the odd chores before supper. They washed and polished the glass lamps, smoky and sooty from the kerosene wick burning inside them. Then rinsed the milk buckets and the separator, readying them for the hot sudsy scrubbing they would soon get.

"Mother can't keep up with all this work when we're gone," Jessie worried out loud.

"Why can't Byron and James learn to do this?" Frances replied.

"Let's get them," all three cried at once, "and teach them to accept this job regularly." The three girls shooed the unwilling boys, toward the house, like driving a flock of chickens to roost. The boys tried to elude their older sisters, to no avail. Once inside, the lessons began. There was a lot of clowning and horseplay to contend with, but within an hour the boys were finally made to understand that Mom can't do all this alone anymore. The separator was the worst chore for them. Their big hands had much difficulty taking each separate, little disk apart to wash them one at a time. After they washed all the apparatus, the two boys carried the separator and buckets back to the barn to begin the milking cycle over again. It would all be rinsed with fresh water after the evening chores and left in the cool air until morning chores were finished. Then the men would carry it all into the kitchen to be washed and rinsed again. This finished, the girls snatched little Morris and Don, like a predator catching his prey. The girls insisted they learn to

CHAPTER 35

gather eggs, feed the chickens and help clean the hen house. When they told Minty, she could barely believe that these younger boys were willing to take on these "girlie" chores. It was a great relief to her though, to have help with these dreaded jobs.

Later that fall, Ern and Minta received a letter from Charlie with his latest news and another newspaper clipping. He said he received a telegram from the Kansas City Blues minor league baseball team saying he had been recommended as a prospect for professional baseball. They asked him to report to their training camp next spring at their expense. The newspaper article was from the Kansas City newspaper and said that Charlie was going to tryout at the training camp in Lake Charles, Louisiana. It also said that in addition to the eight athletic letters Charlie had received at Washburn, he had made two letters in baseball at K.U. as pitcher and outfielder. Charlie said the timing was perfect because he will finish the school term in February for his four year college degree plus his first year of medical school. He was looking forward to playing baseball and taking a break from school.

CHAPTER 36

After teaching in small rural grade schools, Frances finally had a three year teaching certificate and was offered a job teaching at Esbon High School. This was a raise to $90 per month, but it meant she would be teaching two of her younger brothers. She was not sure how this would work out. They will probably try to take advantage of me, she considered. Well, I will worry about that next fall and, with that, she threw her worries away and made a pledge just to enjoy the summer.

As the young Kennedys began to return home for the summer, Ern presented his family with an idea.

"What if I were to rent a house in Esbon?" he began. "Frances needs a place to live while teaching and Kenneth and Lyall can live there while going to school. I will put sister Frances in charge of the house. She will be the head of the household and you boys would have to mind her."

Everyone agreed this could work, so Ern set about finding a proper house for his nearly grown-up children. Late in July, the Kennedy family started working on the house that would be the home for Frances and her brothers. It was far from luxurious but cozy and comfortable.

Vivian finished high school this year and wanted to teach and follow Frances in attending summer classes at Hays.

There were many ball games that summer. Both Moose (Byron) and Pete (James) were tall, lean, and sinewy. They were well matched and were terrors in the infield. When the boys were in a game together, it was rare another team could beat them. Kenneth had become quite a fine pitcher. Lyall was a good outfielder. Young Don played right field most of the time. These fun-filled games fueled the fire of a sports mania that remained with the boys the rest of their lives.

As fall arrived they settled into the little house. Before long, they established a routine. The experiment seemed to be a success. It made living expenses much less costly for all and helped Ern and Minty with their high school students.

Frances's worries about teaching her younger brothers turned out to not be a problem. She found Lyall was a pleasure to teach. He had an interest in learning and appreciated ideas that would serve him well if he decided to apply for college. On the other hand, after six weeks of high school, Kenneth became sick and could not play football. He decided high school was not for him, dropped out, and started working.

At the end of the school year, Frances announced she had a new job teaching high school English in a town school in western Kansas. "It is in a town called Rexford. Western Kansas is so desolate," she complained. "It's treeless, dry, flat and endless. There is nothing there but immense wheat fields," she said. "I may get lonesome there, but the pay is much better than here. The schools are bigger because there are fewer of them."

Three days before Christmas, Charlie Kennedy sat alone in his room at the Gates City Hotel in Crawford, Nebraska thinking about his life. As the end of the year approached, he recognized that he had been diverted from his goal of medical school long enough. It was time to regroup and get back on track.

After pitching and playing outfield with the Kansas City Blues for two months, he was released by the team and had gone to Crawford to play on their baseball team in the Northwest Nebraska league. He had stayed after the season ended in September. Like always since he left home, he had taken any job he could get and worked many different jobs. In Crawford, these jobs had included unloading merchandise and produce at Star Grocery, deliveries to a nearby fort, working at the mercantile, loading and unloading heavy freight including cars, delivering ice (referring to himself as the iceman), helping the Maytag man with deliveries, laying linoleum, driving the laundry truck, working evenings at the movie theater, and more.

The best place to go to regroup was back to his home on the farm. In the personal journal he kept, he wrote "in eve decided to go to Kansas. Left at 9:50. Thanks — Off for new start".

He stayed home through the rest of the winter and into spring. Besides helping around the farm, he did some hunting with his brother Kenneth. When summer came, he went to Oshkosh, Nebraska and played on their semi-professional baseball team. Then, in the fall he went to Denver and began completing his last three years of medical school at the University of Colorado.

Kenneth and Charlie Kennedy hunting, probably in 1927.

CHAPTER 37

Lee and Georgie had been seeing one another this past year steadily, but each was uneasy about this unusual relationship. They were primarily best friends who brought out the best in each other. When Lee was with Georgie, he felt an inner peace and he liked the feeling, but he was unsure whether Georgie was interested in him romantically. She had rejected him long ago, maybe she would again.

Georgie, however, loved being with Lee. His mischievous nature made her feel alive and vital. She was fearful though that he would not want her permanently since she had broken off their summer romance long ago—that he could not trust her again. They had enjoyed being together this past year and had attended all the ice cream socials, some movies, and ball games throughout the summer and fall.

Right after the semester ended, Francis returned to help Lee get crops planted in the spring. He despaired at times about the years passing by and his relatively small crack in the four-year regimen. This summer with Lee would be a time to regenerate his exhausted energies.

The spring work was finally finished, giving Lee a short break before the haying season and wheat harvest. Then the cycle would begin again. He must plow the wheat field, work it down with the disc, then replant in the late fall.

He finished his chores early, cleaned up, and drove into Mankato to see Georgie that afternoon. He found her finishing her day's work in the store and she seemed delighted to see him. She was more than ready for some entertainment that evening and informed Lee that there was a bingo party and dance combined. It was to be a fundraiser for the city park. He felt exhilarated at her obvious enthusiasm at seeing him again, yet about the time he began to feel that she was interested in him as more than a friend, she seemed to withdraw emotionally. There was a subtle mannerism that warned him to not be too familiar, a small nuance that gently encouraged him to keep their friendship on an impersonal level. In fact, Georgie was protecting herself from further torment, still vulnerable from the distresses in the past that she had recently worked through and finally put behind her. She did not want to have such a wretched predicament again.

Lee had fully intended to suggest a steady courtship this evening, but again felt put-off by the vague, protective wall Georgie had recently built between them. He felt positive that Georgie was the girl he wanted to live with for the rest of his life. She, like him, loved farm life, loved the animals and the freedom rural life allowed. He walked her home as he customarily had done this past year, then softly placed a little kiss on her cheek. She did not stiffen, nor did she respond. They said their good-byes, and Lee walked away, discouraged and bewildered. Maybe she was just one of those fickle girls that like to lead men on and then dump them, he thought. No, Georgie is not that kind of girl was his immediate rebuttal to his inner self. Maybe her elusiveness is just a game, maybe she is playing hard to get. I doubt it, was the answer from the inner voice. Then what, he asked this voice. No answer came this time.

Lee returned home before Francis this evening. He has probably gone to a local get-together he decided with a little annoyance. He really felt like he needed someone to talk to right now. He picked up a newspaper and browsed through it, hoping his brother would be back soon. Just as he hoped Francis returned shortly and was surprised to see Lee home so soon.

"That was an early date," he observed.

"Stub, I need to talk to you," the older brother admitted, feeling a little humiliation. It should be the other way around. My little brother should be asking advice from me, he thought to himself.

"I have been taking Georgie out for nearly a year now, and I don't feel like we have progressed in our time spent together since the first day. We have become very good friends and there is nothing that we can't discuss between us, but I can't seem to bring out even a slight encouragement that gives me an opening to talk to her about making these casual dates a steady affair. I would even like to ask her to become engaged to me."

"Lee, I remember Georgie from school. I think she is sensitive and has been hurt a few times before. I would call it a defense mechanism. We learned that in school," he grinned. "Probably the thing to do is just take a deep breath and ask her. If she isn't interested in something permanent, you need to know now anyway."

Lee nodded as if taking this under deep consideration then as if an afterthought said, "Stub, if you'll stay through the fall semester and help me harvest, I'll pay your share. It will help you pay for the next semester."

"Agreed," he answered with no consideration.

The country had broken the spell of droughts and had enjoyed fine crops these past few years so Lee could afford to help this time.

"Lee," Francis started his sentence timidly. "I still feel that I have been unjust to you. You have always stayed behind and worked so that I could go to school. It's unfair to you and I feel guilty."

"Don't Stub," Lee assured him. "I love being outdoors. I love farming and working with livestock. I would never be happy at an inside job. I don't enjoy school like you do." He slapped him on the back affectionately and said, "Let's go to bed."

Lee limited his trips to Mankato to see Georgie during the busy time in early summer. He did, however, keep contact with her. He wrote her letters occasionally, called frequently and would stop to see her when in town. He wanted her to not feel pressured and he hoped she would see that he would never hurt her.

However, Georgie's reaction to Lee's efforts to keep his distance was to begin wondering if she had been wrong to let herself become so close to him. Even though their relationship was still basically as good friends, she feared that Lee was losing interest in her, just like Paul Morgan had a few years ago. I should have held to my original plan and stayed away from men in the first place, she thought with some regret.

Towards middle of summer, Lee finished early, cleaned up and told his brother he was leaving for Mankato.

"Tonight is going to be 'do or die' night," he informed Francis. "I'm going to give Georgie a chance to either accept me or reject me. Either way, I have to know."

He found Georgie still at work, and waited until closing time.

"Georgie, I would like to take you to supper and a movie," he gave her little choice. It was more a statement than a question.

"That would be nice, "she answered uncertainly.

Once seated in the little downtown cafe, Georgie's demeanor changed, her eyes lit up and twinkled as she remembered her news, "I have a new little niece, Lee. Forrest and Goldie have a new baby girl. She is the sweetest little thing, Lee. All the aunts and uncles just adore her."

Lee chuckled, "There's sure plenty of them. They'll probably spoil her to death."

With Georgie in such a tender mood, Lee decided this the most advantageous time to talk about the engagement.

"Georgie, I have cared for you since we were children, you know that, don't you."

Georgie nodded somberly.

"I loved Nita and we had a good marriage until she died," he continued. "I loved Nita in a different way. I have always had you in my heart. You were my first love. Georgie, I would never leave you and I would never hurt you. I want to be engaged to you and I want you to consider being my wife."

Georgie contemplated all the words. I would never leave you and I would never hurt you seemed to be rattling back and forth in her mind. Suddenly, she understood this had been her dilemma for a long time. She had worried that all her steady boyfriends would tire of her and abandon her.

"Lee, I have always cared for you. When you married, I still admired you as a fine person and considered you a good friend. I know you would never hurt me. You couldn't." Her eyes filled with admiration as she answered, "I would be proud

CHAPTER 37   153

to be your girl. If we still care for each other when the farm work winds down this fall, I will marry you then," she smiled at him enchantingly.

Suddenly, all the barriers seemed to fall down. He reached across the table and offered his hands. Georgie this time did not withdraw, but placed both her hands in his. He squeezed her hands, then on impulse, they laced fingers and smiled. All through the movie that evening Lee held her hand, occasionally looking to give Georgie the assurance she needed. It was gratifying to him that each time he glanced in her direction, she returned his attentions with a soft, tender smile.

They began making plans to be married in the county courthouse in Mankato the following fall.

Once Georgie and Lee were married and settled in their home, their popularity as a couple blossomed. Separately they were known as kind and genial, but together they became irresistible—they had visitors almost every evening.

Vivian and Wiley stopped by in early spring for a short visit.

"How is your teaching career going?" Georgie asked Vivian with sincere interest.

"Pretty well," Vivian replied. "There were no complaints last year, anyway," she giggled. Vivian had very modestly under-rated her ability to teach. She had enjoyed a very successful year. Her zany sense of humor and patient attitude made her a favorite with the children. She had a special way of relating to all the students. The parents were quite pleased with her also. She had in fact received a better job offer for next year. She would teach in District 148 for $75 per month.

Georgia and Leo in 1932. They were married in 1927.

CHAPTER 37

"How is Francis doing?" Vivian asked Lee suddenly.

"He started the first semester of his third year," Lee answered. "I would like to help him more, but money has been so hard to come by these past few years."

"He has a part-time job as janitor this semester," Georgie added. "It will help with room and board expenses."

Francis was able to complete the entire third year with his savings and the money Lee paid him, together with the janitorial job. What a good feeling he thought as he entered into the second semester of his third year. After the semester was finished, he applied for the job of assistant groundskeeper for the following summer. It was also available through the fall months, so he decided to keep it a few months longer, thereby he was able to put away a bit more in his savings. But this put him behind another semester. He would have to wait until second semester to start his senior year.

Francis learned that the school saved the best jobs for the upperclassmen. They thought that the students who made it that far would make it to graduation. He did make it through his fourth year relatively easily. He sold hot dogs and peanuts in the stadium on game days and worked in the concession stands during other occasions throughout the year. This allowed more time for study and he earned his Bachelor of Science degree.

Francis had been advised by his professors to apply for Kansas University Medical School. They practically promised him a space if he would apply. This he did and was duly accepted. Now he was back to his original worry: "Where to find the money?"

CHAPTER 38

Mattie wrote to Francis early in the spring of his last year in college that she worried about "Poppy." He seems to be failing and doesn't see well any more she reluctantly voiced her concerns. Her son sensed her apprehension as she was not one to cause alarm without good cause. He had also noticed that his father had mellowed considerably in the past several years. He wrote his parents that he planned to spend the summer at home and help Dad. Both parents were overjoyed as they were aging.

On his return, young Obert instantly noticed with sadness that his parents had indeed failed. Mattie was gray and heavier; Frank was not the invincible man he remembered. He was now increasingly dependent on others because his eyesight had failed considerably.

When his son questioned him he replied, "It seems like the world has closed its doors on me. I run into walls when I turn, stumble over things I can't see. I can see straight ahead, but have no sight to the sides at all. And," he added, "my forward vision seems to be getting narrower and narrower."

Francis worried about this condition and promised his parents that he intended to check on this next year at school.

Later in the evening, when he and Mattie were alone, she confided another worry she had been carrying.

"Mary has become quarrelsome, Francis," she ventured. "She isn't getting along well with her classmates. She claims real or imagined persecutions continually. She is sharp with her father especially, and with me, though to a lesser degree."

Francis crossed his eyebrows and considered this a short time. He too had noticed Mary's sharpness with Lee and himself. He couldn't understand either where her ideas came from sometimes. She had in the past accused her big brothers of unjust treatment and this he knew was not true. They had been good to her. They had always treated her like a little princess.

"What does Lee say?" Francis queried.

"Oh, you know Lee," Mattie answered with a soft smile. "He thinks everyone is OK. 'Mary's all right,' he tells me. She'll outgrow it."

"Well," Francis answered "it could be paranoia. It could even be schizophrenia. I hope not, but the symptoms sound right for it."

"Francis, those words sound so horrible. All these things you're learning in school give you big ideas. It couldn't be anything as bad as those words sound."

"Mom, it is more common than you think. We just aren't familiar with these disorders out here."

Mattie had intended Francis to ease her mind. Instead, he left her with a heart full of new worries, even more perplexing than the ones she had been harboring. This can't be right, she told herself. Mary can't have a problem that frightful. Nevertheless, she now carried more worries than she had before her son came home.

This was also a year of changes for the Kennedy family. In January, Ern was badly gored by a bull that had been considered a family pet. It was a bad wound in his upper leg. Jessie paid the $55.00 medical bill. The doctor wrote on the bill "Your father's injury was a very ugly and bad wound--in fact one of the worst to clean up. Bark, Hay and bits of his clothing had to be removed or pick out, and I did not expect the good results we got--But feared infection or blood poisoning. Fortunately we got good results--better than I expected at time of the 1st visit." Georgie and Leo came to the house daily to take care of Ern's wound. Francis Obert was in town part of the time and was a big help in caring for the wound.

In February, Vivian and Wiley married. They lived at White Mound, with Vivian teaching and Wiley farming.

In June, Charlie Kennedy graduated from medical school at the University of Colorado in Denver. Fred and Jessie had been married almost five years now and drove Ern and Minta to Colorado for Charlie's graduation. They lived in Salina and both worked at Marshall Motor Company, Fred as a salesman and Jessie as a secretary

While in Denver, the family met Charlotte Mevich, the young woman Charlie had been seeing there. Charlie had first met her a few years before when he played baseball in Oshkosh, Nebraska. Charlotte's family lived there, and she was in town during the summer and went to the baseball games. Charlie returned to Oshkosh to play baseball for the two summers he was in medical school, in addition to the summer before. He also assisted the local doctor.

Charlotte had graduated from high school at age 16 and then attended Nebraska Weslyan University Conservatory of Music, majoring in voice. She also did graduate studies at the Conservatory. Later she taught piano and voice at Barber College in Anniston, Alabama and toured one season with the Chicago light opera company. Charlie had heard her sing on the radio and had gone to see her perform in a large city. She and her mother had lived in Denver for a few months before Charlie's graduation.

The day after Charlie's parents and sister left to return to Kansas, Charlie finished his medical board exams at 10:00 AM, drove to the fraternity house where he had been living, loaded his Ford, met Charlotte, her mother and a few people at the Methodist Church at 11:00, married Charlotte, and at 11:30 started driving west with Charlotte to San Francisco for his medical internship. They drove through mud and snow in the mountains to arrive at Steamboat Springs at 6:00 PM. The only room they could find was at a hotel that did not look too good. They took the room for $1.50. Charlie found the bed to be solid iron and the bedding about the same. The only thing modern in the room was a pitcher that did not leak. The toilet was down the hall. They got up early the next morning to continue driving west.

The next night they got to Salt Lake City and stayed in a nice hotel. They finally got the dirt washed off and had good food. The next morning they slept late and then did some sightseeing before continuing west at 3:30 in the afternoon.

*Charlie and Charlotte Kennedy
about 1930*

CHAPTER 39

For the years he was in college, Francis Obert devoted virtually all his time to studying and working to make money to support himself. He had neither the time nor money to consider developing a relationship with a girl. He accepted that some things must wait until later if he was going to get the education he wanted.

During this same time, Frances Kennedy was not postponing her life. She was working and enjoying life. She bought a car that gave her mobility and had curtains, and she happily worked in different places. She took a trip to New York City with some other teachers and sometimes traveled with a bottle of whisky in her suitcase.

Georgie and Lee saw what Francis and Frances did not see—those two had remarkably similar values and interests. Both were in their mid-20s and had focused on obtaining a college education and developing a career rather than trying to get married like most other young people from rural Kansas. Both had interests far beyond farming in Kansas, but both also had strong family roots and were unlikely to permanently leave the small town life in this region.

Francis and Frances were often home during summers and, not surprisingly, it happened that they often crossed paths at Georgie and Lee's house. They both enjoyed visiting with Georgie and Lee and with each other. They did not recognize that some of these visits may have been orchestrated for them to spend time together.

Frances thought of Francis as a bright college student with a good sense of humor. She encouraged him to pursue his education. Francis admired Frances's enthusiasm for life and enjoyed hearing about her latest adventures. They got to know each other and enjoyed talking, but their conversations about what they were each doing seemed to bring out the fact that they were in different stages of life, as well as living in different locations. There was no effort to flirt or develop a romantic relationship. Francis felt that he needed to stay focused on school and did not see himself as being involved with a girl now. But he sometimes thought to himself, "When I am in a position to have a girl, I hope I can find someone like Frances."

CHAPTER 40

After she had been teaching at Rexford for three years, Frances spent part of the summer at home with Minta and Ern. Francis Obert was also home after graduating from college and was trying to scrape money together to start medical school in the fall at the University of Kansas in Lawrence.

Lyall was staying in Esbon that summer and working on the railroad. He and a friend were planning to become partners in buying a restaurant. Lyall lived in a house with Byron and David. Byron was working in a restaurant in Esbon.

In August Lyall got the flu and it seemed to hang on. Frances told him to go to the doctor but he said he needed to work. Frances left to return to Rexford before Lyall got over the flu. After about three weeks of the flu, he started feeling worse. He went to the doctor's office in Esbon three times on one day, but the doctor was out on house calls. That evening he ate at the restaurant where Byron worked could only eat a few peaches and said his back hurt. Later, at their house, Byron rubbed his back and David stayed up with him when he could not sleep.

The next morning Lyall could not find the doctor in Esbon and got a ride to his parent's farm. He arrived just as Georgie and Lee were arriving. They saw how sick he was and took him to the doctor in Lebanon. They were so relieved to find the doctor in and requested Lyall be seen at once due to his extreme illness. This request was granted. Once into the inner sanctum of the doctor's office, the nurse began the preliminary work for the examination ahead. She noted his temperature was unusually high, his reflexes quite slow, and a general weakness over his entire body. This she related to the doctor as he entered the room.

He conducted a cursory check, looked at the boy and asked, "Where did you get it, son?"

"Get what?" Lyall answered in confusion.

"The bad liquor," the doctor answered with some condemnation.

"Doctor, I haven't had any liquor at all," Lyall answered in irritation.

"Well, I think you have," the doctor insisted. "Now you go home, rest, and take this medicine until you are well." Lyall had to ask the doctor to fill out the check for the medicine because Lyall's fingers were so paralyzed that he could hardly sign the check.

Georgie and Lee were by this time completely bewildered. They helped the sick boy back into the car and took him back home to Ern and Minty.

Minty fussed over him, put him in their downstairs bedroom and became totally dedicated to his care and comfort. Lee talked to Ern out of hearing distance, in the front room.

"The doctor thought he had gotten into some moonshine," he explained. "Lyall insists he did not, and I believe him," Lee continued.

"I know Lyall wouldn't do that either," Ern replied. "At least, that must mean that the doctor doesn't think it is anything too serious. It's probably a bad case of flu," he comforted himself.

That evening the family was becoming increasingly worried and asked Francis Obert to come to the house. When he arrived, he had a calm presence that brought comfort to the family. He focused on providing whatever help he could. Lyall told Francis and Lee that he believed he had infantile paralysis. He said the doctor had not told him that but he just knew it. He also said he thought it would be fatal but asked them not to tell anyone.

Unfortunately, Francis thought that Lyall's diagnosis may be correct. The symptoms of infantile paralysis were well known, and Lyall was increasingly showing those symptoms. Francis stayed that night.

The next morning Lyall's legs and arms became increasingly paralyzed. By mid morning, only his head, heart, and upper lungs were functioning. It was clear now that Lyall had infantile paralysis. There was nothing that could be done. Those in contact with Lyall needed to be quarantined. Contact with other family members was limited because the phone was in

CHAPTER 40

the same room as Lyall. Family members who could not be quarantined, such as Vivian who was teaching, needed to stay away.

That evening Lyall seemed to feel a little better, but about midnight he became worse. He became partially delirious and wanted his father nearby. At one point he said to Minta "Well, what do you say, Mother?" Some stray turkeys had begun roosting in their barn that day so Minta said "I say we have lots of turkeys in our barn, what do you say, Lyall?" He said "I say let's sell 'em."

Early the next morning, Lyall said to Ern "Dad, did you see them?" Ern tried to appease him by saying "yes," but Lyall said "No, you don't—you don't see them like I do—you're just telling me you do. But I see everybody up there. They seem glad to see me." He died shortly after. He was 19 years old.

The funeral was held the next day as a grave-side service. County health officials asked that only immediate family members attend. However, over 100 people drove to the cemetery and stood at a distance along the road during the service. The family members who were not quarantined also stayed at a distance. Friends and neighbors left gifts in the Kennedy's mailbox, but did not approach the house. Those who were in the house with Lyall could not write letters during the quarantine period.

Lyall Kennedy, graduation picture in 1928, two years before getting polio

164　　　　　　　　CHAPTER 40

The man who was selling the restaurant to Lyall arrived in Esbon on the day of the funeral, expecting to sign the contract for the sale. He had not heard of Lyall's illness.

The entire county was quarantined for 8 days. No school, church, or public gatherings of any kind. Children under age 16 could not leave the premises of their homes. Francis Obert could not return to his home and stayed with Leo and Georgie.

CHAPTER 41

The death of a young person in the prime of life can change things. Priorities in life can shift and feelings can change. Lyall's death caused some changes.

Minta was devastated, but made a strong appearance at the funeral for the sake of the family. She knew she had been lucky—thirteen children and this was the first time she had to face the death of a child. But, Lyall died in her bed, and she would not sleep in that bed again. She also began following the news about polio and donated the little that she could to support research on polio.

Tears would roll down Ern's face when he told the stories of Lyall's last hours.

Lyall's death was hardest on Kenneth. He and Lyall had always been the closest of brothers. This was almost impossible for him to endure.

For Francis Obert, Lyall's death brought the realization that he did not want to wait to meet someone like Frances in the future. He wanted someone exactly like her now.

For Frances Kennedy, Lyall's death brought into focus the importance of family. And, it showed her a different side of Francis. Her sister Jessie and other family members described Francis's great compassion and generosity in helping the family during these difficult times. They said that the family could not have gotten along without him. Frances developed a new appreciation for Francis's drive and confidence, and began to see him now as more than just a bright, entertaining college student. She had a flash of insight into what his life was going to be like, and she liked what she saw. When Frances wrote her a letter describing the events with Lyall after she had left, she was ready to respond to his letter—and to him.

They both went home for the Christmas holidays and hoped to spend time together exploring new possibilities for their relationship. Francis was still plagued by the problem of no money. He knew he was not prepared to support a wife. He also worried that instead of taking jobs over these holidays to save for next year's school, he was devoting time to a girl. He could not continue this or there would be no money to finish his education. He explained to her that he did not have any money to take her out and they would have to spend time at Georgie and Lee's, or other friend's houses. He carefully watched her reaction.

"Francis, that is fine with me," she answered with a sincerity he did not doubt. "I'm not used to fancy movie shows and restaurants. I'm just a country girl from a big family."

"What about that fancy trip to New York City?" he mocked with a devilish grin.

"Oh, you know better than that," she snapped.

Lee and Georgie became their social life, and their place of refuge for the holidays. By the end of the Christmas vacation, Georgie and Lee could see that the seeds they had planted over the past few summers were clearly bearing fruit. They took a break from their card game and Frances and Georgie went to the kitchen to fix a light lunch. Georgie was pregnant and due in a month.

"Lee is afraid for me to have a baby" she whispered to her sister. "He is afraid I will die like Nita did. He says he couldn't bear to lose me."

"Tell him we're Kennedys and are made to have babies" she counseled. They both had a good, long laugh over this bit of facetiousness. "I think Francis wants a permanent relationship, Georgie, and it would be good for him, but he is afraid that it would be too difficult while he finishes school. I would probably have to give up my teaching career."

"Would you mind?" Georgie probed gently.

"No, Georgie, no I wouldn't," she said emphatically.

"Well, then just tell him you wouldn't mind and that you would like to help him finish any way you can," she advised.

Frances took this under consideration and decided to have this conversation, either in a future letter or at the next vacation.

CHAPTER 41

Francis returned to finish his first year of medical school. He thought he had never felt so alive. The classes and lectures were stimulating. He was vitally interested in all the things he was learning and could not wait for the second year. Still, the same old problem persisted—money. He made a conscious decision to return home for this summer vacation, find work and save money. But his main objective was to settle the matter of his newfound romance. He and Fanny Kennedy would have to have a serious talk about their future.

His train arrived at the Esbon depot in late afternoon on a lovely spring day. The prairie wind was blowing from the south, bringing up moist warm air, but not a steady harsh wind like early spring. It was more a pleasant soft breeze, dying down then suddenly rising up to gain your attention again.

He suppressed a temptation to walk to the house where Fannie lived, and decided to go home first, get settled, and think things through. He hitchhiked to the highway and then walked the remaining distance. His thoughts were captured with the loveliness of the high plains all around. He had learned to appreciate the beauty of eastern Kansas with its woodlands and green meadows, but as the train traveled toward home, he had to admit that he loved the prairie most of all. The land graduated into uplands and rolling hills with their valleys narrow in places and grassy slopes leading to the creeks. Once upon the rise of a hill, the panorama that came into view was breathtaking. Nothing interrupted the great view of windy grasslands that supported a varied wildlife system. The rabbits, mice, skunks busily ran about with their errands. Squirrels chittering among the groves of trees were busy putting food away for winter.

It was twilight as he neared the Obert land. His mind had cleared as he walked the road home. He was ashamed of the Spartan way he was forced to live and humiliated that he would have to ask Fanny to share this austere life. Still, he knew he must ask. It was not for him to decide what she would or would not like. He had to give her the opportunity to decide her future. He would give her a choice, to marry now and

CHAPTER 41

suffer the discomfort of college life with no money, or to wait until he was finished with school and then marry. After forming this plan, he entered the house with a sense of relief.

Frank and Mattie had become frailer since he was last home. His father's eyesight continued to decline. It was apparent now that he would someday be blind. It seemed impossible that he could actually save his farm. He was not physically able to keep up the required work.

His little sister Mary was also home for a short visit. She had been enrolled in the business school in Salina but the general atmosphere around her betrayed what she was trying to portray. Her many real or imagined persecutions were becoming increasingly hard to believe. Her manner was agitated and her disposition was for the most part sour. Francis decided that his method of coping would be to agree with her, detach and go on. Mattie, he knew, was disturbed by her daughter's obvious change in personality. Mattie had decided to try to convince her daughter of reality versus imagined injustice. Lee, on the other hand, accepted Mary philosophically. If we can't change her, he decided, we'll just learn to live with her. He was aware that she had become increasingly difficult as she passed from adolescence into adulthood. Maybe it's a phase and she will outgrow it, he hoped without much certainty.

Later in the week, Francis borrowed the automobile his parents had recently purchased. It was an economically priced model, but sturdy. He had previously set a date with Fanny to go to the free show and festivities that evening in Esbon. He parked the car at the house where she lived with all her brothers, telling her it was such a pleasant evening to walk a bit. She agreed, and the two ambled about the small, farming village with the trees and flowers all in bloom. The quiet early summer air held the fragrance of the freshly budded flowers from the yards of every home as they walked along. He reached down suddenly, picked a few fresh flowers and handed her the bouquet with the outrageous manners of a medieval knight from King Arthur's court. Frances curtsied coyly, accepted the bouquet, then feeling more at ease curled her fingers in

CHAPTER 41 169

the curve of his elbow and continued the stroll in congenial silence. She withdrew her arm as they neared the main street of the village.

Wooden benches had been built alongside the big brick building that would be used as the screen for the movie this evening. They took their seats, became engrossed in the movie, and before the show ended Francis timidly took her hand. She did not resist. As their fingers curled and locked, she knew positively that when this young man with such determination asked her to marry him, her answer would be "Yes." She felt so safe and secure when she was with him. There was something about his confident attitude that made her feel protected and sheltered.

When the movie ended, they walked to the local drug store to enjoy a soda and then began their slow, intimate walk back to see her safely to her door. "Fanny, I have three more years of medical school left, then one year of internship. There will be no pay during the last year. It will be a little easier because I won't have to pay tuition and books, but on the other hand, there will be no time to work to help with living expenses. Do you think you could bear to live that way for three years?"

"Yes," she answered with a certainty even she wondered at. "I would like to help you finish your education any way I can. I think you will make a fine doctor."

She had turned to him and when finished looked directly into his face—her eyes so sincere, her smile so benevolent. He placed his arms around her, gently kissed her.

"You have made me so happy, Fanny," he whispered. "It will be a hard three years, but when it is over, I promise I will make it up to you."

The playful daytime breezes had died down with the twilight. The night became still and damp. These long summer nights added an atmosphere of romance to their courting. They worked during the day and spent evenings together, but never seemed to tire and had the invigorating natural high that young lovers experience.

CHAPTER 41

They spent many summer nights visiting Lee and Georgie and told their parents of their plans. Mattie was delighted. Little Fanny had always been a favorite of hers. The matter of religion was never mentioned—each family remembered the trouble it had caused before. Francis Obert, especially, did not want the problem spoken of just yet. His intention was to handle it just as his brother Lee had. He had not attended Mass regularly since starting to college anyway. He would just slowly stop attending his church, but never intended to join another. Fanny could attend where she wanted and as often as she wanted, but he would not join her.

Throughout the summer, the people in Esbon watched these two walk through town or amble down the country road between their two family homes. Frances, with her dignified manner, walked very ladylike. Francis Obert sauntered nonchalantly along, his slim, slightly bowed legs carrying him jauntily beside the pretty girl. Now and then he would have to do a hop and a skip to make things a little more interesting. The restless energy of his childhood still bubbled up in him on occasion. They would say, "There goes the Obert boy and the Kennedy girl from Odessa again," or "I hear the Obert boy is trying to be a doctor."

"In a pig's eye," would sometimes be the retort. "Oberts don't have enough to live from week to week, let alone finish all that high-powered schoolin'."

During the first week of August, final plans were made for the wedding. Francis would return early to Lawrence, register for fall classes, find an apartment, and then during the weekend ride back to Esbon. They planned a small wedding, with just Georgie and Lee standing with them. They would go to the county courthouse in Mankato to be married. Then they would immediately pack what few possessions they owned between them and board the train back to Lawrence to start the beginning of his second year in medical school.

The ceremony did not take long. Frances wore her only special occasion dress, a lovely soft pink with shoulder straps. She carried a bouquet from Georgie's flower garden and wore her

CHAPTER 41

inexpensive wedding ring with great pride. The groom dressed plainly in one of his two pairs of black dress pants and one of his two white shirts, the required dress code for school. Georgie and Lee helped them load their few possessions into Lee's automobile, took them to the train station, and watched them leave. Georgie waved as the train chugged slowly out of the station, with tears in her eyes.

"Lee," she whispered, "they are going to have some hard times. I worry about them."

"I know, I do too," he answered, trying to comfort her. "Since the crash on Wall Street in '29, jobs are impossible to find. She will never find a teaching job there. Everyone is taking any job they can get. Even educated people have to take menial jobs to exist. I have never seen anyone so determined to finish a goal, though. I have no doubt that he'll make it through."

Lee and Georgie returned to their small farm with no regrets about the choice they made with their lives. They were happy and loved the farm chores and the great outdoors.

The train picked up speed soon after leaving Esbon, the engine puffing dark smoke to keep its momentum. Frances watched the vista change as the train took them further eastward. She expressed a delight in the green beauty of eastern Kansas.

"It's so different from western Kansas. I can't believe it's the same state," she whispered in wonderment.

The train slowed and stopped at the Lawrence, Kansas depot. The young couple unloaded their belongings and started slowly for the university area. Frances was a bit taken aback at the size of this city. This will take some getting used to, she mentally noted. She enjoyed the slow evening stroll through the residential area of Lawrence and wondered at the green grassy lawns, trees and flowers.

"They must have more water here than we do back home," she mused.

"They have more rain here," her new husband answered absently.

His mind was not at ease. He worried about the next year especially. He privately wondered at the wisdom in asking this lovely woman to share his misery. Maybe I am just selfish, he scolded himself.

They reached the old Victorian home that had his apartment, walked up the stairway to the second floor, and stopped at door #2, a former bedroom. Francis grandly took out his key, unlocked the door, and threw the door open as though he were tour guide for the Taj Mahal. They entered; the young bride stopped to look over her new home. It's dark and dingy she noticed first of all, a bit small and cramped. The room was kitchen, dining room and living room combined. A sink against the far wall, the stove next to it, an old icebox, and small counter finished the cooking area. A small table and three chairs completed the kitchen. The rest of the room was strewn with old dirty overstuffed furniture. Behind the door of the adjoining room was a small bedroom with an antique bathroom, presumably made from a former closet. This guy wasn't kidding when he said he had been living a Spartan existence, she mentally noted.

But aloud she said, "Well, at least we don't have to cut wood to cook and find the outhouse when we need it. If there is running hot water for baths, we'll be comfortable. We can cozy this up quite a bit later on when we're settled and I find a job."

He adored her at that moment. She had dispelled his worries about how she would accept this life and had given him peace of mind to begin his second year of training. After they had put away their few things and straightened the living space a bit, they luxuriously soaked in the old bathtub and prepared for their first night together.

Francis put his arm around his new bride, pulled her close and kissed her with undemanding control.

"We can't have a baby for at least two years, you know," he explained.

"I know," she nodded. "We won't."

Their first day together was spent working around the apartment, rearranging furniture and cleaning. Monday

CHAPTER 41

morning the student hurried off to his classes. Frances stayed in the apartment and continued cleaning and rearranging furniture. She wandered outside in the afternoon to find a few groceries for their evening meal. She brought all the money she had saved from her teaching career, and intended to use it to help support them this year. However, she was taught to be frugal from childhood, so did not intend to spend it too quickly. She chose a beef bone and some vegetables to make a soup for the evening. I will get a small piece of ice for the icebox to keep the leftover soup fresh for maybe two meals more, she planned mentally. Then later, Francis can bring in a larger piece that will last longer. The following day she planned to start looking for work to help pay the rent and groceries.

Francis returned home from his second day of classes to find his new bride sobbing at the kitchen table. His heart took a leap then tumbled to the bottom of his chest cavity with an aching thump. He knew she wouldn't be able to stand this life. She is probably going to go back home he decided with a heavy heart.

"What's wrong, Fanny?" he asked with trepidation.

"I found a job today," she sobbed into her hanky.

"Well, that's good news, isn't it?" he asked completely bewildered. "What is the job?"

"It's in a tailor shop. I will work as a seamstress," she answered with a choke in her voice.

"You are probably disappointed, being an experienced teacher to have to take a job like that," he probed further.

She shook her head.

"Then what is bothering you?" he finally asked in exasperation.

"I can't sew-oo-oo," the word trailed off like an echo in a canyon.

At this he took her in his arms, patted her shoulder, pushed the wet hair from her face and chuckled a bit. He could not help it. She was so comical in her misery.

True to her word, she lasted only a few weeks at that job. She had predicted this outcome from the start, so to Francis

174 CHAPTER 41

she only reported, "I couldn't stitch fast enough to suit the boss and he fired me. I expected it," she shrugged.

"You will find another job that you like better," he comforted her.

This she was able to do. She accepted two small jobs throughout the semester, clerking in a dime store and working in a bakery.

She considered their life in Lawrence to be settled and stable, so when Francis related his new plans, she was taken by surprise. He suggested that he transfer to the KU Medical Center in Kansas City.

"But what could be the advantage in that, Francis?" she questioned with wide astonished eyes.

"They tell me that there are more job opportunities there, for you as well as me, though tuition is higher in Kansas City," he explained without wholehearted conviction. "Mostly, though, Fanny I've been hearing that the training is more extensive and that I will stand a better chance of doing my internship there if I graduate from Kansas City."

"Well, then, "she answered, "we'll go to Kansas City."

Thanksgiving arrived before they realized it. Instead of celebrating with a holiday dinner, they rode the train to Kansas City to look for an apartment and inquire about jobs. Money was again becoming a problem with them, so the dimes they spent on train fare were hard to come by. Even so, they felt the trip was an unfortunate necessity. The train ride into Kansas City was uneventful, but interesting. They enjoyed the changing scenery and the woodlands, which they considered to be forests having come from the high plains where trees were only seen along the creeks and rivers. The land became increasingly hilly, with heavier forested woodlands each mile they traveled eastward.

"We have to find an apartment with a shower, Fanny. That is the first requirement," Francis murmured, his thoughts turning to words of their own accord.

"A shower," she turned with a startled look.

CHAPTER 41

"That is going to be a requirement when we start our sterile procedures," he explained. "Our professor gave a lecture on sterile procedures the other day and said, 'You must start with your own personal hygiene in order to follow sterile procedures.' He stressed that in order to be sanitary, you must keep your hair clipped short because a lot of organisms live in the hair, and it must be washed every morning. He prefers his students begin each day with a hot shower and shampoo. Only then will you be able to begin sterile procedure. If your hair or body is dirty, all the sterile procedure in the world will do no good," he finished explaining to his puzzled wife.

The school allowed them to sleep in visitors' quarters and eat in the school cafeteria, which enabled them to finish their business and return to Lawrence for classes.

Francis had to finish final exams before the end of the semester and needed his free time to study. Fanny intended to begin packing so the job would not be enormous at the last minute. In the meantime though, she intended to acknowledge the fast approaching Christmas holiday in some small way. She insisted the Sunday before Christmas that they find a small tree for the apartment. She had never missed a holiday at home until this year, she reminded her new husband. Francis crossed his eyebrows a bit in irritation, but did agree to help her look that afternoon. They rode a bus to the outskirts of town, then walked slowly along the open fields. Francis noticed a loose limb from an evergreen tree, reached up to loosen it, when it broke away. He brought it down, sat it upright and was surprised at how like a small tree it stood.

"What do you think, Fanny?" he asked.

Fanny was delighted, "It's perfect," she answered in a soft whisper.

The happy couple hurried home with their treasure where Francis immediately returned to his studies and his happy wife began setting her limb into a container of dirt and sand. When the angle suited her and the tree looked like a genuine Christmas tree, she spent the remainder of the evening making ornaments from common household products. A star from tinfoil, a snowman from cotton balls, snowflakes from pieces of lace and a little angel for the top. When she was finished, she called Francis, who was by this time deep in concentration and barely heard her. He looked up from his books, a bit bewildered, and finally understood what she wanted. As the two gazed at their first tree, in the glow of the streetlights below, it slowly transformed into the most gorgeous decoration either had seen.

The lights from the window behind picked up light in the little metallic ornaments. They sparkled and twinkled in the darkened room. The angel seemed to be descending in an effervescent cloud.

"It's beautiful, Fanny," he breathed softly in total sincerity.

"It's the prettiest tree I have ever seen," she replied equally sincerely. She considered it one of the many miracles that the Christmas season presents century after century.

"Fanny, we need to talk about Christmas this year. Come over here," he patted his lap.

He placed her comfortably on his lap and tenderly looked into her eyes. "We can't afford gifts for one another this year," he began hesitatingly. "We will save the money for getting settled in Kansas City."

Fanny nodded her agreement. "What about Christmas dinner?"

"Fanny, we'll make it peanut butter sandwiches or something like that this year. Someday we'll have a turkey with all the trimmings," he smiled as he made her this vow.

She agreed, just happy that they were together and able to follow through this far with their coveted goal. When the semester tests were finally over, the young couple at last allowed themselves a few days of complete relaxation.

Christmas morning Fanny rose first, put on her robe and slippers, and started for the kitchen to make coffee and begin their breakfast, but then noticed a small package underneath the little Christmas tree. What could that be, she wondered, as she hurried toward the tree to make a closer inspection. Why, it's a box wrapped with a bow with my name on it, she mused.

CHAPTER 41

Suddenly, she understood the meaning of this little box. Francis had tricked her. He had slipped the present under the tree before going to bed last night. Tears suddenly gathered in her bright eyes and a lump constricted her throat. The tears she could not control started flooding over the brim of her eyes and a soft sob slipped from deep inside without warning. She opened the box to find a lovely watch and then the sobs wracked her whole body. She lay her head in her arms across the table and sobbed uncontrollably. Francis entered the kitchen in time to watch the scene unfold before him. He thought his heart would break to see her so distressed and could hardly control his own tears.

He leaned over her and gently said, "Fanny, I thought the watch would make you happy."

"Yes, it does, dear," she answered, "but I feel so bad that I didn't get anything for you."

"That was my plan, Fanny. I wanted you to have the watch, but did not want you to spend money on me. Please, it made me happy giving it to you."

She whimpered a small sigh, shuddered and hugged him tight. "I'll always remember this Francis," she promised.

After the holiday ended, the test results were announced and Francis was relieved he had done well. In the meantime, he had been accepted at Kansas City for the second semester. The young Oberts finished packing and took the train from Lawrence for the last time to begin their new venture.

Once again, Fanny was only able to find small, part-time or temporary jobs. She cheerfully took them, but it was only enough to eke out an existence. Their savings began to slowly diminish. They felt the third year would be entirely possible, but worried about the last year. They calculated all their savings would be gone by the end of the third year and Francis had no time to work now. There had been no mention of the coming predicament, but the realization was heavy on both their minds.

Fanny received a letter from home after returning early from her downtown job. She was sitting at the kitchen table reading the letter intently when Francis entered the apartment.

"It's a letter from Mom," she told him as she looked up. "She says that Charlie has finished his internship and is starting a practice in Paso Robles, California. Mom says it's a perfect place for him because the Phillies spring practice is held there. That brought him to his final decision to go there. He says the weather is beautiful. She also says the weather this year looks good so far for crops. The prices are down though, so that they can't make any money even if they do raise a good crop. Something about the tariff trade."

"Yes," Francis answered, "the government, in all its wisdom, has put a high tariff on imports. Well, of course, foreign countries answered with a high tariff of their own. Now, we can't sell our products to Europe and can't afford to buy their products. With unemployment growing every day, I don't see how this country can continue. There will be a terrible depression," he predicted. "Well, at least Charlie has finished." He fell into a dejected state of mind when these thoughts became words and were spoken.

"I'm so happy mom and dad got to go to Charlie's graduation in Denver last year and meet Charlotte. They have been so shackled with their big family that they have never had a trip out of the county. Vivian and Wiley kept the teenage boys and Georgie and Lee kept the two younger boys," she reminded him.

"It's payback time and Ern's older children know it. I admire the respect they show your parents and they deserve it. They've been extraordinarily good to their family and now the family wants to show their appreciation. Someday, Fanny, when we're setup, we'll do something nice for Ern and Minty, too."

CHAPTER 42

Francis and Fanny took the train home for an early summer visit. They found Georgie in good health and the baby strong. Lee was mostly over the fears that remained from his first marriage.

"Georgie," she smiled, "now I have three little nieces and two little nephews. Forrest and Goldie are going to be hard for you to keep up with. Three little girls, one little boy and another on the way."

"Vivian and Wiley are expecting too, Frances," Georgie answered with a grin. Poor Ern and Minty. They will start all over again with grandchildren now." Both girls laughed and knew that Ern and Minty would enjoy the grandchildren, no matter how many they had.

Francis slipped over to see his parents one afternoon during the weekend. Frank and Mattie had continued to decline since his last visit. Frank would soon be blind. Mattie had lost her youthful strength and energy, but remained cheerful. He left with a worried mind and did not see how his father could make the payments on the farm. The weather had cooperated unusually well he knew, but the depression made it hard to sell the crops for any profit. His father's failing strength, together with the state of the economy, only added to his concerns about the future.

He also worried that the short-term prosperity in his life with Frances would soon come to an end. It was true their savings would pay tuition for the third year, and that Fanny would find a job of some kind to help with their living expenses. But it was obvious that next year would finish their small savings accounts. He kept these dismal thoughts firmly locked in his mind with a conscious effort never to divulge his worries to Fanny. She had been so supportive through these tribulations, with never a word of complaint. He knew he could never have found a finer wife if he had looked the world over, and to think he found her across the field—the girl next door, with whom he had grown up.

He returned to Kansas City in a dejected state of mind. If I don't shake this attitude, I will never keep my grade average up and I won't make it, he rebuked himself on the way to his class the following week. As he passed from class to class he still carried with him this black, unproductive mood.

His latest change in temperament had not gone unnoticed by Frances either. She mechanically managed her morning chores and started for the streets to find another job, with uneasy acceptance of this new side of her husband. Though her mind was heavy, she did manage to push her worries back and concentrate on finding a job. Toward late afternoon, she saw an encouraging sign in the window of a hardware store, "HELP WANTED." The owner liked her quiet charm and mild manner as he asked the required questions. He considered that this young couple did indeed have a basic integrity and persistence so hired her on the spot. She hurried home feeling a new exuberance for the upcoming year. She was working in the little antique kitchen of their apartment when Francis came home, whistling a happy little tune. She looked up in surprise at this sudden change in mood and smiled brightly at him. His usual happy-go-lucky disposition had returned. He winked back at her welcoming smile with his trademark impish grin.

"Fanny, I've just met the most interesting guy I've ever known. We were partnered together in the science lab today. He's not one of the rich boys but he is better off than we are. He is still living at home here in Kansas City. His father is a railroad conductor, so you know that they are comfortable enough. His parents help him, but he has had to work along the way as well. He has a girlfriend named Berniece and wants us to get together next weekend. He says they can't get married until he is finished because he is afraid his folks will withdraw their help."

"That would be fine," she exclaimed with excitement. "I haven't had a girl for a friend since we were married."

The weekend arrived and Herb Beauchamp brought his girlfriend Berniece to their apartment for an evening of diversion. Before the first hour had ended, the two couples were completely comfortable with one another and well on the way to a lifetime friendship. Herb Beauchamp was indeed an "interesting" person. His continual wisecracks and booming bolt of laughter kept all his friends happy when he was around. He was short and mildly stocky, built a little like Lee, Francis noticed. His hair was light red, and he had a cheerful round face and an eternal grin. His manner was determinedly puckish and drew people to him like a magnet. He and Berniece together were like a comedy team. She would cackle at his jokes as if she were a paid audience. His nature was always cheerful and Berniece was likewise good-natured. Francis and Fanny loved being with them. Their special relationship blossomed as the last semester drew to a close.

The holiday season was again drawing near with little hope of this Christmas being any different from the last for the Oberts. They could not avoid the bleakness that would occur when Christmas Day finally arrived. There would be no presents for either of them this year, and worse, the only food in the house was an onion and some bouillon with a small piece of cheese leftover.

"We'll have some onion soup," Fanny announced grandly, with a grin.

"I feel like such a failure, Fanny," he replied.

She was able to allay his feelings of failure quickly, by insisting he help make the soup.

Early in the afternoon, Beauchamp and Berniece dropped by for a visit. They felt so ashamed that they had not invited Obert and Fanny to have Christmas dinner with them at Beauchamps' parents.

"Mom always has enough food for the whole biology class," he admitted. "Dad has a good job for these days and we at least always have food. Next time, you're coming home with me for holidays."

At this time, there was a knock on the door. A good neighbor in the apartment house had "suspicioned" there would be sparse fare for this couple, so they shared their dinner with them. Placed before them on the table was a bountiful meal: turkey, gravy, cranberries, rolls and all the other accompaniments.

"Beauchamp, Berniece, come share with us. Eat what you can. It will make Christmas dinner more festive for us," Francis begged.

The two new friends had tagged one another with last names as a show of their special camaraderie. Francis had never felt such a comfortable familiarity with another living being outside his own family.

"Obert, I can always find room for a little bit more Christmas dinner," Beauchamp chortled.

The four friends were soon enjoying this wonderful meal and the kind thoughts of the neighbor, a stranger to them until this day.

"Fanny, weren't you a teacher before you were married?" Beauchamp suddenly asked.

"Why, yes," she answered, startled.

"Well, girl, there's an opening in the children's ward for a combination tutor/nurse. It would be a perfect job for you. You better get in there and apply first day school opens."

"Fanny, if you could get that job, it would make life so much easier," Francis breathed. He could barely allow himself to hope for such a wonderful break. Fanny was as apprehensive as he. She did not dare to become too confident, in case she did not get this job.

On the day school reopened she was waiting at the personnel office. She asked if it was true that the job was open and was elated to learn that it was. She immediately applied for it. Her resume looked good to the personnel manager. He liked her manner and appearance and hired her without further ado. She left the office, her eyes sparkling with tears of happiness. She could not believe her good fortune. Maybe our luck is turning, she thought hopefully.

CHAPTER 42   183

That evening when Francis returned from classes she was so excited for him to know, she just blurted, "I got it, Francis. I got the job," and ran to hug him in her great euphoric happiness.

He too, silently wondered if their luck had changed. This was indeed a cause for a celebration. He called Beauchamp and arranged for the four of them to go out for hamburgers. Nothing was too extravagant for this occasion, he reasoned, and in this way justified his impulsive action.

Frances loved her job. She loved working with children and these little sick children were especially endearing. They soon loved their teacher/nurse in turn. Everyone admired her expertise in this difficult job and her job security was gratifying to her.

The second semester was much smoother with her higher salary. Both of them working in the same building complex and her meals provided by the hospital made life much easier. They finished the semester happy in their newfound fortune.

True to his promise, Beauchamps' parents invited them to Sunday dinner every week. The meals were sumptuous, and Mrs. Beauchamp insisted they take home leftovers each Sunday evening, which provided much needed food for the next day or two.

Spring was approaching and final tests for the third year of school. Neither could believe they had accomplished this much since their marriage. One more year, both thought independently, and we'll be finished with the hardest part. Both felt exuberance to be so close to attaining their lofty goal.

They planned to spend their summer vacation at home with Georgie and Lee. Francis could spend time helping his parents and Frances could spend some time with Minty and Ern. They could both help Georgie and Lee, who had helped them so much. They hoped too that they could maybe earn a little money somewhere during the long summer months. Fanny had the summer off from her job at the hospital, but was assured it would resume next fall. The packing began with a feeling of confidence by both partners. It would be wonderful to be home again, to be in the old familiar neighborhood and to be without

CHAPTER 42

all the stresses and worries that had become part of their daily life. They knew they did not have quite enough money for tuition for the last year of school, but Francis predicted confidently that he could easily get a loan for the senior year. He would see a banker later in the summer.

As they had hoped, the summer was one of the most carefree, blissful periods they had ever spent. As the end drew near they felt mixed emotions. They hated to leave the peace of the quiet countryside with their families close by, yet they were anxious to finish this trying episode in their lives. They were close to the finish and exceedingly anxious to go out in the world, make a home and go to work.

Francis planned a trip into town the following day to get his loan for the last year of school. While he was gone, Fanny would begin packing and preparing for their trip back to Kansas City. He arrived at the bank in early afternoon, entered the door nonchalantly, asked to speak to the president and waited patiently in the front part of the bank. Presently, a young woman motioned him to follow her.

"Mr. Childers will see you now," she told him, rather haughtily.

Hmph!, he thought. Who does she think she is. Just a small town clerk in a small town bank. He entered the office of the president, smiled and extended his hand. The bank president was a short, rotund man with a round head that sat at a downward angle, neckless on his shoulders. He gave the impression of a prehistoric man as he strutted about his little domain in the little country town.

"Hello, Mr. Childers. You probably don't remember me, but I'm Francis Obert, Frank Obert's second son."

"Hello, there young man," he replied. "What can I do for you today?"

"You may know, or you might not," Francis began, "but I've been in school for the past ten years. I've just completed my third year in medical school and can't quite put enough money together to pay my tuition for the last year. I have eighty-five dollars saved, but need thirty-five dollars more in order to

CHAPTER 42

finish. I wondered if the bank would make me a loan for the remaining thirty-five dollars? I will pay you as soon as I get out of school and get to work," he finished in a sincerely humble manner.

Mr. Childers leaned back in his chair, studied the young man as though he were a feudal lord deciding the fate of a peasant on his estate. His manner was uncomfortably pretentious as though he were enjoying this power he held over his fellow mortals.

"Money is hard to come by these days, as you know, Mr. Obert. A depression is sure as the world on the way. I have an obligation to my patrons to make careful decisions on the loans I give. I think at this time you would be considered a poor risk. I'm sorry."

Then he excused Francis as though he were a flea on his collar. Francis' usual confident demeanor had just been shattered. This rebuff brought him down to the depths of despair. The shock was traumatic. He left the building with the appearance of complete humiliation. What am I going to tell Fanny, he wondered. How will I explain this to all my classmates and friends? He rode slowly home in deep contemplation. He unhitched the horse, led him to the barn, and slowly returned to the house after caring for the animal.

Once inside the house he took Fanny aside and told her in a whisper, "He refused me the loan, Fanny."

Horrified, she blurted, "What will we do?"

"I don't know, Fanny. Go out and try to find a job somewhere? Go back to school to become a teacher. I just don't know," he was in such a state of dejection she did not have the heart to question further.

She whispered this development to Georgie who gasped in complete disbelief and immediately ran out to find Lee to give him the message. Lee started for the house on the run, his normally happy disposition gone. His face revealed seething anger. He threw the door open and demanded, "Is it true, what Georgie told me?"

"Yes, Lee, it's true. He refused me the loan," was the cheerless answer.

"That #$%*@jackass," Lee exploded. "Bankers think they are God. I feel like going in there and knocking him right on his fat kapoot."

"Leo Obert," Georgie hissed, her face red with surprise, "I've never heard you talk like that."

"No, Lee, don't get yourself in trouble. I'll figure something out. I'll find the money someplace or go on and make a different career. Either way, I'll get back at that pompous baboon someday."

This time, both Kennedy girls put their hands to their mouths, blushed, and then collapsed in uncontrollable giggles.

"I knew things were going too good," Francis complained the first morning after they arrived in Kansas City. "You have a good job at the hospital, and I don't have the money to return to school. I don't know if I should try to get a teaching certificate or just look for a job. One thing sure though, I have to go talk to the Dean of Medicine this morning and formally resign. Then we'll decide what to do. Maybe he can guide me into another career."

They left the house together, she to begin another year in the children's ward and he to begin the resignation process. They walked in silence with downcast eyes. To speak now would only open the painful wound. He gave her a quick, friendly peck as she turned toward the hospital ward and he continued straight toward the Dean's office. Once there, he dreaded the encounter. He went over the possible words in his mind, but could not find the right phrasing. He became more nervous and agitated as he waited outside the door to his office. Suddenly, the secretary opened the door and invited him in.

"Good morning, Mr. Obert," the Dean greeted him warmly. "I hope this isn't about some problem you are having."

"Dean Miller," he started feebly, then cleared his throat. "At the last minute, I was unable to get a loan to finish school. I wasn't able to put together the entire amount for tuition. I was hoping you could direct me to a job, or maybe to a different career altogether."

The Dean leaned back in his chair, trying not to show the surprise and disappointment he felt. After some thought, he began to speak.

"Obert, I've watched your progress during your college career. I admire your perseverance and your endurance. You would make a fine doctor. That much I know. Your professors all speak well of you. We can't afford to lose the prospects of a good doctor now. I'll tell you what I'll do. I'll make you the loan, whatever it is. It will be a private loan and you need not repay me until you are finished and set up in your own practice."

"You would do that, sir?" Francis whispered in disbelief.

"Yes, I would be happy to do that. How much do you need?"

"Thirty five dollars, sir," came the instant reply.

Dean Miller allowed a small, slightly amused smile, wrote out a check and without fanfare handed it to the astonished young man.

"I can't thank you enough, sir," the young man stammered. "Someday, I'll make this up to you."

He rushed to the business office, paid his tuition and enrolled for classes. Next, he hurried to the ward where Fanny was already working with the children.

"The Dean made me the loan," he told her breathlessly. "My tuition is paid and I am enrolled in my senior year."

Her head jerked upward involuntarily. They grasped hands, put their foreheads together, then squeezed hands in a mutual victory celebration.

"I have to get registered in my classes," he told her as he released her hands. "It will take most of the day. I'll see you this evening, after work."

188 CHAPTER 42

CHAPTER 43

The first day of school Beauchamp and Francis requested they be lab partners again. As they set up their lab work for the day Francis casually told Beauchamp his experience the past few days.

"I just about wasn't here today," he related. "The obdurate &*$# in the bank in my home town turned my loan down. I'll remember him though, he's filed away on my special list."

Beauchamp looked up at him, surprise in his eyes and something more. Francis thought he saw a worried look in his friend's face this morning.

"Everything's OK now, though," he reassured him.

"No, Obert, it isn't that," Beauchamp answered. "I have some troubles of my own."

Francis straightened, looked directly at his buddy and waited. Beauchamp seemed distracted and agitated today, he noticed—more upset than he had ever seen him. Still he said nothing.

Finally, Beauchamp quit his aimless puttering, looked directly at him and explained, "My wife's pregnant, Obert."

Francis' mouth dropped, a startled look overtook his whole face. "What wife?" he answered, dumbly. "You don't have a wife."

"It's Berniece. She's pregnant. Don't look at me like that. We've been secretly married for a few months now, but if my parents find out, I'm afraid they won't help me anymore. It's enough for them to support me, but now if I burden them with a wife and a baby—Obert, I'm afraid I'm done for now."

The two friends talked this over a short while before class began. In the end Beauchamp knew there was nothing for him to do but to go to his parents and tell them everything. He knew that it was up to them now to decide what they wanted to do about his situation.

The semester progressed smoothly. Francis and Fanny had by now recovered from their traumatic period. Beauchamp and

Berniece had been easily accepted by his parents. They took Berniece in with open arms and anxiously awaited their new baby. Fanny told Francis that she knew they would accept them.

"They are such wonderful people," she marveled. "We could not have gone this far without their help."

"They have been about as good to me as anyone I have ever known," Francis agreed.

He then told Fanny about the deformed baby delivered in OB today. He said it was taken away without even allowing the parents to see it. They brought it over to the lab where he and Beauchamp were working and let them examine it. "That crazy Beauchamp came up with another of his lunatic ideas. He stuck a pencil under the window in the lab so that we could open it from the outside tonight. He wants to take you and Berniece in to see the baby. Do you want to risk it?"

"What would happen if we were caught?" Fanny asked with her usual caution.

"We would be in a lot of trouble," he answered matter-of-factly.

Over the course of the evening, he talked her into this risky venture. She had much apprehension about this open violation of the rules. On the other hand, she had never been involved in anything so daring and thought that defying the rules one time in her life would be kind of fun. They cleared the table after supper and cleaned the kitchen together. As they left the apartment, Fanny's heart was accelerated with nervous excitement.

They met Beauchamp and Berniece outside the hospital building and stood around casually watching for witnesses. When they considered it safe, they all slipped toward the side of the building. There, just as he had left it, the window was slightly open. The pencil could just barely be seen from the outside. Beauchamp lifted Francis a bit until he could get the window open and then bent over and let Berniece stand on his back to gain entrance into the building. Next, they pushed Fanny through. Then Beauchamp pushed Francis through the window. Last, they pulled Beauchamp through. Beauchamp shut the window tight, then all four started tip-toeing through the dark, quiet room. Berniece was in the lead, with Beauchamp guiding her with his hands on her shoulders, followed by Fanny and Francis bringing up the rear. Beauchamp had a flashlight but dared not use it yet—not until they reached the back rooms where the light could not be seen from the outside. Suddenly, Berniece stumbled over something, dropped over with her hands and let escape a blood-curdling scream. Beauchamp clamped his hands over her mouth,

"Shhh!" he whispered coarsely. "Are you trying to get us arrested?"

He slowly pulled her up, flashed his flashlight on the corpse of a young woman, a Jane Doe brought in from the streets. She would be used in lab class tomorrow.

"Hello, Ramona," he whispered, and headed the group along. Frances and Bernice followed with mindless distraction, their heads turned back to watch the corpse as if it were going to rise and follow them.

They finally reached the back room where the monster baby was kept. Beauchamp flashed his light, Fanny and Berniece gasped, clasped their hands to their mouths and averted their eyes. The body was round and animal-like, with fur all over. The face was less than human and its hands were more like paws. It was more than disturbing to look at.

"The poor mother," Berniece exclaimed. "How could she stand seeing this."

"She didn't," Beauchamp answered softly. "They took the baby away, told her it was deformed and she was never allowed to see it."

"How sad," Fanny murmured. "The poor little baby. It's a blessing it didn't live."

The four adventurers slipped quietly back to the window, where they crawled out in the same stealthy manner they had entered. They closed the window completely when they left, leaving no evidence of their foray, and then went to the

CHAPTER 43

campus cafe to celebrate their successful mission with pie and coffee.

The year seemed to advance very rapidly. The practical jokes and pranks the two med students kept inventing, together with the expectation of the Beauchamp's baby, made the time pass quickly. In early spring, Berniece presented Beauchamp with a son. They named him after his father and grandfather, Herbert Earl Beauchamp. Francis and Fanny adored the new baby. Fanny was anxious for the time when she could have a baby of her own.

They made plans to spend this summer at home just as they had the last, except this year would not have the worry of money for tuition. They were not so naive as to think their money worries were over, however. They knew they had a year to live in Kansas City on just Fanny's paycheck alone and that it would not be an easy year. They had depleted their savings and Francis could not possibly work during the internship period.

Toward the end of the semester, after the lecture period in obstretics, the professor called Francis to stay a minute after class.

"I want to talk to you," was all the explanation he gave the apprehensive student. As the class filed out, Francis remained in his seat nervously pounding his pencil on the desk.

The professor took off his glasses, looked through the light, absently wiped his nose and cleaned his glasses. "Obert, you show promise as an obstetrician," he began. "I've watched you and you have the basic ingredient that makes a baby doctor, whatever that is," he grinned. "It's something elusive, a quality you can sense. If you'll stay an extra year with me in my practice, I'll teach you everything I know and when I'm ready to retire, I'll turn the whole practice over to you. What do you say?"

He pursed his lips, crossed the brows until they met at the bridge of his nose and thought profoundly about this marvelous offer. It was tempting. He could hardly resist, but after long consideration he answered, "I'm extremely tempted by this offer, Professor Brewster, but I have been poor since I graduated from high school. My patient wife has been living from hand to mouth ever since she married me. I have just got to get out, start a practice and make some money. If my situation were different, I would agree to the offer in a minute. Thank you, for the chance anyway. I consider it a real honor."

He left the classroom full of mixed emotions. As he walked away, he realized that his experience studying medicine had been like that—always mixed emotions.

Graduation day approached with none of the young wives in the group owning a decent dress to wear. The women were all concerned about attending without being properly dressed. At the last minute, a package arrived from the aunt of one of the wives. She was a wealthy woman and had been told of this predicament of the young people. She sent an assortment of dresses with matching hats and gloves for the wives to use. The dresses were on loan and were returned after the ceremonies. It seemed to Fanny as if they must have a guardian angel. Every time we meet an obstacle, some kind soul appears to help. She picked a soft, powdery pink, tiered dress with a bow at the neck. The matching round hat and gloves completed the outfit.

"I feel grander than the day we were married," she told Francis as she finished primping and whirled to face him.

"You look terrific," he answered with approving eyes.

They left early for the ceremonies as he had to get into his cap and gown and get lined up.

Francis was especially delighted with the choice of William Allen White as the main speaker for the program. He had long admired him. He read all his editorials as well as his books. This promised to be one of the finest days of his life. He couldn't remember when he felt so content and lighthearted. During the ceremony the students listened intently to the Dean and to the minister, and especially to the main speaker. Like the lectures they had heard in ethics classes, White admonished them to treat each patient as though he were a member of their own family. The theme of his lecture was from the ledgers of an ancient Chinese doctor, many centuries ago. He finished by quoting the old doctor:

"If your patients can't afford to pay you, treat them anyway. Treat them free of charge. Money is not so important as to be loved and remembered."

The slightly emotional ceremony was finished with the young graduates taking the Oath of Hippocrates. With constricting throats and shining eyes, they repeated:

"I swear by Apollo, the physician, and Aesculapius, & Health & all the Gods & Goddesses, that according to my ability & judgment, I will keep this Oath & this stipulation: to reckon him who taught me this Art equally dear to me as my parents, to share my substance with him & relieve his necessities if required to look upon his offspring in the same footing as my own & to teach them this Art if they shall wish to learn it.

Without fee or stipulation & that by precept, lecture, & every other mode of instrument I will impart a knowledge of the Art to my own sons & those of my teachers & to disciples bound by a stipulation & oath.

According to the law of medicine but to none others, I will follow the system of regimen which, according to my ability & judgment, I consider.

For the benefit of my patients & abstain from whatever is deleterious & mischievous, I will give no deadly medicine to any one if asked, nor suggest any such counsel, & in like manner I will not give to a woman a pessary to produce abortion.

With purity & with holiness I will pass my life & practice my art. I will not cut persons laboring under the stone, but will leave this to be done by men who are practitioners of this work. Into whatever houses I enter, I will go into them for the benefit of the sick, & will abstain from every volunteer act of mischief & corruption. And further from the seduction of females or males of freemen & slaves. Whatever in connection with my professional practice or not in connection with it, I see or hear, in the life of men, which ought not to be spoken of abroad, I will not divulge as reckoning that all such should be kept secret. While I continue to keep this Oath unviolated, may it be granted to enjoy life and the practice of the Art respected by all men in all times. But should I trespass & violate this Oath, may the reverse be my lot."

The new doctor and his devoted wife walked slowly and thoughtfully home that warm spring evening. The birds were singing as they always had. The spring breeze blew as it always did. Yet nothing was the same. In fact, after the graduation ceremony, the repeating of the Oath of Hippocrates, the whole past eleven years, life had changed forever. Never would things look the same way again. They clasped hands, swinging them joyfully as they walked. The world suddenly seemed bright and carefree.

"Fanny, we have one more year ahead of us. Can you stand another hard year?"

"One more year seems a flash in the pan now," she answered happily.

CHAPTER 44

Georgie and Lee were waiting at the depot when they stepped off the train. They had come to their place of refuge for a brief rest before the internship began.

"Hello, Doc," Lee offered his hand, his face alight with pride.

"Lee, did you ever think we would get this far?" Francis grinned back.

He would be known as just plain "Doc" from now on. Georgie grabbed little Carroll's hand and waved it.

"Say hello to Uncle Doc," she told the smiling boy.

They all settled in the little rattletrap car and bounced down the country roads toward the Obert home—now a family of three. A radiant glow beamed from Lee's face when he looked at the little boy that sat happily between his father and his uncle.

"Last year was dry and dusty, Doc. We didn't raise much, barely enough to feed the livestock and a little to keep for seed. But this year has been the worst I've ever seen. The winds started in March and have never really let up," he continued. "If the rains don't come and the dirt doesn't quit blowing, a lot of farmers are going to go broke. I'm glad we're only renting for now. If I had payments to make, I would be out of business myself."

Francis shook his head sadly and looked out the window at the dry, burned earth.

The dry, gusty winds kept the dirt swirling ahead of them, giving the illusion of smoke filtering through the sky. Farms, machinery, houses and buildings were only a vague outline in the ever-constant melee of hot, blowing dust.

In the back seat Frances looked out one window and Georgie the other, each thinking her own thoughts. Frances was suffering an aching nostalgia as the car passed field after field of slowly withering stalks. What has happened to Kansas, she wondered. She was reliving the carefree days on the homeplace with Dumb Old Donkey, the baseball games, and the girls' games—when the pastures were green, the crops straight and tall, and the wind only a breeze that cooled the face and body. She remembered when the air was clean and pure.

Georgie interrupted her reverie, "I don't know what's going to happen to Ern and Minty, sister. We had two years of low prices and now two years of drought. The depression makes it impossible to sell what we can raise. Frances, they're even killing hogs and calves north into Nebraska because we can't feed them and no one can afford to buy them. I just don't know what will become of them." She shook her head in deep concern.

"We'll visit both our parents this week," Lee promised as they turned toward home.

Mercifully, the wind died down during the night. Morning dawned murky with dust still suspended through the sunbeams rising from the east. Now and again, Lee and Georgie explained to their guests, the wind gives us a break.

"A day without wind is such a blessing to us," Georgie added.

Lee had not verbalized his concern, but privately worried a bit about his younger brother. He noticed he had become too thin this past year, his color was pallid. He knew these last years had been hard, but why would he look so haggard now after the worst of the hardships were over.

"Let's get outside, Doc, get some fresh air while the wind and dirt isn't blowing. You look like you could use some fresh air." He rose from the breakfast table, put on his hat and led the way to the back yard.

"Lee, how are you going to make it?" Francis inquired without warning.

"Like I said, doc, I don't have a bank loan to pay and Georgie is not a demanding wife. I am helping her with the garden, expanded it and we are milking more cows. We can live on our cream and egg money if we have to."

They walked toward the garden, where Lee showed his brother his ingenious method of irrigation. He had cobbled together with pipes, baling wire and furrows, a watering system from the windmill directly to the garden. It would of

CHAPTER 44

course not produce a luxurious bumper crop of vegetables he explained, but would give them something to eat during the winter. The two men continued to walk through the dry, brittle stalk fields, kicking big clods of hard, dried earth as they went. The stalks clung tenaciously to life, still green at the bottom, but the tops and leaves were wind-whipped, frayed with dry yellow and bronze tips. Lee led his brother toward the lowland fields and creek valleys. He showed him where he had begun to plow in the bottoms of gullies and ravines. The earth turned up rich and damp there. What little moisture remains, he explained, will be here.

"If I can raise a little bit of feed in these low spots, I can hang on, Brother. I plan to cut the corn stalks before they die and use them for cattle feed. We'll get through this," he grinned. "It'll rain again someday. Nothing lasts forever."

Francis raised his eyebrows in wonderment at the indomitable spirit of this remarkable man. Lee only clasped his brother's shoulder, grinned at him—his blue eyes shining jolly as ever—and suggested they start back toward the house.

CHAPTER 45

As expected, the winds began again. Small gusts whipped uninvited over the fields early in the morning, then later changed to steady surges. They brought with them dirt from miles away, rolling and swirling, infiltrating into every crack and cranny it could find. People fought grit in their teeth, grit in their food, dust and dirt between their sheets. The winds not only brought misery with them, but sickness as well. Many were down with dust pneumonia, a sickness of the lungs. Some were intensely ill.

The two couples planned a visit with their parents on this dirty miserable day. Doc and Frances intended to leave the following day for the return trip to Kansas City. The surging wind was rearranging one field into another as the car passed along the murky road. Minty was fighting the dirt with everything she had. She had blankets and rugs tucked under the door jams and wet blankets and towels covering windows and doors. Still, the gritty dirt found its way inside her little rock house. She had soup on the stove, but warned her guests there would be dirt in it.

"We can't keep the dirt and grit out of our food," she explained simply.

Her table was set with the silverware underneath the overturned plates, the glasses set upside down and a napkin covering each service. Then, a sheet covered the whole table.

Even then, the dishes were covered with the intrusive relentless dirt that seemed to be invading the prairie homes like an incessant barbaric army from distant ages past. Ern did admit to his daughters that the threat of foreclosure was increasing, but he did not allow his concern for his and Minty's future to be discussed in the conversation. This was a matter for him alone to worry about. These young people had enough worries of their own, he reasoned.

Minty was waiting for a more pleasant time to present her news.

"Charlie and Charlotte have a new baby boy," she grinned. "Now with Forrest's five little girls and one boy, Georgie's boy and Charlie's boy, and Vivian's little girl, we have six little granddaughters and three little grandsons. Little Viva Jean is down in bed sick with dust pneumonia, though," she told them with a worried look. "Forrest and Goldie are discouraged with farming in this country," she continued. "If the rains don't come soon, they will seriously consider leaving for Oregon."

As soon as the short visit ended the two young couples drove on to visit Frank and Mattie Obert. Lee was aware that his father would soon be blind. He also knew that both parents were frail and unwell. Sometime in the near future a decision would have to be made, but for now he intended to let things ride as they were. Neither Francis nor Lee was in a position to help financially. There was no money to save the farm or to situate them elsewhere.

To make matters worse, both boys knew that Frank Obert blamed them for his plight. Though he said nothing, it was clear he felt if they had not left him, he would have saved his farm and expanded the operation. He was certain that if they had all stayed together, all would have become prosperous by this time. Instead, Frank had been warned of foreclosure. He told his boys the news with downcast eyes and a quiver in his voice. Nothing in the world could be as tragic to this once proud man, so strong and determined. Both boys only looked downward, muttered appropriately and changed the subject.

"Something will come up," they hedged, or, "the rains will start again soon."

Sadly, Mattie was fighting the dirt in the same manner as Minty.

"These have been miserable times, children," she told them as they arrived.

They eagerly listened to the stories Francis and Fanny had to tell of their adventures in Kansas City and of their son's graduation from school. He explained that he had one more year of internship before he would be able to open his own practice.

"I will be interning in the hospital there in Kansas City," he explained. "Fanny will keep her job and that will help. We don't know yet where we will locate, but we do know it will not be in the Kansas City area. It seems so rundown and decadent compared to our quiet, peaceful little towns out here. The drought is not as pronounced there, though," he did admit. "It is windy and there is dust in the air. The grass is dried and the yards have turned brown, but it is nothing like here."

Early in the evening, Lee and Francis rose to bid their parents good-bye. They needed to get home to finish the evening chores, and Francis and Fanny needed to pack for their return trip to Kansas City. Mattie shed a few tears as she kissed her expanded family good-bye.

CHAPTER 46

Fanny had noticed the weight loss in her husband, as had Lee. She also was aware that he did not seem as energetic as usual. He was pale and generally did not appear to be well. She did not confront him with these cares because he seemed a bit agitated and preoccupied of late. The relentless adversity seemed to be finally catching up with him. The stress of the past years had at last taken its toll. She intended to keep her own counsel on this matter, and perhaps things would improve this year. They were preparing for his first day on the job at the hospital that evening. She was pressing his shirt and pants as he frantically reviewed everything he had learned about medical care in the hospital. His nerves were on edge. He had never felt less confident in his life. This was the single most frightening thing he had encountered in his whole student career.

Francis entered the building, freshly showered, his white shirt pressed, his black pants clean and ironed, his shoes newly polished. He had an air of confidence that belied the self-doubts within. He signed in at the desk and was immediately given his duties for the day. He shuffled the records of the first patient nervously, then dropped them clumsily as the patient related his symptoms. The patient eyed the young doctor sideways a bit hesitantly, looked at Miss Fisher, the nurse who had been around for many years and was imperturbable, then continued with his complaints. Francis cleared his throat, looked at the nurse a bit bewildered, and said, "Let's get a urinalysis on him," more a question than an order.

The older nurse was used to training these young doctors. She had been doing this for many years now. They were all alike, she thought. Study for years, come out of school and go to work at the hospital, but can't remember the first thing they learned. She would not allow a smile to soften their first day jitters as that might make it a bit easier on them. She only answered, "Yes, doctor, and would you like an x-ray of the wrist?"

This brought the med student back to reality a bit. He said, "Oh, yes. Let's get an x-ray to see if the wrist might be broken."

How stupid, he thought. What could I have been thinking. Then, he remembered each patient's visit should start with a check of the vitals. His own personal opinion had always been that a check of the urine was as vital as temperature and pulse. He intended to add urinalysis with every patient checkup. The day stretched longer and longer. He knew it had to be the most difficult day of his life. The old nurse is certainly not making things any easier for me, he thought unhappily to himself. She stood over him, looking down her long, crooked nose. Her close-set eyes peered birdlike from the narrow face. She was tall, thin and ramrod straight, like a marine sergeant. She was studying him, as if to decide if he were worthy of her trouble. Her face was rather like a hawk, Francis thought wryly, for now he was beginning to gain a small bit of confidence. He did not realize it, but she not only intimidated the young interns, but the older, more experienced doctors as well.

The new doctor and the older proficient nurse slowly passed from patient to patient throughout the day, with the nurse helping him subtly more than he realized. "Would you like to place the patient on an elevated bed," or a little too respectfully, "Doctor, would you like the patient taken into room two for a clamp?" Slowly the information learned from the books started coming back to the bedazzled young man. His natural air of confidence was returning, along with his marvelous mind full of medical data now ready to be put into use.

His final stage of training began in this way as he moved from shift to shift and ward to ward. The twelve hour shifts were exhausting and he was becoming increasingly thin and pale. To add to his worries, their financial situation had recently declined.

He returned home one night late with an armful of laundry. Fanny was asleep and did not hear him come in. He shut the door to the bedroom, quietly tiptoed to the kitchen and started running cool sudsy water in the sink. He slowly rinsed each piece of clothing one by one, wrung them gently and placed on the draining board. Then, just as carefully ran rinse water and rinsed them one by one, and then wrung and hung them across the kitchen on a string from the cupboard to the refrigerator.

"What are you doing?" a voice behind him demanded.

He jumped, more from fatigue than from fright, "I picked up silk nightclothes and under things from the rich patients today and brought them home to hand wash for some extra money," he answered a little feebly, knowing a scolding was forthcoming.

"You get right to bed," was her answer. "Next time you want to do this, we'll rinse them out together at a decent time of day." She knew he was worn out and needed rest.

The weeks passed and the grueling internship did not ease. He worked in the OB ward, the long-term care ward, the emergency ward, and all the other wards until his mind was in a state of constant confusion as to all the different treatment methods. They rarely saw Beauchamp and Berniece as Beauchamp was enduring a schedule just as demanding, but at different hours and shifts.

Frances received a call one evening from the hospital relating that her husband had collapsed while working on the pediatrics ward and was now in the hospital himself. She rushed to the hospital expecting the worse. He had not looked well lately and was thin and pale with poor appetite, lack of sleep, and low energy. He was not at all the resilient, energetic young man she had married. She told the nurse at the desk who she was as she hurried into the wing where he was staying. They directed her to his room and she was alarmed at the sight of him as she entered.

"What is wrong with him, doctor?" she asked directly without any preliminary courtesies.

The doctor attending him turned slowly, "He has been selling blood and has given more than he should. He is smoking too much and sleeping too little," was the curt answer. "These young interns never learn. They try to burn the candle at both ends. If he is going to be worth a hill of beans as a doctor, he will have to realize that he needs rest and decide how to find time for it in an extremely busy schedule. Mrs. Obert, your husband has a collapsed lung and will need bed rest for at least a week. When he returns to work, I urge you to see to it that his lifestyle is somewhat modified."

"Yes, doctor," was her meek answer. "We will. We'll certainly do that."

Dr. Obert returned home, chastened and wiser. This hospital stay had put him behind in his internship. He would have to stay a few weeks later in the summer to finish. Adding to his worries, he did not know where he would set up practice or how he could afford it.

"We have to have some money to start up with," he nearly shouted in exasperation. "It seems like it has been money, money, money my whole life."

"You have this blown out of proportion," she told him. "My goodness, if we have to, you can work a while in a hospital until we can afford to set you up."

He slowly began to realize the merry-go-round he had allowed himself to get on. He learned from this experience that he needed to pace himself and take life as it came. He had been borrowing from the future and he had enough in the present to take care of for now.

He stayed home to rest a few days, thought things through a little more clearly and considered many decisions that needed to be made. One evening when Fanny returned from work at the hospital, he motioned her to come sit by him on the couch.

"We aren't getting any younger, Fanny," he told her gently. "It's time we started a family. I would be finished with the internship by then and we would be nearly ready to support a baby."

She looked at him in astonishment. "I am so anxious for a baby," was her only answer.

He raised his eyebrows up and down in a mock grin of lechery. She blushed charmingly, and smiled. His playfulness assured her that he was again the same man she married and things would return to normal.

Summer arrived and brought the usual heat with it. Even in Kansas City the air was dry and dirt-filled. It must be terrible at home they thought. Francis had slowly gained confidence and been able to practice his skills without the self-doubts that plagued him the first few weeks. He was now ready to take on a shift without supervision. The first day on his own would be July Fourth. He did not at first realize the significance of this date, but before the day was finished he would learn. He had drawn the second shift: middle of the afternoon to after midnight. He entered the hospital, went directly to the nurses' station and signed in. He was unnerved to see that Miss Fisher was the nurse assigned to him for this day. It's bad enough that I am on my own for the first time without having her to breathe down my neck all day. The early part of the afternoon went somewhat smoothly. There were only the normal complaints entering in an orderly regular schedule. A middle-aged man with gastroenteritis, a child with fever, and another child who had fallen from his bike and received cuts and abrasions were easily cared for and released. Then, late in the afternoon, things started happening. The emergency ward seemed to go out of control. A young boy was hurried in on a stretcher with a bloodied face and claimed to be blinded. A firecracker had gone off too soon. He was hysterical, "Help me," he begged. "I can't see. I'm blind."

Miss Fisher, instead of her usual critical attitude, this time, pulled right in to help.

"I'll take him into Room 7 doctor," she advised. "You go ahead and see the comatose in Room 3." When Doctor Obert arrived in Room 7 she had the young boy quieted and ready for treatment. He examined the boy quickly, determined that he did not need stitches, but cleaned the wounds and dressed them.

"Take him up to pediatrics and call Dr. Miller," he ordered with no self consciousness. Dr. Miller was the eye specialist and he felt the child needed a specialist right away.

"Yes, doctor," was the respectful answer from nurse Fisher.

"What about Room 3?"

"A drug overdose," came the confident reply. "We'll admit him and try to bring him out of it."

At this time, two stretchers were rolling into the ward. The slightly distressed young doctor and the nonplussed nurse both looked at the scene at the same time. She smiled, nodded in a manner that bespoke, you can do it, and left with the injured boy.

"What have we got?" he asked as he approached the new crisis.

"A knife wound," came the instant reply, "bar fight, somewhere. And a father with burned hands—another fireworks injury."

He examined the knife wound first, satisfied himself that the wounds were not deep and ordered he be taken into the minor surgery ward and readied for suturing.

"He hasn't been stabbed," he explained, "looks like just slashed."

Meanwhile, the father was examined and taken into the burn ward.

"Let's give him a little morphine for the pain and dress the burns," he ordered.

Before he finished this grueling night, he had seen victims from a car wreck, a broken back and many more injuries due to fireworks.

Fortunately for Francis, the scheduling department did recognize that after working the Fourth of July shift, a day off was in order. He slept late the following morning. Frances arose quietly, closed the door and encouraged a long uninterrupted sleep. She washed the expensive, silk things he had again brought home to be laundered. She did this without complaint. She did make it clear though, that she did not wish him to sell blood again. Midmorning he came yawning and stretching out into the kitchen, looking refreshed and tousled like a small boy. She poured coffee and sat down to hear about the experiences of the night before.

CHAPTER 47

Summer turned to fall, and fall into winter. Francis felt his medical skills were nearly ready for his own practice. He now had confidence as he saw patient after patient. He had developed a fine bedside manner and his diagnostic skills were admired by all the nurses who worked with him and by the staff doctors. The holiday season was again approaching and again they would not be able to properly celebrate. He and Beauchamp had both drawn Christmas Day on their working schedule. He arrived home and sat down at the kitchen table wearily this Friday evening.

"Fanny, I am so disappointed that you will not have a decent holiday again. After this year, I promise you we will celebrate Thanksgiving and Christmas in a grand manner."

She only smiled and nodded. "Berniece and I have been invited to eat with the Beauchamps so we will have a wonderful Christmas."

"Fanny, I feel like I have finally become a doctor," he confided. "I feel in charge of myself and situations for the first time since I started interning."

"And I feel like I have finally become a mother," she smiled back at him.

Christmas Day, Beauchamp and Obert took a break in mid-afternoon. Both filled their coffee cups and sauntered away to a quiet place where they could talk privately. Francis could not suppress a grin when he revealed his news to his good friend.

"The baby will come next summer," he told Beauchamp. "I hope I have a place to practice by then. I'll need some money for sure if we're to have a new little person in our family. Not to mention the money I owe the Dean here at Kansas Med School. We'll have to have a car, too," he added forlornly. The more he talked, the more depressed he became. Beauchamp, in his characteristically happy frame of mind told him to not be so easily discouraged.

"Don't get morbid with me," he grinned at his unhappy friend, "we're going to find a place to practice," and slapped Francis' knee as he arose to finish his rounds.

"It's not good at home, Beauchamp," Francis persisted. "Both our parents are facing foreclosure if the draught continues. Fanny's brother lost a little girl with dust pneumonia and they are moving to another state. Forrest is her brother's name and he said he could not live in an area where children died from the weather. Lots of young farm families are packing their things and leaving, most for the west coast. There won't be any patients left for us to take care of if this drought continues."

Beauchamp only shook his head sympathetically, "Nothing lasts forever, Obert. Just remember that, even the weather will change again."

CHAPTER 48

The winter passed and spring grudgingly appeared. Not with its usual soft warm air but with a vengeance. The wind blew mournfully, stirring dust in the air like a smoky haze. Heat was permeating so early in the season that it was frightening. This year promised to be even worse than last. The drought had not abated nor had the winds calmed. Why do people live in this harsh unforgiving land, Francis wondered silently?

Maybe we should move on to the west coast too. The future weighed heavy on his mind, especially with the baby soon to arrive. Fanny had been unusually sickly with the pregnancy and that was an added worry. It was a good thing that her teaching would soon be finished at the hospital so she could rest a bit before he finished his internship. He arrived home to the apartment late one evening in April to good news for a change. Fanny waved a letter in his face with a broad, cheerful smile.

"Read this first, Francis," she ordered benignly. "It will make you feel good."

As he read the letter his eyes began to twinkle like she hadn't seen in the past two years. He began to grin, then it spread into a broad, contagious smile.

"Damn," he almost shouted, "I can't believe we have good luck for a change."

Then as though he were ashamed at his inconsideration, he asked in a more subdued tone of voice, "How do you feel about living in Lebanon, Kansas, Fannie?"

"I love Lebanon," she answered. "I would be very happy there."

The relief he felt was complete. She had never let him down yet. She could be happy anywhere, he decided. She is the type of woman who can make her own happiness anywhere you put her. She has been a big part of my achievement. He really did not believe that he could have finished his education without her help and her undying support. He called Beauchamp immediately to tell him of the good news letter.

"Beauchamp," he began. "I have received a letter from Dr. Scott in Lebanon, Kansas. He has offered to turn over his practice to me as he wants to go to Topeka and get into politics. We're going to accept as it will be a great way to start."

"That's just great," Beauchamp answered. "I received an offer from Sterling, Kansas a few days ago. An older doctor wants help with the calls, especially at night. He said he can hardly manage the nighttime hours and work all day anymore. When he retires the practice can be mine, if I want it. We will be leaving right after I finish interning. We'll keep in touch, though, Obert, won't we?"

"Sure we will," was the instant answer. "We'll come to visit you on weekends and you come visit us."

The two friends reaffirmed this commitment when they parted later in the summer. Beauchamp left a few weeks earlier as Francis had to stay and make up his sick time.

Early in July Franicis finished and the couple began to pack for the journey home and to their future. Fanny was in complete misery, so large it was hard for her to get around, even to walk. She had been ill throughout most of the pregnancy and, as a result, was weak as well. Her husband felt so sorry for her discomfort that he splurged and ordered a cab to take them to the train station. He then loaded all their belongings onto the train and helped his wife up the steps. After he was satisfied that she was at least as comfortable as she could be, he settled back in his seat, relaxed completely and slept.

When the train arrived at the depot in Lebanon, Kansas, there was a large group waiting for them on the platform. Of course, ever faithful Georgie and Lee were in front with their little Carroll waving happily at the train. Fanny's younger brother David was there with his wife, Alma. Alma was a petite lady with black curly hair worn short and a permanent smile that had created charming smiling creases on either side of her mouth. Her eyes were large and dark and her quick, easy laughter created a pleasant atmosphere wherever she went.

CHAPTER 48

Also waiting were the town druggist and his wife, Charlie and Florence Arbuthnot. The new doctor would be located above his Rexall pharmacy and would, no doubt, bring him a nice income. Last, but certainly not least, was the town's leading society ladies, Tess Bunker and her daughter, Clara Bunker. They owned and operated the only hotel located in Lebanon and used it as the center for social meetings as well as renting hotel rooms.

Doc and Frances, as they had become known in Lebanon, stepped off the train to this treasured welcoming party. The men picked up the baggage and started for the main street area where the new couple would take up residence. Georgie grabbed her sister's arm and walked affectionately down the street, slowly to accommodate her awkward gait.

"This year has been worse than last," she confided, "the wind blows continually, the dirt is swirling in the air. We do everything to keep it out of our houses, but it is in our beds at night, in our food throughout the day, in our hair, our teeth. Last March 17, St. Patrick's Day, the dirt blew from the south so bad that it obliterated the sun. The day turned dark as night. The following day after the dirt had settled, there was a thick coat of red dust over everything". Lee said he thought most of Oklahoma had moved into Kansas. I don't know how long we can keep going if the rains don't come again, soon."

Frances patted her hand and encouraged her, "The drought can't last much longer, Sister," she said consolingly.

Georgie laughed and changed the subject to a more cheerful note.

"Poor Minty," she chuckled. "Charlie and Charlotte have a little boy now, we have a little boy, Forrest and Goldie with their four little girls and Rex, Vivian and Wiley have a little girl and you'll soon have a child. When we all get together it will be mayhem all over again just like it was when she was raising her own family."

"Minty will love it," Frances laughed.

Meanwhile, Doc was worrying aloud to his brother Leo.

212   CHAPTER 48

"I've got to start making some money right away. I have debts to pay off and I'll need a car first thing."

"I'll go with you to the bank," Lee offered, "then we'll go over to the Ford garage here in Lebanon. They'll give you a good deal."

They reached the doorway to their new home where the men were carrying their belongings up the wide dark stairway. Frances stopped for a moment to look at the steep stairway and dreaded the climb.

"You take the rail with your right hand, sister," Georgie suggested, "and I'll help you on the left side."

Frances nodded but to her the long, steep, wide stairway looked like the ascent to a Mayan Temple. Well, at least we're finally home, she thought as she took the first step into her new life.

Epilogue

The extraordinary hard work and persistence of Francis Obert and Charles Kennedy, combined with the support and sacrifice by their families, allowed them to leave farming and become medical doctors during very difficult times. Their success placed them in positions to help others.

Francis Obert stayed in the area and was the primary physician for the extended family for many decades. When people were having financial difficulties, he neither expected nor received payment for his services, particularly among family members. When Frank Obert's farm was foreclosed, Francis bought his parents a house in Esbon. Leo and Georgie also helped Frank and Mattie with living expenses.

Charlie Kennedy established a successful medical practice in California, but had the intention of providing financial support to his family. When the drought eventually caused the well on Ern and Minta's farm to dry up in 1937 and water had to be hauled by horse-drawn wagon for all farm and household uses, it became apparent that they would not be able to pay off the debt on their land. Once again, Ern was foreclosed and lost the final piece of the farm owned by his father. Charlie, with the help of Wiley Sloan, found a more habitable 80-acre farm north of Esbon with a nice small house, farm buildings, and good well. Charlie bought the farm as a place for Ern and Minta to live. Six years later when they were no longer able to manage a farm, he bought a house in Esbon for them.

APPENDIX

Sources of Information

Most of the significant events described in this book are based on family stories that I have heard. The dialogue and details are my surmise or imagination about what could have happened associated with those events. A few of the stories are fiction to illustrate life at that time. This Appendix gives the sources for the major stories in each chapter, and also identifies the events that were fiction. Unless otherwise noted, all information about Charlie Kennedy is based on family records held by his son John.

Chapter 1. My father, Francis Obert, was widely known as Stub when he was growing up. I learned the story about him being ornery in grade school when I was working at his doctor's office. A very elderly lady was waiting and when it was her turn I said, "Margaret, you can come in now." My dad was sitting at his desk and looked up as she swung her cane at him and said, "there's that naughty little Francis." He blushed and was visibly unstrung because nobody wants their children to hear about their misdeeds. She said that he got his school work done fast and then bothered everybody. He had to stay in for recess nearly every day. Margaret said she told the teacher she would stay in for him if he could go out and play, but the teacher said no. Margaret was in 8th grade when dad was about a second grader. My cousin Carroll told me the story of my dad and the marbles and the manure. He got the story from Uncle Lee. The other boy's name was changed for this book. My uncle Kenneth said the Kennedy's played baseball every Sunday afternoon.

Chapter 2. Guy McCarty told me the story of pulling the pump. McCartys lived around the bend from the Oberts and were among the neighbors helping pull the pump. He said grandpa hollered, "poll Stubb, poll."

Chapter 3. My mother, Frances (Kennedy) Obert, told me that they took the old push washing machine out in the yard to wash in the summer and made the little boys push it back and forth. She also told me how they played house with bottles. When one was broken they had a funeral and buried it with her as the preacher. The story that Ern's father Charles Kennedy had a melon patch that thrived and was watered by overflow from the horse tank was told to me by many people from the community.

Chapter 4. Frank Obert tried to be on the school board or a similar position, but he was illiterate and didn't see any reason for school or book learning.

Chapter 5. Mattie Obert's mother was married and had two children in Quilty, County Clare, Ireland. Her husband came to the U.S. first in 1886 and she came a year later. The records showed that she boarded the boat with two children and arrived with one.

Chapter 6. The children walking to school through their grandpa's land with a special gate he made for them and stopping at his house is a well-known family story told to me by my mother and by her brother Charlie.

Chapter 7. There are different family stories about how David fell and broke his hip when he was 5. This version that he fell off a corncrib while trying to put salt on the tail of a bird is from his daughter Irma. The accident actually happened several years earlier than the timeline in the book, but fits better here than as the first chapter. That Georgie delayed her school and worked helping take care of the younger children while the other children played is a well-known family story that was told to me by my mother as well as others.

Chapter 8. This is my surmise about farmers putting up hay at that time.

Chapter 9. The kids trying to sleep in the barn is fiction to illustrate how life was before electricity, air conditioning, and fans. According to family records held by Charlie's son John, Charlie graduated the 8th grade at Lone Tree School in 1911, and then stayed home for three years, which was when Forrest graduated the 8th grade. Forrest told his children that his working on the farm allowed Charlie to go to high school and college.

Chapter 10. After hearing the family stories of Frank shooting at the man, I obtained the transcript of the trial from the county court records. The description of the shooting incident is based on the transcript. My cousin Carroll (Leo's son) told me that Frank was put in jail and that Mattie carried my dad and pulled Leo along all over the neighborhood talking with the neighbors. The neighbors helped get Frank out. The man's name was changed for the book. Uncle Jim was one of Mattie's 10 siblings. She and Jim were very close.

Chapter 11. My father said he always loved poetry but did not want anyone to know. When I was a child, he would read poetry to me, or have me read poems to him.

Chapter 12. Wilbur Obert told me the story of the boys letting the horse go across the field plowing.

Chapter 13. This is my surmise of a trip to town for young boys.

Chapter 14. My dad told me about barn dances and that his mother was the best square dancer. This is my surmise about the birth of Byron.

Chapter 15. According to family records held by Charlie's son John, Charlie attended Lone tree for the 9th grade in 1912-1913 and started high school in Mankato in 1914. He was a star athlete in high school and was class valedictorian when he graduated in 1918. He rode the train to Mankato and stayed at the YMCA. The story of him getting recognized his freshman year and the family's response is my surmise about what could have happened as he began moving away from the farm. I'm not certain that he lettered in all sports his first year at Mankato, but that is likely. The baseball game is fiction, but was a way to illustrate how they lived, what they did for fun, and what was important to them. My father told me about baseball in those days. Dave was a strong hitter to compensate for his hip handicap and sometimes had his younger brothers run bases. My father played catcher.

Chapter 16. Jessie told me how Charlie took my dad under his wing. My mother said she thought Mattie talked Frank into letting Francis go to high school, but no one is really sure why Frank did not object.

Chapter 17. My mother told me dad got through all the levels of Latin in high school and was so good that they called him Caesar. Charlie wrote a book that described his grandfather initially arriving in Red Cloud on the train with Ern and then taking a wagon to Kansas. The book also described Charlie digging potatoes with his grandfather the day before his grandfather died, and the clock stopping on the day he died. My mother later wrote a letter describing how inconsolable the children were when their grandfather died.

Chapter 18. Jessie told me that Lee and Georgie initially separated because of religion. My mother also spoke of that, and Forrest told his daughter Reta a similar story. Georgie's grandmother Kennedy was said to be very opposed to Protestants marrying Catholics. Of course, the specific details of how the separation happened are my surmise. Nita's obituary states that she was a teacher in Jewell and Smith counties. She signed Jessie's report card for the 7th grade at Lone Tree School in 1916.

Chapter 19. My mother and Jessie attended Esbon high school for two years while Charlie and my dad attended Mankato. The Mankato yearbooks verify this. I heard once that Georgie worked in a store in Mankato when she was single and later heard that she did housework. However, I do not remember the sources and have not found anyone who could confirm either story. For the book, my surmise was that she worked in a store.

Chapter 20. Jessie told me about Dumb Old Donkey.

Chapter 21. I originally wrote the story of Minta's reaction to Charlie joining the army based on my surmise. Later Vivian told me what happened, and it was practically the same.

Chapter 22. Jessie told me about Georgie's romance at this point. The man's name was made up for this book. My father told me that they had a contest in high school to see which class could drive the most music teachers out in a year, and how they did it. My father meeting with the school principal is my surmise and seems likely because he was such a good student with no direction.

Chapter 23. My father graduated from Mankato High School in the spring of 1919. My mother and Jessie started at Mankato High School in the fall of 1919. They both told me they lived with an elderly widow and helped with housework for room and board. The woman's name and characteristics are my surmise.

Chapter 24. Lee and Nita married in August, 1922, but the details here are my surmise.

Chapter 25. Vivian did not actually start going out with Wiley until a few years later than the timeline in this book. For purposes of the story here, it was simpler to introduce him at this point while describing going to a dance. Frances and Jessie graduated from Mankato High School in the spring of 1921. Jewell County records show that Frances began teaching at Odessa School #130 in the fall of 1921. Jessie told me her parents thought she should become a teacher and strongly opposed her study of business, but at the last minute Ern said he'd drive her to Fairbury. After she was in her small room, her room-mate told her a man was crying outside the building. Jessie looked and saw Ern sobbing by the car. Jessie wrote the letter to Charlie in November, 1921 describing her experiences at Fairbury Business College. The quotes are from the letter.

Chapter 26. Jessie told me about Georgie's relationship ending when a jealous person stole the mail. The story of Charlie switching from Washburn to Kansas University is from an article in the *Topeka Capital* newspaper February 8, 1922, and another article about the same time.

Chapter 27. Kenneth told me about Don falling out the window. When they got to him he clapped his hands and said "do again."

Chapter 28. Forrest's daughter Reta said that Forrest loved to dance and he could have met Goldie at a dance. She also said that Forrest liked working with his hands outdoors, and worked with his Uncle near Otega before he got married. Charlie taught and coached in Esbon High School for the school year 1923-1924. Frances attended summer classes at Hays, and county records show that she had a one-year state teaching certificate in the fall of 1922 and a three-year state certificate in the fall of 1926. Ern was widely known among the family to have a knack for math and to help his children with their math problems. The story of Jessie and her horse Queen and the war whoop incident are from Jessie's daughter Ruth. As noted before, Vivian and Wiley actually started going out later than the timeline in this book. In the picture of the people on horses, the young man on the horse behind Jessie was a friend of Vivian at the time.

Chapter 29. My mother told me that Ern put his head on the table and cried when he learned that Minta was pregnant for the 13th time.

Chapter 30. The story of Minta's struggle with her 13th pregnancy is my surmise. My father told me he asked his father for payment for working on the farm. When he got nothing, he left and lived with his brother Lee.

Chapter 31. According to Nita's obituary, she died of acute appendicitis in February, 1924 after Glenn's birth in November, 1923. She was ill less than a week. The details of the story are my surmise. Glenn's obituary says that he was raised by Nita's parents. My mother told me there was tension between Lee and his in-laws about who was going to raise Glenn.

Chapter 32. My father told me that he slept on a park bench for two or so nights when he first went to Lawrence, that he waited tables, and that he dropped out more than one semester to make money for the next.

Chapter 33. Ern and Minta losing the farm and moving to the rock house in 1924 or possibly 1925 is a well-known family story that has been verified with deed records. The name of the man who bought the farm and then died was changed for this book. For the eighty acres and rock house that Ern and his siblings had inherited from their father, the county deed records show that Ern's siblings transferred ownership to him in 1924 and that he had a debt of $1200.

Chapter 34. My father told me he once drove mules on roadwork when he was in college.

Chapter 35. Vivian's daughter Pat had the information (and a photo) of the Esbon girls' winning the district championship in basketball in 1925. The Mankato yearbooks show Jessie on the girls' softball team for both years she was in high school there. Her daughter Ruth said she was a left-handed pitcher. County records show that Frances taught at Odessa #130 1921-1924, at Otega #157 1924-1925, at Esbon Township Union 11 1925-1925. The records give her salary. She later obtained a three-year teaching certificate from Hays that required she attend summer classes for at least three years. Jessie told me she lived with Fred's family for awhile while she was the bookkeeper for their business. Fred would slip notes under her door. The information about Fred being a playful scallywag in a religiously conservative family and playing footsie with Jessie during their rather formal meals is from Jessie's daughter Ruth. Ruth also said that Ern would say he had nine boys, three girls, and Jessie, and that Jessie insisted on hunting with her brothers and shot rabbits from her horse. The description of common wedding practices at that time is from Kenneth's wife Gladys, among others. Jessie told me that Fred's family was impressed with her manners. My mother also said that manners were emphasized at the Kennedys when growing up. The story of Kenneth breaking his arm twice and becoming a switch hitter is also from Gladys. The story of James getting the nickname Pete is from his wife Elta. Charlie's personal records had the original telegram from the Kansas City Blues in September, 1925, the newspaper article from December, 1925, and the information about finishing school at K.U.

Chapter 36. My mother taught in Esbon High School for the school year 1926-1927. County school records indicate she had a three year state teaching certificate. She went to Rexford the next year. Kenneth told me that Ern rented a house in Esbon for my mother, him, and Lyall. They were told that she was in charge and they were to mind her. My mother told me that she was worried about teaching her younger siblings because they might try to take advantage of her. The story of Kenneth dropping out after six weeks when he got sick and could not play football was from his wife Gladys. I'm not certain Kenneth's 6 weeks in high school occurred the year my mother was teaching there, but it would have been close. The story about Charlie is from his journal, including the jobs in Crawford, the hotel where he stayed, the quote from December 22, 1926, returning home, going to medical school, and playing baseball with the Kansas City Blues, Crawford, and Oshkosh.

Chapter 37. This is my surmise about how the relationship between Leo and Georgie could have developed.

Chapter 38. Frank Obert became blind with glaucoma. I remember strings all over the house so he could follow them from bedroom to kitchen, to bathroom, to living room, etc. My father and others told me stories about Mary's increasing mental health problems. Ern being gored was described in a letter he wrote his son Charlie. The doctor's comments on the receipt for the medical bill are a quote. Jessie kept a travel log of the trip to Colorado for Charles's graduation. The information about Fred and Jessie living in Salina and their jobs is from the 1930 census. The information about Charlotte and Charles is from newspaper articles and other family records that their son John has. The story of the day of their marriage is from the journal Charlie kept. The entry for June 21, 1930 gives the events, times, and locations, including the comments about the bed, pitcher, and the toilet down the hall. For June 22 the journal also has the comment about finally getting the dirt washed off at the hotel in Salt Lake City and sleeping late etc. for the 23rd.

Chapter 39. Mother told me about her trip to New York. Jessie told me that my mother had a car with curtains and sometimes had a bottle of whiskey in her suitcase. I do not have exact information on when and how my parents became romantic partners in their late 20s. They did not attend high school together and lived in different locations much of their adult lives prior to their marriage. The story told here seems likely given what is known about them. My mother and father and Leo and Georgie were very close after marriage, and probably before.

Chapter 40. The story of Lyall's death in September, 1930 is based primarily on detailed letters Jessie and Vivian wrote at the time, including the quotes of Lyall's final words to his parents. Jessie told me that the doctor in Lebanon initially thought his illness was from bad moonshine. Jessie also said Minta called my dad, who was home from school. Kenneth told me my mother was home when Lyall initially became ill, and she tried to get him to go to the doctor earlier. The letters indicate that my mother had left by the time Lyall actually died.

Chapter 41. Jessie told me that my parents became interested in each other romantically when Lyall was sick. My cousin Jim has a hazy memory of talking with my parents many years ago about how they got together. In this hazy memory, my father said that at one point he was fascinated with my mother, but she viewed him more as a student rather than as an adult that she would be interested in romantically. The specific stories in this chapter are my surmise about what could have happened. Kenneth told me that Lyall died in Minta's bed. Kenneth had to switch rooms and beds with Minta after Lyall's death, and she would not sleep in that bed. My mother told me the story of the watch at Christmas. The description of their apartment is my surmise. The various jobs my mother had in Lawrence and Kansas City for the remainder of the book are all based on stories she told me.

Chapter 42. The Beauchamps were life-long friends with my parents and visited us regularly. I heard many stories of their medical school years as they reminisced during these visits. My mother once said they couldn't have made it without Beauchamp's parents, who had them for Sunday dinner every week and sent home leftovers for a few days. The story of the banker refusing the loan and the Dean offering a loan is true. I have the documentation.

Chapter 43. Herb Beauchamp's father told me the story of his son being secretly married when his wife became pregnant—however, now I wonder if it was actually true. My mother told me about sneaking into the hospital to see the deformed baby. My mother also told me that a wealthy aunt of one of the wives loaned them an assortment of dresses and accessories for the graduation ceremonies, which they returned after the ceremonies.

Chapter 44. This is my surmise of family conversation during the great depression.

Chapter 45. My father said that Frank always believed that his failure to be successful was due to his sons not staying on the farm with him.

Chapter 46. The story of the nurse when my father was an intern is my surmise based on things my father told me. It was common knowledge that my father gave blood for money in medical school, and got a collapsed lung.

Chapter 47. This is my surmise of conversation during this time.

Chapter 48. My father took over the medical practice in Lebanon in 1935.

Epilogue. My father's lenient expectations about payment were well known. My father bought the house in Esbon for his parents and paid the taxes and maintenance. Leo and Georgie helped them with other expenses. Deed records show that Charlie Kennedy bought the 80-acre farm in Highland Township north of Esbon in July, 1940 for $1000 and sold it in May, 1947 for $3700. Ern and Minta moved to the house in Esbon in 1946.

MATTIE OBERT'S CHOCOLATE CAKE

6 tsp cocoa
1 cup boiling water
1/2 cup butter
2 tsp soda

2 cup sugar
1 cup milk
2 1/2 cup flour
2 eggs

Cream butter and sugar. Pour boiling water over cocoa and cook til thick.

Add soda to flour. Add egg yolks to butter and sugar. Add hot cocoa, add flour and milk. Fold in whipped egg whites.

Made in the USA
San Bernardino, CA
15 April 2016